Alex quirk[ed...] secretly in[...] know how [you feel.]

Someone like...me?

Apparently oblivious to his growing interest in her, Kate hesitated. "More like...wondering if I'm waiting around for a fairy-tale life that may never materialize."

He ignored the twinge of something tightening inside him.

She shook her head, as if suddenly realizing if her folks were right—she was wasting every day that passed. That she would likely never get the loving husband and kids she wanted.

And that would make him unbearably sad for her.

Kate straightened. "What I do know—" she met his eyes "—is that being around the boys has made me realize how much I do want a home and family of my own. Sooner rather than later..."

Alex feigned an ease he could not begin to feel. "You're talking kids?"

"Oh yes." Her eyes shone with hope and faith that she would get what she wanted. And maybe she would. It was Christmastime, after all. A holiday when wishes miraculously came true. The urge to take her in his arms and kiss her grew stronger. He relaxed in his chair, his knees shifting beneath the card table, nudging hers.

"What about a husband?" he asked. "Do you want one of those too?"

Dear Reader,

Do you wonder what makes people happy at Christmas? For parents of young kids, I think it is simply that their children have a merry Christmas holiday full of love and free from strife.

This is exactly what Alex McCabe has planned for his quadruplet kindergarten-age sons. They want a Shetland pony for their ranch? He has his eye on one. They love bugs? He knows about a fancy new insect catcher that will allow them to observe to their hearts' content and then set the insect free. The one thing they really need, however, is a mom to love and care for them. That is a little harder to arrange.

Until Kate Taylor shows up on his ranch. Alex hasn't seen her since they worked together at a shelter during a hurricane eight years before. The fast friendship and fierce attraction they felt then went nowhere because both were pledged to others. Now she magically appears for a chef gig on his ranch. They quickly find out their chemistry is stronger than ever. His boys adore her, too, and want her to be their bonus mom.

Can she marry without romantic love? Kate hadn't thought so. Now that she is happier than ever, she wonders. Are hope and faith, love and giving enough to build a marriage—and happy family—on? Only time will tell.

I hope you enjoy reading this book as much as I loved writing it! Have a wonderful holiday season!

Merry Christmas to all!

Cathy Gillen Thacker

A COWBOY'S CHRISTMAS GIFT

CATHY GILLEN THACKER

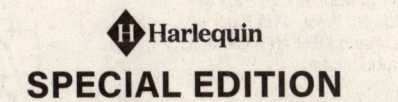

Harlequin
SPECIAL EDITION

If you purchased this book without a cover you should be aware that this book is stolen property. It was reported as "unsold and destroyed" to the publisher, and neither the author nor the publisher has received any payment for this "stripped book."

Harlequin® SPECIAL EDITION™

ISBN-13: 978-1-335-18008-7

A Cowboy's Christmas Gift

Copyright © 2025 by Cathy Gillen Thacker

All rights reserved. No part of this book may be used or reproduced in any manner whatsoever without written permission.

Without limiting the author's and publisher's exclusive rights, any unauthorized use of this publication to train generative artificial intelligence (AI) technologies is expressly prohibited.

This is a work of fiction. Names, characters, places and incidents are either the product of the author's imagination or are used fictitiously. Any resemblance to actual persons, living or dead, businesses, companies, events or locales is entirely coincidental.

For questions and comments about the quality of this book, please contact us at CustomerService@Harlequin.com.

TM and ® are trademarks of Harlequin Enterprises ULC.

Harlequin Enterprises ULC
22 Adelaide St. West, 41st Floor
Toronto, Ontario M5H 4E3, Canada
www.Harlequin.com

Printed in Lithuania

Cathy Gillen Thacker is a married mother of three. She and her husband reside in North Carolina. Her stories have made numerous appearances on bestseller lists, but her best reward is knowing one of her books made someone's day a little brighter. A popular Harlequin author, she loves telling passionate stories with happy endings and thinks nothing beats a good romance and a hot cup of tea! Visit her at cathygillenthacker.com for information on her books, recipes and a list of her favorite things.

Books by Cathy Gillen Thacker

Harlequin Special Edition

A Marrying a McCabe Romance

Stand-In Texas Dad
A Double Christmas Surprise

Lockharts Lost & Found

His Plan for the Quadruplets
Four Christmas Matchmakers
The Twin Proposal
Their Texas Triplets
Their Texas Christmas Gift
The Triplets' Secret Wish
Their Texas Christmas Match
A Temporary Texas Arrangement

Visit the Author Profile page
at Harlequin.com for more titles.

Chapter One

"Are you our mom?"

Not the question Kate Taylor had expected to be asked upon her arrival at the Rocking M Ranch in Laramie County, on the Monday morning before Thanksgiving.

Never mind by four adorable little cowboys standing on the front porch of the sprawling prairie-style ranch house. Although not identical, they were all pretty much the same height, with similarly cute faces, sea-blue eyes, and curly dark hair. Quadruplets, she presumed, as the fluffy gray and white sheepdog accompanying them strode closer, too, as if wanting her answer.

Guessing the boys' ages to be about five or so, she moved away from the driver side of her shiny red pickup truck, smiled at them kindly and said, "No. I'm not."

Before she could introduce herself further, they peered at her suspiciously. The leader of the group stepped closer, followed quickly by his little comrades. "Are you sure?" He fingered both plastic water pistols holstered at his side.

The others did the same with their bright orange toy water guns. She could see, from the moisture dripping from the toys, that she had interrupted what was about to be an epic water fight.

"'Cause our mom probably could be coming to see us *right now*," another child added.

All of them frowned, in the gloomy autumn light. The scent of impending rain hung in the air. Washing over them.

"Yeah, maybe you just forgot us," a third added, as they all narrowed their gazes even more.

"And just *now* remembered we was here, on the ranch," the fourth stated soberly.

Wondering how anyone could apparently abandon such darling boys, Kate smiled kindly at them. "I'm sure I would remember if you were my children," she said, stepping curiously closer. How long could it have been, since parent and children had seen each other, if these cute little boys mistook her for their mom? Her heart going out to them, she asked, "Is your mom *supposed* to come and see you today?"

"If we knew, we would be in trouble," the leader of the group told her, "because then we would be eavesdropping and we are not allowed to do that."

"Who are you anyway?" the most extroverted kiddo, asked. Striding closer, his western boots clicked on the stone porch that spread across the front of the elegant prairie-style ranch home.

"I'm Kate Taylor. And I'm here to see Alex McCabe, who I assume is your dad…?" At least she hoped so!

"Yep!"

"He sure is!"

Another suspicious squint. "How come you want to see him?"

"He's looking for someone to cook for the cowboys in the bunkhouse," Kate explained as the front door opened and a gorgeous man strode out to join his sons. At six foot four inches tall, he had the same sturdy build, short dark brown hair and ocean blue eyes as his sons. His chiseled features, square jaw and strong nose were even more familiar.

Hauntingly, amazingly so…

OMG. Could fate have brought them together again? Could it really be…?

Looking just as stunned as she felt, he came to an abrupt halt, just short of her. He gave his head a slight shake and squinted. "Kate…?" he said hoarsely, as if unable to believe she was there. On what was apparently his ranch. With his sons.

"Alex?" Kate croaked back, her knees suddenly trembling as badly as the rest of her.

She hadn't seen the handsome cowboy since Hurricane Inga, eight years prior. A familiar thrill swept through her, followed by knee-buckling shock. This really was a blast from the past! She stared at him, too. "I had no idea your last name was McCabe." Or that he was one of the legendary Texas McCabes.

Volunteers had been on a first name only basis at the Houston shelter where they had labored for three intensely long days and nights. Working side by side to assist all those who had been displaced by the category four storm.

He nodded in the affirmative. Adding ruefully, "And I didn't know you were the Kate Taylor who owned Chuck Wagon Catering!"

That made sense, she guessed.

After all, they had only communicated through e-mail about the job that had brought her to the Rocking M Ranch.

"Wow…" he murmured. "And here I thought we would never see each other again."

Kate had figured the same. With good reason, she recalled. They had both been engaged to others when they had met before. Both fighting the chemistry simmering between them, as they worked for seventy-two long hours, helping hurricane evacuees. Determined to stay honorable, they hadn't talked about exchanging phone numbers or emails when the storm passed. They simply stated how much they had enjoyed being on the same rescue team, said a properly platonic good-bye and returned to their normal lives.

And that had been it.

Except for all the times when she had remembered him and wished they had met at a time when both were unattached...so they could have seen if there was something to those sparks she was certain both of them had felt.

Another silence fell. This one fraught with long-repressed emotion. And that made her wonder—was he still feeling the same now? Pondering about what might have been, too? Had their circumstances been different, of course...

Clearly, their previous relationships hadn't worked out all that great for either of them. Otherwise, she would not still be single without the husband and kids she had always wanted. And his precious little boys would not be on the lookout for a mom they weren't sure they were going to recognize.

Alex broke the silence, the personable charm she remembered in evidence. "It's so good to see you!" he stated sincerely. He stepped even closer, wrapping his arms around her and giving her a hug she couldn't help but return in kind.

Damn he felt as good as she had always imagined he would. Big. Strong. Capable. And he smelled wonderful, too, like brisk soap and shaving cream.

Kate drew a breath, hardly able to believe they were here together now, holding each other. *Talk about Christmas coming early!* "You, too," she murmured, her feelings swirling crazily with lust. Need. Hope.

When he finally released her, their gazes meshed again. And the magic was back, simmering between them, more potent than ever.

Alex had thought his morning couldn't get any crazier. First, the boys had been hard as heck to get ready for school.

Then, before he could wrangle all four of them into the Navigator, to take them to kindergarten, the phone had rung and it was Tiffany calling, of all people. With an ask that was as outrageous as her behavior had been since their children had been born.

And now, the chuck wagon cook he'd been planning to interview—Kate Taylor—was here. Early. Unexpectedly turning out to be a real blast from his past. Looking pretty as could be in a pair of boots, figure-hugging jeans and a dark brown turtleneck sweater that brought out the amber of her eyes.

He'd always been attracted to the honey-blond beauty.

However, for a lot of reasons that no longer applied, at least on his part, he had always considered her off limits.

Was she still…?

He didn't see any kind of ring on her left hand that would have signaled a romantic commitment.

Kate drew a breath, stepped back.

"I see you've already met my quadruplets." He moved away, too, still taking in her full lips and beautiful smile, fit athletic body.

She nodded. "Yes. I have."

Sensing something highly unusual going on, his boys all crowded closer. "Aren't you going to tell the lady our names, Daddy, so we can shake her hand?"

Where were his manners? Alex wondered. The fact Kate was just as stunning as she had been the last time he had seen her was no excuse.

"Ah, boys, this is Kate Taylor. She's an old friend."

"Is that why you were hugging her?" Michael asked.

"Um, yes."

Not sure whether Kate was amused or taken aback, he continued with the introductions. "Kate, this is Michael." Alex pointed to the most studious one of the bunch. "And Max..." Who, as always, had a mischievous smile and a twinkle in his eyes. "Marty..." The most boisterous and athletic one. "And Matthew..." Who was charming and charismatic.

Unlike himself these days...

"It's good to meet you." Kate went down the line, offering her hand to each child. They clasped it dutifully. Then she stopped and turned back to him.

"Daddy!" Michael chided.

"Manners!" Max said.

Wincing inwardly, Alex stuck out his hand. Kate's fingers were as soft and delicate as they looked. She shook his hand warmly, looking him straight in the eye.

He felt a wave of heat, similar to the one he'd experienced when they had hugged hello. Another unexpected tingle of awareness.

"I'm sorry for all the chaos this morning," he began. "But we're going to have to..."

He stopped as the sound of a vehicle speeding quickly up the lane roared behind him. He turned to see a white BMW Z4 sports car zipping up the circular drive, finally coming to a screeching halt behind Kate's fire engine red pickup truck that was parked in front of the ranch house.

His ex-wife wasn't alone.

As she had indicated on the phone, her new husband had come with her. And was getting out of the sports car, too.

He was a good half decade younger than Tiffany. Mid-twenties maybe. Italian. Very debonair and sophisticated, in that slicked back black hair, European playboy kind of way. He wore expensive loafers, no socks, tight pants, a partially unbuttoned silky shirt and fitted blazer.

His boys gaped at their new stepdad like he was an alien who had just landed from Mars.

And in Laramie County, where they resided, he kind of was.

"Everyone, meet Paolo Delucca," Tiffany said.

Although the boys had been eager to shake hands with Kate, they kept their arms at their sides. So tense and wary, Alex's heart went out to them. Since they hadn't seen her in over four and a half years, or had any contact at all, and hence, wouldn't recognize her now.

"Is this lady our mom?" Max demanded curiously.

"Yeah, the lady you were calling Tiffany on the phone!" Marty added.

Alex looked at his boys and gave a brief nod. Instinctively, they seemed to shrink back even farther. He could hardly blame them. His ex was not the least bit maternal. Which was why they needed to get a few things straight before any further potentially damaging interactions ensued. "Boys, why don't you go inside with Reckless and give the grown-ups a few minutes to talk, and then you can come back out in a few minutes," he said.

Not surprisingly, his ex didn't dispute the vanquishing of their sons. Nor, he noted, with renewed disappointment, did she seem the least bit interested in personally greeting or getting reacquainted with any of them.

His boys didn't need to be asked a second time. They called for their sheepdog to go with them and hurried inside. Slamming the glass-paned door after them.

Tiffany turned to Kate. "You look awfully familiar for some reason." She squinted suspiciously. "Have we met?"

Kate froze, as if bracing for an attack.

"Don't tell me you're Alex's latest lady friend," his ex-wife snarled.

Alex had to credit Kate.

Though she paused momentarily, giving Tiffany an odd look he couldn't quite decipher, she quickly backed up and smiled the way waitstaff did when confronted with a difficult client who could easily get them fired. "I'm Kate, the owner of Chuck Wagon Catering. Just here to speak to Alex about a job. But since I can see this isn't a good time for that, perhaps I'll just leave and come back another time." She started to go.

"No," Alex said firmly, holding an arm out to waylay her. "That won't be necessary." They needed to get that contract signed so she could begin today.

He turned to Tiffany, his temper rising the way it always did when his ex created havoc in his life. "As I told you on the phone, you can't just show up here without warning," he told her grimly. "Not. Anymore."

Kate had dodged trouble when Tiffany had failed to recognize her. Although, unfortunately, *she* remembered the mean-spirited Houston socialite all too well. She just hadn't known that Alex McCabe was the wealthy rancher who had been Tiffany's first husband. The one who viper trash-talked all the time to their mutual private school alumni.

And she certainly hadn't been aware that Tiffany had had quadruplet sons!

Especially since Kate couldn't recall a time when the woman hadn't been rail thin, with a super model's pampered glow and an oil heiress's elegant attire.

Even now, Tiffany had a glamour that was newly European in nature, with her sleek, straight, ebony hair cut in a Cleopatra style, her makeup perfectly applied, from her kohl lined eyes to her ruby red lips.

Gone was the southern belle vibe that she'd had when Kate had seen her last.

Over a decade before…

"You can't keep me from seeing my sons, Alex!" Tiffany insisted.

He folded his arms and glared at her, looking about as movable as a brick wall. Grimly, he reminded his ex, "You waived all discussions of possession and physical custody of our sons when we divorced."

Wow, Kate thought.

That was hard to understand, especially given how adorable the boys were.

Still focused solely on Alex, Tiffany nodded. She stepped closer, leaving a waft of expensive perfume in her wake. "Because," she tilted her face up to Alex's, as she reminded him, "our attorneys told the court that because I was going to be travelling abroad for an unspecified amount of time, that it wasn't going to be appropriate to set up a formal custody and visitation schedule dictated by the court, at the time our marriage dissolved. When we knew at the outset I would not be able to honor the terms. Instead, you and I promised the judge that we would work together to parent our children by agreement, according to their best interests. Until such time, as things changed." She shrugged, elegant as ever. "If they changed."

Like now? Kate wondered. Still feeling like there was a helluva lot more to this than Tiffany wanted Alex, or anyone else, to think...at least at the moment.

His handsome jaw set, Alex harrumphed. "Right. Only problem with that, Tiffany, is that you were a no-show. The entire time. Nor did you even call or email or text even once, to see how the kids were doing."

Talk about bad mothering, Kate thought.

"For four and a half years," Alex added grimly, for emphasis.

Tiffany shrugged, as self-centered and unapologetic as Kate recalled her being way back when.

Her old nemesis flashed a sweet smile that did not quite reach her eyes. "That was then. This is now. I've grown older, wiser, and changed my mind." She stepped even closer to

Alex, while her new husband lingered at the edge of the porch. Looking as if he wanted to be a part of this as much as Kate did, which was not at all.

"The holidays are coming up, after all." She waved a lecturing finger at her ex. Adding smugly, "And before you try to tell me no, that I can't have what I want, remember I still have joint legal custody of the boys. Just as you do."

Uh oh, Kate thought.

"Which gives me equal input into every detail of our boys' lives," Tiffany concluded complacently, "including where—and with whom—they spend their holidays!"

Tiffany was right, Alex admitted reluctantly. As it stood right now, she had the same amount of say in where the kids lived, and went to school, or what they wore and ate, and the time they went to bed at night, as he did. But only because, Alex thought, his ex had refused to voluntarily give up her parental rights to the kids when they split up and he hadn't wanted an ugly public fight. So he had given her what she wanted. A no-strings divorce. Her freedom. And the money to travel and live abroad. With no expectation she would ever have to take physical custody, or care for the boys.

For a while, he had left the door open.

Thinking with time Tiffany might change her mind about having a relationship with the children. Or at least come to see them now and then. Try and bond with them emotionally.

When she hadn't, he had realized the separation was for the best. And as for the boys, they hadn't missed what they could not remember...and had never had. A mother's love.

"And because there are no court orders in place, you can't keep me from seeing them," Tiffany continued triumphantly.

His brother Gabe, who was also his attorney, had warned him about this. When there were no court orders in place, there were no rules for visitation, and both parents had equal rights to the children.

Neither parent could force visitation to happen, if the other parent did not agree. Unless they went to family court. Would she do that? File a petition and try and force the issue? There was no way to know.

"So I want to see them for the holidays," she continued firmly.

If he thought she had their sons' best interests at heart, it would be one thing. He didn't. "Thanksgiving is in four days," he reminded calmly, still trying to do what was best for everyone. And she and the boys were complete strangers to each other! Add too much holiday stress, and their reunion could be a disaster. Which would benefit no one.

Tiffany scoffed and waved off the information. "I'm not talking about that."

Recognition dawned. Finally, he saw where this was going. "Well, you are not taking them for Christmas," he shot back wearily.

"I don't see why not," Tiffany returned carelessly. "When I'm here to give you *plenty* of advance notice of my plans!"

Kate could see plenty of reasons why not.

Judging from the set of Alex's jaw, the handsome rancher was of the same mindset.

Holidays were really for kids.

Parents…good ones anyway…had an obligation to do their best to make the celebrations good, for their children.

Whereas Tiffany was all about her own happiness. Needs. And wants. And that selfish, self-centered attitude could be disastrous for her and Alex's sweet little boys.

A fact which made Kate sad.

Although, she reminded herself sternly, this wasn't really

any of her business. So, she should just stay out of it. The way Paolo seemed to be...

"You've had them for the last four Christmases," Tiffany continued, even more aggressively.

Alex's eyes were filled with a resentment Kate could easily understand. "That was your choice, if you remember," he shot back at his ex.

"Which makes it my turn now!" Tiffany grew even more petulant. "I want to reconnect! And spend the holidays with my boys! And if you were any kind of father at all, you would support that and let me have them with me for Christmas!"

Didn't really seem like she wanted to be with the kids, Kate thought. It appeared more like she wanted to use them to get under Alex's skin. Which she was doing very well!

His fury growing, Alex stared at his ex.

Tiffany stared right back.

Kate would never know what the Houston socialite was going to say next, because the four boys and their dog chose that very second to burst out of the front door, yelling wildly, water pistols spraying.

Their target?

Their mother. And her new husband.

That quickly, Tiffany was soaked from head to toe. Her cashmere dress, makeup and hair ruined. Paolo's clothes were splattered with water, too.

It seemed eight water toys, activated all at once, could do quite a bit of damage. "We're not going with you!" Michael shouted belligerently.

"Yeah, that's not what we're doing for Christmas!" Marty said.

"We're staying here with our dad!" Matthew declared.

"So you just need to go away!" Max hollered. "Right now!"

"Boys..." Alex warned. Not about to tolerate his sons'

out-of-control behavior any more than he was his ex-wife's. "Apologize!" he told them all sternly. "Now!"

"Nooo!" they all screeched in unison. Then they turned and ran inside the house, once again slamming the door behind them.

Paolo—who had managed not to get nearly as drenched—went up to Tiffany. He took off his jacket and gallantly put it over her shoulders. "Darling," he murmured softly, "I am so sorry."

Tiffany turned back to Alex with an accusing look on her face. Clearly blaming him for the melee.

"If you had given me time to prepare the boys, for your visit, this wouldn't have happened," he said.

"Somehow I doubt that," his ex-wife snarked. "In any case, you have not heard the last of this, Alex McCabe! One way or another, I am going to lay claim to my boys. And there isn't a darn thing you or anyone else can do to stop me!"

She turned on her heel and headed for the low-slung sports car. This time Paolo got behind the wheel. Alex moved to stand next to Kate as they drove off. His tall body tense. Lips compressed. "Sorry you had to witness that," he muttered.

Kate nodded mutely, equally sorry it had happened.

The holidays were almost upon them.

And it looked as if nothing but trouble lay ahead for Alex and his sweet little boys.

Then she turned so they were standing toe to toe. "No worries," she murmured back, tilting her face up to his. "I'm here for whatever you need. At least for the next three days."

Chapter Two

Alex wasn't surprised Kate had offered to help. She was the kindest and most generous woman he had ever met. "Thanks," he murmured as Tiffany's car sped onto the highway, disappearing, and another vehicle turned into the drive.

The vintage pickup truck, with the Lavender Ridge insignia on the side, rolled to a stop in front of the ranch house. His sister, Sadie, got out. A look of concern on her face, she headed straight for him and gave him a great big hug. "I passed Tiffany's car and saw her expression. I can't imagine what just happened. But we're all here for you, big bro," she said thickly. Drawing back, she continued, as fiercely protective as ever, "The whole family's got your back!"

Alex nodded appreciatively. Catching his little sister's curious glance, he introduced Kate. "This is the cowboy chef I was telling you about."

Sadie smiled and extended her hand.

Before she could say anything else, all four boys and Reckless barreled out of the front door again. She held open her arms. "Who wants Aunt Sadie to take them to school?"

Figuring it was best she stay as much out of the way as possible, Kate waved off Alex's offer to go inside and took a seat on the front porch while backpacks and lunches were gathered, car keys were exchanged and the four boys were loaded into Alex's luxury eight-passenger SUV.

Sadie took off with a jaunty wave.

Looking only slightly less stressed, Alex moved to the bottom of the porch steps and gazed up at her. Eliciting a shiver from her. He was still the same tall, sinfully sexy Texan that she remembered. All muscle. As ready for anything as ever. And head to toe gorgeous. She stared at his ruggedly chiseled features and strong masculine jaw, wishing he weren't so damned confident and imposing.

Pretending that he hadn't haunted her dreams for the past eight plus years...

Not that she had ever imagined she would see him again.

Especially since they hadn't even known each other's last names.

Never mind for a short catering gig, that would get him through a pinch, while he looked for a permanent live-in cook for the Rocking M. Instead of a travelling chef like herself. Who enjoyed the challenge of different gigs in different places, and owning her own business.

Still watching her intently, he asked, "Ready to get those contracts signed?"

She was.

Her heart racing, Kate retrieved them from the silver stream trailer that was attached to the back of her pickup.

He had been giving her a wide berth. Now, he came to stand beside her. Close enough she could see just how broad his shoulders were and feel the heat emanating from his body. She drew in another breath, taking in the scent of him, so intoxicatingly male.

Aware that she really was drawn to him, *embarrassingly so*, Kate forced a smile and took a step back.

She was not going to fantasize about what it would be like to feel the force of that much masculine confidence and testosterone. Never mind wonder what it would be like to experience the skill of his big, capable hands and sensual lips, or feel the enticing weight of his body stretched out over hers.

Not when she was here because she was being hired to do a job on the Rocking M Ranch. And then leave.

"We can go over the contracts and get them signed in the ranch dining area." With his mind on business—the way hers *should* have been—Alex escorted her up the sidewalk that led to the covered breezeway that separated two one story buildings from the main house.

As personable as she recalled him being, no matter what the circumstances, he told her, "The building on the far end was the original ranch house when I bought the place. We remodeled it, and it is now the bunkhouse where the hired hands live during the week."

"They aren't here on weekends?"

"No." He matched his steps to hers. "They all go home to their loved ones."

Nice. Jobs where you were expected to have a satisfying personal life were the best. She slanted him a curious glance. "Who usually cooks their meals?"

As he exhaled, his wide shoulders tensed, then relaxed. "A permanent ranch employee. Unfortunately, the fantastic chef we'd had for seven years decided he wanted a change and elected to go work at a big outfit in Montana. The cook that followed pretty much burnt everything he touched. The last one gave everyone on the crew food poisoning, week before last."

Kate winced. "Did you fire him?"

Alex frowned, recalling, "He quit."

Curious, she looked over at him. "Would you have fired him?" Their steps slowed as they reached the dining hall entrance.

He reached out to get the door, then held it open for her to pass. "Probably. I mean, mistakes are okay, everyone makes them, but he wasn't all that big on food safety practices, and refused to admit he had to do better in the future." Alex followed her inside the nice open space. "Which left me no choice. Had he not left voluntarily."

Kate sympathized. For bigger jobs, she had to hire temps to help her out. Most had worked out just fine, but occasionally one didn't. Which was always tough.

Alex lifted his arm in a sweeping gesture, explaining, "This middle building contains the ranch kitchen, dining hall and hang out area."

Which appeared to be one connected space, with powder rooms on either side, Kate noted.

"I'll show you the kitchen." He strode across the terrazzo floor to a galley style culinary workspace, with a commercial stove, sink, dishwasher and fridge located along the back wall, with a long stainless steel work table fronting the other.

She could see how easy it would be to set up buffet style meals and keep them at the perfect temperature in warming or cooling dishes.

"This is where you'll cook and set up dinner and breakfast for the men. Lunch will be packed up to take with them. So it needs to be ready to go as soon as they've finished breakfast."

That would make life easier for them all. "Okay."

Alex returned to the long plank table with wooden benches that could seat a dozen. He sat opposite her and Kate handed over the contracts she had prepared for the week. Which was short, because it was a holiday week. With Thanksgiving on Thursday. Which she had already been told she would not be asked to prepare.

He scanned the pages carefully. "Seven meals over three days. The Rocking M provides all food that you'll be preparing, so your business won't have any of those costs." He paused, dark brow furrowing. "It doesn't say anything about room and board being included for the duration."

Although he had generously made that offer when they'd conversed about the gig via email, Kate hadn't wanted to discuss that until she toured the ranch. As a contingency, she had made a reservation at the motel in town that could be cancelled by this evening. Staying there would require driving back out to the ranch by three thirty in the morning to prepare a hot, filling breakfast for the men as the contract required. Still…

Did she want to be underfoot 24/7?

Especially when Alex already had so much going on? "I'm not sure I would be comfortable bunking with the cowboys," she told him honestly. Although she imagined if the hired hands worked for a man like Alex, they would be perfectly polite.

"Actually, that's not an option." He signed off on the already negotiated financial terms of her standard catering agreement. "The bunkhouse is a guys-only facility. Female guests of the ranch stay in the suite on the first floor of the main house, which is located well away from the other bedrooms that are all upstairs. So not to worry. You'll have plenty of privacy if you elect to stay on the Rocking M, which is what I would advise."

His phone buzzed. "Sorry. Got to get this." He hit the keypad on his cell phone, stood and walking away from her, then began to talk. "Yes, I'm still planning to be there this morning. In about forty-five minutes… All right, see you soon."

Alex ended the call. "I have an appointment to see a Shetland pony I am thinking about gifting the boys for Christmas. So, as soon as I show you where you'll be bunking while you are here, I have to go." He walked briskly in the direction of the main house.

As they stepped into the rear door of the ranch house, passing by a large butler's pantry and the laundry room and mudroom to another hallway, Kate asked, "Any thoughts about what you want me to prepare for dinner this evening?"

He paused in front of the guest room, which was as private and well-appointed as he had said. With its own en suite bath.

Then turning back to her, he led the way out of the house and toward the dining hall again. He paused at the door of the facility where she would be working. "The fridge and freezer have plenty of food. Fix the guys whatever hearty fare you think they'll like. Just make plenty of it. There's only five of them, but you will probably be surprised at how much they will eat after working out on the ranch all day. They'll be rolling in around five for dinner."

He started to walk out. Then pivoted back, when he reached the door, as if only then realizing how abrupt he had been. His blue eyes gentled, seeming more like the co-volunteer she recalled than the man with way too much weight on his shoulders that stood before her now. "I really do want to catch up, Kate," he said softly. "So...maybe later?"

Realizing she wanted that, too, she nodded.

They had been fast friends once. Could they be so again? This time without the sexual attraction that had prohibited them from getting closer then?

Only the next three and a half days would tell.

He gave her another long, regretful look, then headed for his sister's pickup truck and left.

Alex parked his SUV, in front of the ranch house shortly before five o'clock. All four of his boys were out of the vehicle in a flash, racing for the dining hall. Trying to be first through the door, as per usual.

"I told you this was where that cook lady would be," Max

shouted, coming to a dead halt when he saw Kate standing at the buffet line she had set up on the island.

The boys' eyes widened at the big platters of pillowy biscuits and crispy fried chicken, bowls of mashed potatoes, gravy and string beans. Garden and fruit salads.

"It smells so good!" Michael observed. Behind him, the hired hands filed in, freshly showered and shaven. Slim, Buck, Rowdy, Hector and Luis looked as pleased by the spread as Alex's boys.

"Can we eat dinner in here tonight, Dad, please?" Matthew asked.

Alex looked at Kate. "There's plenty," she said with a warm encouraging smile.

Next, he turned toward the guys with an inquiring expression.

"Fine with us," Slim said.

Happy to be getting a good meal, too, Alex got the boys situated and went about fixing them all plates of the hot, delicious looking food.

When Kate held back, Michael and Max slid apart, making room on the bench between them. "You can sit here."

"Yes, please join us," Alex said, surprised by how happy he was to have her here with them. She brought a warm, feminine touch to the ranch that hadn't been there in years. Unless Sadie or his mom or one of his sisters-in-law came around, that was. And their visits here were few and far between. He was usually going to their places for family gatherings.

Kate looked touched. "All right," she acquiesced. "Just let me fix myself a plate."

As soon as she sat down, the questions started. "So where do you live when you're not doing this?" Hector asked.

Kate broke open a biscuit. "I've got an apartment in Fort Worth as my home base. But you're right—I'm not there much. At least during the warm months when people want to throw parties outdoors and feed their crews on the range. Then I am always on the road. Traveling all over the Lone Star State. Although the majority of my jobs are on ranches between here and Fort Worth, at least right now." She sent everyone an interested glance. "So what about you fellas?" she asked the cowboys. "Where do you all live?"

One by one, she got the usually reserved cowboys to tell their stories. Then the boys shared what they had done in kindergarten that day. The only person she didn't question was him. Which made sense. Since they weren't the complete strangers that everyone else was to her. Or *had* been.

By the time dessert was over, the quadruplets were yawning. Alex waited for them to thank Kate for the wonderful meal and then herded them out the door and over to the main house.

It was the happiest he had seen the Rocking M Ranch family in a long time. Because they'd had a woman in their midst.

Actually, he corrected himself thoughtfully, because they'd had Kate.

"Everything okay in here?"

Kate turned in the direction of the familiar, deep male voice. Alex was on the other side of the custom-built silver airstream trailer that served as both chuck wagon kitchen and food truck. Looking in. An evening beard rimmed his jaw and upper lip.

She had just come out of the shower a little bit ago, needing to wash off the grime of the day. Her face was bare of all makeup and her freshly shampooed hair spilled over her shoulders in damp waves. It made her feel oddly defenseless. The situation suddenly way too intimate.

"Yeah." Kate opened the door, ushering him inside. She

was wearing a pair of gray leggings, a long plaid flannel tunic that served as a sleep shirt and shearling lined red moccasins that kept her feet nice and toasty. Even on chilly evenings like this.

He shut the door behind him. Aware he was too tall to stand in there comfortably, she gestured for him to have a seat on the cushioned banquet that lined one end of the silver stream. "I was just making some instant cocoa."

He settled at one end of the table. "You could have done that in the ranch house kitchen."

She shrugged, her pulse kicking up a notch. Then admitted reluctantly, "I didn't want to intrude."

Her sensual lips curved into a ghost of a smile. He tilted his head. "You wouldn't be."

Kate nodded briefly, doing her best to contain a blush. "You want some?" She reached for another packet, showing him there was plenty of the gourmet mix to be had.

"Sure."

It was a lovely evening and the view of the Rocking M was spectacular. Stars gleamed in the black velvet sky overhead, and moonlight spilled over the neatly fenced pastures that were as meticulously kept as the sprawling ranch house, and new state of the art barns and stables. "I was going to sit on the front porch of the ranch house and drink it," she continued.

He watched her add steamed milk and a dash of vanilla to the contents of the packet, instead of the usual water most people used. The intoxicatingly smell of rich chocolate filled the trailer. "I thought you would have been in bed by now." Their fingers brushed as she handed him his mug.

She went about making herself a mug of the doctored confection, too. Then got an aerosol can out of the fridge and added generous amounts of whipped cream and a sprinkle of cocoa powder to both their drinks. She paused to put the can back in the fridge. "I'm too wound up to sleep."

Kate reached for her knee-length coat, slipping it on. He rose graciously, grabbed his mug and held the door for her. "Any particular reason why?"

Yes, she thought. *You. Seeing you again after all these years. Finding out the old chemistry that could easily have gotten us both in trouble, still existed, strong as ever. And that you were one of the Texas McCabes. Father to four adorable sons. Single. Successful.*

And way, way too attractive to me.

It was a good thing her stint at the Rocking M Ranch was brief. She could not share close quarters with him for long, not without something hot and sexy and irresponsible happening, anyway.

She walked with him up the steps of the house to the front porch. He slipped inside just long enough to grab a soft leather jacket, then came back out and joined her on the three-person glider.

Aware she hadn't answered his question yet, she said, "I guess I have become more of a night person since I started my catering business."

He tilted his head, his gaze drifting over her lazily, creating little sparks of awareness. "Most parties occur later in the day?"

"Yeah. Unlike the work around here, I guess."

He flashed her an appreciative grin. "The cocoa's great by the way. As was dinner."

"Thank you." It was always nice to know her efforts had hit the mark.

"So catch me up. Last time I saw you, eight years ago, you were engaged and planning to backpack all over Europe before going to grad school to get your MBA. What happened?"

Another failed romance, she thought ruefully, tracing the rim of her mug before taking a sip. "Fiancé number one—Chad...the guy I was with during Inga—got cold feet while we were in Europe. He said he wasn't ready to get married, or at least not to me, and we broke up. So I went to business school, graduated and worked as an executive." *At my parents' company.* "Hated the corporate life, and being locked inside an office at a computer all day. Meanwhile, my parents were pushing me to marry the son of a colleague of theirs, who I met at business school, and was also an executive."

"And did you?"

"No. But I did let him sweep me off my feet, briefly. And said yes to his proposal. Had I not seen the prenup he was planning to ask me to sign and realized that Thaddeus and I getting hitched was the key to our parents' two retail businesses merging..." *A way to expand and keep both businesses in the family,* "Who knows what might have happened."

"So you didn't want any part of that and broke up."

"Yes." Kate's relief over that was marred by the emotional fallout. She looked over at Alex and saw the understanding and compassion she had wanted from her own family. "My parents still haven't forgiven me. They thought I was a romantic fool. That I should just forget about the infatuation stage, which never lasts longer than six months anyway, and focus on building a future with someone who can give me a good life."

Alex's brow furrowed. Something akin to pity appeared in his blue eyes. "Meaning money?"

Kate sighed. "More like shared goals and values that lead to lasting financial stability. Anyway, I rejected all that at first. But then I got to thinking..." She sipped her cocoa, letting the dark chocolate flavor soothe her.

"I had two wildly romantic relationships. Both flamed

out. Mostly because my two exes and I didn't want the same things in life. I wanted stability and someone I could count on in my life. Work that brought joy to me and the people around me, and the kind of big, loving family I never had growing up. Ultimately, in both situations—with Chad and Thaddeus—it is good we broke up because neither relationship would have lasted over the long haul."

He nodded, then slowly ravished her with his gaze, as if he found her completely irresistible. "I can see that."

The question was, what did he *want?*

She pushed the inappropriate thought away.

His romantic needs and wants were none of her business. Unless he chose to share them with her. And he hadn't thus far.

Kate forced her mind back to the here and now. "So now I have my own catering business. And even though I am not making the kind of money I once did, I am a whole lot happier."

His smile turned soft. Approving. "I can see that."

Trying not to think how good it was to have his support, Kate said, "So what about you? Was Tiffany the same person you were engaged to during Hurricane Inga, when we met?"

Impossible, really, to imagine the kindhearted Alex with the impossibly cruel Old Money heiress from her nightmarish high school years.

"Yes."

Without warning, the front door opened. The quadruplets came tumbling out in their pajamas, all rubbing their eyes and crying. Alex jumped up, rushing to their rescue.

"Dad, I had a bad d-d-dream!" Michael sobbed loudly. His brothers cried, too. "That mean mommy t-t-take-ed us away!"

"That's not going to happen," Alex soothed, gathering his four sons close. He sent Kate a brief, apologetic glance over their heads. She nodded, letting him know she understood. His priorities were with his boys—they had to be. Then she watched as he ushered his children inside the ranch house, where she knew their beloved sheepdog waited to console them, too.

Kate had just finished with the breakfast dishes when she received a text from Alex.

I know breakfast for me and the boys at the main house wasn't part of the contract. Possible to add it this morning?

Sure, she texted back. When did you want me to come over?

ASAP.

Be right there.

Alex and his sons were gathered in the kitchen. All four boys had puffy eyes—as if they had been either up or crying most of the night—and exceedingly glum expressions.

Alex looked worn out.

Her heart went out to them all. Figuring now was *not* the time to get an update about what had been going on, however, Kate set down the box of ingredients she'd brought with her and, getting straight to work, asked cheerfully, "Who wants breakfast?"

Still looking pouty, but interested in food nevertheless, Marty vaulted up onto a stool at the island. "I want pancakes!"

Appearing equally hungry, his brothers followed suit, all watching curiously as Kate broke eggs into a mixing bowl and began to assemble the batter.

Alex began to relax, appearing relieved to have her there. Imagining how challenging it must be to care for his five-year-old quadruplets on his own, Kate sent him an encouraging look. *Not to worry, cowboy. I've got this.*

He nodded, getting her message, and set about making a fresh pot of coffee for the adults.

Alex's stove had a built-in griddle in the middle, so she turned that on to preheat, too. Then set bowls of blueberries, chopped pecans, banana slices and chocolate and vanilla chips, where all the boys could see them.

"Time to place your order, guys!" She waved her hand over the assembled add-ins, like the experienced short order chef she was. "Any of this stuff look good to you? 'Cause I can put whatever you want in your flapjacks. Or make them plain, if you want them that way, too."

For a moment, all was silent.

"I'll take blueberry pecan," Alex said.

"Coming right up!" She added his to the griddle, then went down the line with his boys. Soon, she had orders for double chip, blueberry only, banana only and chocolate chip.

Alex poured glasses of milk and brought out the butter, syrup, confectioner's sugar and whipped cream.

By the time their plates were in front of them, the boys seemed to have forgotten all about their troubles. They dug in along with their dad. All eating voraciously.

"Aren't you going to eat?" Alex asked.

Thinking about how satisfying it would be to do this for the handsome rancher and his boys every morning, Kate poured herself a cup of coffee and lounged against the counter. "Already did. The crew insisted I join them, since I am 'temporarily part of the Rocking M team.'"

Michael finished his short stack. He pushed his plate away from him.

"What do you say?" Alex asked gently.

"Thank you, Kate."

The little boy's sincerity was as genuine as his tired smile.

He turned back to his dad. "Do we still get to stay home from school today?"

"Yes," Alex said. "You do."

Kate accepted thanks from the other three boys, while their dad went off to call the school to let them know the boys weren't coming in.

With their tummies full, all four kids were fading fast. Matthew yawned, "Can we watch TV, Dad?"

Alex nodded. "I'll turn it on for you."

Abruptly, Max was by her side. He took her hand in his. Held it fiercely. "Come and watch with us," he said.

Kate wanted to.

But...this was definitely not part of the contract. Not sure how Alex would feel, she turned to him.

He nodded imploringly.

Not about to do anything that would propel his children into a state of unhappiness again, after all they had been through in the last twenty four hours, Kate let Max lead her to the large U-shaped sectional sofa. He swept up a stuffed animal and snuggled next to her. Matthew was on her other side. Then Michael and Marty brought Alex over to sit with them, too. Soon all six of them were cuddled together. Looking as weary as everyone else in the family, Reckless curled up at their feet.

Alex turned on the TV mounted above the fireplace. An animated show featuring talking dogs appeared on the screen. More yawns and fiercely blinking eyes followed. One by one, each of the boys fell into exhausted sleep.

And Kate finally knew—this was what it would feel like if she ever had that big, complicated, loving family she had always wanted.

Which was why she had to extricate herself from this situation as soon as possible. Before she got even more emotionally entangled.

Chapter Three

Alex knew he had been taking advantage by calling Kate over to the house the way he had. She didn't seem to mind. But that didn't necessarily mean she was okay with it, either. Especially when he caught the somewhat troubled expression on her face as she followed his lead and eased away from the sleeping children on the sectional.

When they were out of earshot, she said, "I'll get the dishes cleaned up and be out of your way in no time."

So. She *had* thought he had crossed the line this morning. Damn. He needed to make it up to her, fast. He could start by being as self-sufficient as a single dad was supposed to be, and he usually was. But that was before Tiffany had barnstormed back into his life.

He flashed Kate an apologetic smile. "You don't have to do that."

She remained perfectly still.

He lifted a hand. "It was enough you came over here to make the pancakes."

An even more awkward silence stretched between them. "Why did you need me to do that?" she asked softly, a myriad of emotions filtering over her face.

Because, in that second, oddly enough, I needed you and only you. Figuring she really wouldn't want to hear that particular nugget of truth, he offered a one-shouldered shrug.

"I was desperate for a change of pace, I guess. Something to help them forget their nightmares last night." And he was happy to see that spending time with Kate had quickly put the kids in a better frame of mind. It was like she was the kind of mother that they needed, had *always* needed.

Kate came closer, her amber eyes full of compassion and maternal concern. "They all had bad dreams?"

Alex noted she still smelled like the lavender soap he kept stocked in the guest bathroom. "Multiples are so close, when one hurts, they *all* hurt." He stacked the sticky plates with the silverware on top and carried them over to the sink. Then after rinsing off his hands, he returned to the table to put the small amount of leftover food away.

Kate watched for a moment, then, apparently unable to help herself, began to pitch in, too. "Anyway, whenever they started to fall back to sleep last night, one of them would wake up crying, and then the others woke and started sobbing, too."

She spritzed cleaner on the island and wiped it with paper towels. "And you couldn't comfort them." It was more a guess than a question.

Reckless wandered in, went straight to Kate to be petted, then ventured over to his water bowl.

"Not as much as they needed, apparently." Alex watched as Kate moved around to clean every speck of the granite island, her motions both graceful and purposeful.

He let out a huff of frustration.

"Anyway, I thought a woman's touch just might do the trick, but they didn't want to go and see their grandmother."

Their go-to person for female comfort since they had been born.

"Even though it was only seven a.m. and my mom wouldn't have left for work yet."

Kate sent him a curious glance. "What did they want then?"

Appreciating her willingness to talk about this, Alex cleaned the griddle on the center of the stove while Kate began loading the dishwasher. "To stay here and have breakfast with you and the fellas, like last night."

"Except the cowboys eat at four-thirty, and were already gone."

"Which of course made them more furious and out of sorts. They said I should've woken them up, because," he mimicked their sulky voices, "they don't want to miss it when you're here."

Kate paused, clearly pleased. "They really said that?"

Alex returned her smile. "They really did. Anyway, my mom is always telling me I need to think about putting myself out there and getting married again, because the boys and I need a woman in our life."

She studied him as if trying to decide how much further she wanted this discussion to go. "You don't want to do that?"

He felt the barriers go up around his heart. "I don't know if I could go through another divorce. Never mind put the boys through one," he told Kate honestly.

Sighing wearily, he went over to get another cup of coffee. Gestured to see if she wanted one. She shook her head. "But, on the other hand, my mom is probably right," he said, as he poured steaming coffee into his mug, before lounging against the opposite counter and facing her. "We do need a woman's loving touch around here. And the boys would benefit greatly from having a mom who really cared about them."

All he'd had to do was see how they had responded to Kate, as opposed to Tiffany, to know that.

She studied him for a long moment. "It shouldn't be that

hard to find a wife, if you choose to go that route. You're attractive, single and the boys are freaking adorable."

He chose to focus on what she'd said about his kids, not him. "You think my boys are adorable?"

She squinted at him like that was the stupidest question ever. "OMG...*yes*! Who wouldn't?"

Deciding the coffee had been set too long on the warmer, Alex put his cup aside. The sludgy taste still in his mouth, he rummaged around in the catch-all drawer for a roll of mints. Finding one, he said, "Well, lots of people, actually. Especially when they misbehave in the grocery store."

Kate rolled her eyes and took one of the peppermints he offered. "Well, then those people are idiots. Of course the boys will have their moments. And act out from time to time. It's their only way of expressing their emotions when they are truly upset, after all. And let's face it, since Tiffany came back on the scene, demanding they go with her for the Christmas holiday, they've had plenty to be upset about."

"You don't think she should have a turn?" Alex asked curiously. He was fully aware a lot of people, including some Texas family court judges, would automatically take the mother's side.

But apparently, Kate was not one of them.

She folded her arms in front of her. "Not until she's earned one, no."

Realizing she was starting to get way too involved in a situation that she didn't belong in, Kate lifted a staying hand before Alex could ask her anything more. "Listen, I'm sorry for giving my two cents. I shouldn't have."

He shrugged, looking as intrigued by her as she was by him. "It's okay. I asked."

And he shouldn't have done that, either, Kate thought.

Not when the boundaries of their professional relationship were beginning to blur a little too intimately, just the way they had during Hurricane Inga. Whatever this was hadn't worked out then. And it wouldn't work out now. She needed to remember that before she jumped in to help him and his boys and ended up getting her heart broken.

And it would happen, because his was the kind of family she had always dreamed of.

She forced an officious smile, pretending a tranquility she couldn't begin to feel. "I promised the cowboys I'd make Tex-Mex for dinner, so I better get a move on."

He nodded, his expression suddenly inscrutable. "Thanks for helping," he said.

The rest of the day passed swiftly.

Alex texted mid-afternoon to ask if it would be okay to include his parents, himself and the boys in the crew dinner that evening. Would there be enough food? Something not too spicy for his kids to eat?

Kate assured him there would be, then hustled to put together kid-friendly chicken and cheese quesadillas, sliced veggies with ranch dip and fruit cups to go along with the big pans of jicama salad, red and green enchiladas and the rice and refried beans she had already made.

At five o'clock, everyone piled in to the dining hall.

The kids seemed happy to be with all the cowboys. And their grandparents. And the ranch hands dug into the food with zeal. Chowing down on the main courses and then lingering over the tres leches cake as well as the sopapillas with honey that she made especially for the boys.

Only when the meal was winding down, and Mitzy and Chase took the kids back to the main house, did the cowboys ask to speak to Alex outside.

Trying not to wonder what had them suddenly looking so grim, Kate focused on cleanup.

She was halfway done when the men filed back in.

"We'll take over here," Rowdy told Kate. He and the other four hired hands looked soberly at Alex. "The boss has something he wants to talk to you about."

With a formal nod, Alex gestured to Kate, indicating she should accompany him. Together, they walked outside, into the breezeway that connected the main house from the ranch kitchen and dining hall.

"What's up?" she asked, feeling suddenly nervous. Even though the men seemed to enjoy the feast she'd prepared, was there something wrong with it? Had the food been too hot? Not spicy enough? Worse, not the variety of Tex-Mex the guys had expected?

Alex stood, legs braced apart, arms folded over his chest. In that instant, he looked like one of the Titans of Laramie County. "You're the best chef we've ever had at the Rocking M."

Her heart pounded. "Really? That's good to hear. Then what's the problem...?"

"The fellas don't want you to leave tomorrow evening. And neither do I."

Her mouth was so dry she could barely speak. "That's very flattering, but—"

Disappointment came and went in his blue eyes.

Kate realized that he had been expecting her to turn him down, while the men who worked for him expected him to find a way to keep her on.

Poor guy. More stress and pressure heaped on him when he least needed it!

"I get it," he said brusquely. "You have a traveling chef business to run..."

"Right. Even though I'm not all that busy this time of year, the gigs will pick up, come February. And I'll likely have a full plate all through the spring, summer and early fall, if last year was any indication."

He listened to everything she was saying, then blurted, "Would you consider extending your contract with the ranch and staying on another week? Or better yet, till December 23, when the cowboys head home for the holidays?"

December, here? With Alex and his boys and all the cowboys?

An enticing proposition.

His glance narrowed. "That would give me more time to find a permanent chef."

She understood the bind he was in. Plus, it was hard for her not to help someone in need. "Same hours?"

He nodded. "Room and board and anything else you require included. Just name it. If you help me out, I'll throw in a Christmas bonus of twenty-five percent, too."

Kate laughed and shook her head. She was used to appreciative clients, good online reviews and repeat bookings. But this offer was hands down the best one she'd had so far! "You must really want me to stay."

His sensual lips compressed. "We all do." Arms still folded, he leaned toward her persuasively. "So what do you say? Will you continue to help us out?"

Kate knew the smart thing to do would be to pack up her things, cut ties with Alex the way she had years before and head out tomorrow evening as planned.

But the thought of cooking for all the residents of the Rocking M Ranch and having a warm and inviting place to stay, at least during the lead up to the loneliest holidays of the year, tugged at her heartstrings. Before she knew it, she was nodding back at him. "Yes. I'll be happy to stay."

* * *

Wednesday was as busy as expected. Telling himself he hadn't made a mistake by furthering his business relationship with Kate, when what he really wanted was to pursue something of a more *personal* nature, Alex stopped by the ranch dining hall to drop off the signed extension to their contract that Kate had emailed him the previous evening.

"Daddy said you're staying until almost Christmas!" Michael said happily. His siblings grinned in delight, too.

Kate gathered them into her arms for a group hug. "I am."

"Yay!" The boys danced around, accepting the frosted pumpkin cookies she had baked for them.

Alex would have liked to stay and hang out with her, too. Unfortunately, he had a lot to do. Which meant they had to get a move on. Kate smiled as Alex shooed them out the door. "You-all have fun today!" she called after them.

Alex drove his sons to his parents' ranch, the Knotty Pine, for a day with their cousins. When he returned, he caught up with the cowboys and worked to make sure all the cattle were healthy and the winter feed was put out.

Anxious to be on their way to their various destinations for the Thanksgiving holiday, the cowboys had elected to take their dinners packed, for the road. By the time Alex had showered and changed, all their pickup trucks were gone and Kate was in the ranch kitchen, tidying up.

Unlike the last time he had seen her, she seemed exhausted, which wasn't surprising given the hours she had been keeping since arriving at the Rocking M. But, he noted with a pang, she also seemed depressed. Like she expected tomorrow's festivities to be anything but joyous for her.

As if feeling his sympathy, she straightened, slipping back into business mode. "I forgot to ask. Did you and the boys want brisket sandwiches, too?"

Taken aback by her cool tone, Alex shook his head. He had hoped they were starting to reconnect. That she might be ready to move on from her failed engagements. Maybe even take a chance on him?

He swallowed hard. Yeah, this situation was…complicated. He knew they both had baggage—being a good dad to his kids would *always* be his first priority—but there was something raw and palpable between the two of them. Was he crazy to think Kate felt it too…? Even after all these years?

As if reading his mind, she blew out an annoyed breath. Letting him know with a glance that she wasn't the kind of woman who could handle sex with no strings.

He backed off reluctantly, all Texas gentleman once again. If he wanted her—and he did, he realized—then two things were going to have to happen. First, he was going to have to be patient. And second? It was going to have to *mean* something. "The kids are playing with their cousins. They won't be back until later."

"Right." She seemed to recall the day before Thanksgiving was a school holiday.

"They'll eat dinner at my mom and dad's. But if there's extra, sure, I'd love a sandwich for later."

She took the platter of sliced beef out of the fridge and reached for the rolls. "Coming right up."

He lounged against the counter, enjoying the graceful way she moved around the kitchen. The manner in which she really seemed to enjoy what she was doing.

How could her family not see this was what she was born to do? And expect her to enter a marriage based on a business merger with a guy who was never really going to love her? Or care for her, in the way that he would, if she were his wife…

Not, Alex swiftly derailed his thoughts, that he planned

to tie the knot again. One miserable union had been enough. Plus, he had his boys' happiness to consider.

In an effort to get the conversation—and his thoughts—back on track, he asked, "What about your holiday plans? I realized I never asked when you were planning to leave to see your family."

Kate glanced up with a stricken look. Realizing he had just stepped in it, he winced. Clearly this was a sore subject for her. He scrambled for a way to rectify the situation, but then she shrugged amiably, letting him off the hook.

"No plans, exactly." She paused to layer meat onto the sub-style roll. "My parents are retail executives. November and December are incredibly busy for them. So we've never really done much to celebrate the holidays."

That sounded bleak, Alex couldn't help but think. "But you have dinner together on Thanksgiving, surely. With extended family?"

Kate shook her head matter-of-factly, as if it were no big deal. "I'm an only child, as are both my folks. When I was younger, they were usually at the store, prepping for Black Friday sales. And then when their roles in the business began to really expand, they were busy reviewing sales figures and trying to find ways to increase profits, and so on. So until I was seven, I usually spent any time I wasn't in school with my maternal grandmother and we went to a cafeteria near her house for the buffet for all our holiday dinners. Which was pretty nice, actually," she admitted with a fond smile. She straightened, inhaling, "After she passed, I stayed with sitters, and Thanksgiving and Christmas dinners were just Chinese takeout, delivered, whenever my parents did get home."

He could hardly imagine it. Especially when compared to the festivities his family put on. "And that's still what your folks do?" he asked, curious.

She wrapped his sandwich, abruptly looking weary to the bone. "Work like crazy through the holidays? And focus on their own dreams and ambitions? Yes." A hint of bitterness and hurt edged her low tone.

It was all he could do not to cross the room and pull her into his arms, hold her close. Offer what comfort he could. He knew—from his failed marriage—what it was like when family let you down. Staying where he was, with effort, he said quietly, "I'm sorry."

She shrugged and put the food away. Evidently done talking about her family situation.

He could hardly blame her for that, either.

"So what do *you* usually do for the holidays, then?" he asked, more curious than ever.

Letting out a slow breath, she walked over to give him his wrapped sandwich. Being careful not to touch hands in the process. "If I'm seeing someone, I spend it with him."

Good opening. "Are you currently dating anyone?" he asked gruffly, acutely aware that a beautiful, kind, hardworking woman like her wasn't going to be single forever. She was a real catch, and any man would be lucky to have her.

Including him?

"No boyfriends."

Well, that at least was good news. Great news, actually. Glad they were two equally empowered business owners, under contract with each other, and not boss and employee, which would have made asking her out unacceptable, he asked, "So. No plans for tomorrow…?"

"Except for driving back to my apartment in Fort Worth?" She lifted her chin, and in that moment, he sensed the wall around her heart go back up, as resentment flared in her pretty amber gaze. Maybe because she seemed to think he was pitying her?

Inhaling deeply, she squared her slender shoulders before retorting, "Not to worry, cowboy. It's a big city. I'll find something holiday-ish to do. And then come back Sunday."

He hated the idea of her all alone. And more importantly still, he wanted her with him.

He spread his hands wide. "Or you could just stay here and spend Thanksgiving with me and the boys and my family," he said.

Chapter Four

Kate stared at Alex, momentarily speechless. "You don't have to do that," she said finally. "Unless...you're asking me to *cater* the dinner...?" Which would put an entirely different spin on it.

He shook his head, letting her know, with exasperation in his mesmerizing blue eyes, how far off her assumption was. "The invitation is purely social," he corrected. "The kind I would have given you years ago, when we first met, had we not been involved with other people at the time."

Kate tensed. She went to turn off the lights in the kitchen, then grabbed her phone and headed toward him. "What will your family think?" In her experience, holidays were difficult to maneuver, in one way or another, in most every clan. So she could only imagine what kind of reception she might receive if he brought a last minute guest to the dinner.

He walked with her to the dining hall exit. "They love meeting and making new friends. Same as me."

Relieved, Kate felt herself begin to relax. Even as the hopelessly romantic part of her was disappointed the gesture didn't mean more than that. But then, what had she expected? They were former acquaintances, whose businesses were under contract. Nothing more. "Um... Sure. I'd love to go." She forced herself to feel good about the casual invitation. And he was right. It had to be better than spending the holiday alone.

She paused as he reached for the door. "Where are the festivities going to be held?"

Alex held the door so she could walk through it onto the breezeway. "My parents ranch, the Knotty Pine. It's about fifteen minutes or so from here. You can ride with me and the boys."

Sounded simple and uncomplicated enough. She had met Mitzy and Chase McCabe, the other evening. They were the epitome of the happily married couple who doted on their children and grandchildren. She'd also met Sadie, Alex's sister, who was a delight. She imagined everyone else in the family was just as charming.

Beginning to feel excited about the gathering, she asked, "Is there anything I can bring?"

He shook his head and held the door that led into the main house. "My mom will have the menu covered. Although I have to warn you, it'll be our entire immediate family—as well as a few other friends—which will probably number at least thirty guests. So when it comes to getting dinner ready to serve, it's all hands on deck."

Alex wasn't kidding, Kate found out the next day.

The turkeys and hams were being smoked on outdoor grills manned by Alex's father and his attorney-brother Gabe. Kate watched with amusement as another one of his siblings, Zach—a well-respected physician—was riding herd on his three preschool-age triplets that he shared with his cardiologist wife, Claire. Alex helped out by leading the triplets and his four kindergarteners in a series of yard games that enthralled and entertained them all. Meanwhile, Alex's third brother, Joe, was talking to a few friends and watching over his and Ellie's two toddlers, Jenni and Jaime, in the family room.

In the kitchen, Mitzy was in charge.

Never one to stand around idle, Kate volunteered to dice celery and onion for the stuffing.

"So how does your business work?" Ellie, who owned the Sugar Love bakery in town, asked.

"I know you're filling in for the ranch cook at the Rocking M until Alex can find someone to take the job permanently," Claire said while crumbling cornbread into big bowls.

"But do you have a set area of the state where you work, or just go from place to place, as requested?" Sadie, who had recently started a lavender farm of her own, chimed in while adding thyme and sage to the mixture of butter and chicken broth simmering on the stove.

Enjoying the female camaraderie and the laid-back atmosphere, Kate explained, "Most of my gigs have been at ranches around Dallas and Fort Worth, although I'm starting to do a few roundups and small rodeos in the Panhandle and west Texas, too."

Mitzy smiled. "Do you cook out of your silver stream?"

Kate nodded. "Unless the party-givers have a vintage chuck wagon or big outdoor fire pit. Then I'll use that. But most of the time, the hosts want me to take my trailer to the site of the party so we'll have refrigeration for the items that need it. Not to mention, I can do much of the cooking and food prep in air conditioning without worrying about spoilage."

Mitzy smiled again. "Sounds challenging."

It could be. And it was nice to be respected and admired for what she did. Instead of asked why she wasn't putting her business school degree and corporate and retail experience to better use.

Without warning, Alex breezed in. He put his hands on his waist and comically surveyed Kate up and down. "Isn't this a familiar sight."

Every female eyebrow lifted. "Us cooking?" his sister asked drolly.

Looking happier and more relaxed than she had seen him

since they had reconnected mere days before, Alex shook his head, correcting, "Kate in the thick of things." He went straight to the fridge, retrieving seven juice boxes with straws attached.

He stationed himself next to Kate. Sort of like they were a couple. "You all should have seen her during Hurricane Inga, cooking up a storm for the victims for three days straight." His glance swept over her admiringly before returning to linger on her face. "She was quite the heroine."

Kate felt herself flush at the memory of that unforgettable experience they'd shared together. He'd been a sight, too, looking like a real Western cowboy in a long yellow rain slicker, Resistol and boots. Not to mention ruggedly handsome enough to make all the single women swoon!

But he hadn't seemed to notice anyone but her back then.

Nor she anyone but him.

Which had proved a problem for both of them, since they had both been otherwise engaged.

Pushing away the desire she had felt then, *and now*, she pointed out as serenely as possible, "You helped out at the shelter, too." She also doubted he had boasted about it. The way he had just bragged about her.

Wanting everyone to know what a hero he had been as well, she turned back to his family and said, "If it hadn't been for Alex and his buddies, taking their pickup trucks around to collect the donated food, the volunteer chefs and I wouldn't have had anything to prepare."

The grooves on either side of his sensual lips deepened. He seemed to be remembering things, too. "I guess it was a joint effort," he allowed finally.

"And a life-changing time," Kate couldn't help but admit with a grateful sigh. "At least for me."

That crisis had changed her. For the better.

"Me, too," Alex murmured thickly. Their glances meshed. Reminding her how intensely emotional those three days had been for everyone, storm victims and helpers alike.

"Sounds that way..." Mitzy murmured with the approval of a veteran social worker who had spent her life helping others.

Sadie's phone buzzed. She pulled it out of her pocket and looked at the screen. Shoulders slumping in disappointment, she pressed the end button and slid it back in her pocket.

"No word from Will yet?" Ellie asked sympathetically.

Sadie shook her head.

Silence fell.

Alex walked over to put a comforting arm around his only sister. "I'm sure he'll call if he can," he murmured.

"Exactly," Sadie said, a mixture of sorrow and defeat in her low tone. Tears filling her eyes, she informed everyone, "I'm going out to see if Dad and Gabe need anything..."

Ellie stopped what she was doing. Lifted a hand. "I'll go," she said, hurrying after her sister-in-law.

Kate glanced at Alex, wondering what was going on. His lips thinned. "Will is a soldier with the Special Forces. He's deployed at the moment. No one knows where, exactly. Or what he is doing. Or when he will be coming home."

"Just that his mission is likely dangerous," Kate guessed, admiring the courage and sacrifice the military made to keep the country and its citizens safe.

Mitzy nodded, looking as worried about Will as her only daughter was. She brought two pans of roasting sweet potatoes out of the oven to cool.

Claire helped mix all the stuffing ingredients. "Ellie's husband, Joe, had a career in the Special Forces, too, before he left to raise his kids and start a climbing gym here," she explained upon seeing Kate's concerned expression. "Since she went through that herself for twelve long years, she gets what it's like to have someone you care deeply about ostensibly in harm's way." Claire paused, reflecting. "So I'm sure she'll be able to make Sadie feel better."

Kate imagined that was so, especially if Ellie had weathered that kind of relationship challenge herself. "So Will and Sadie are a couple?" Kate murmured, buttering four large casserole dishes.

A shake of heads, all around. "No. Just very good friends," Mitzy said. "Since Will and Joe went to basic training together when they were both eighteen. And we all got to know and love Will, too."

Kate supposed that made sense, although in her opinion Sadie wasn't acting as if she and Will were just family friends. It seemed like way more than that, she thought as she watched Alex walk back out, juice boxes for the kids in hand. But then again, what did she really know about the kind of deep and everlasting ties the members of the McCabe clan had with the people they cared about? For all intents and purposes, they were strangers to her. So she shouldn't jump to conclusions about Will and Sadie without knowing all the facts.

Even if her gut was telling her there was much more to their story than the family was letting on.

She had no more time to think about it, though, as work on the sweet potato casseroles assembly began.

The pecan crusted delicacies were just being put in the second oven when a ruckus could be heard. Seconds later, Alex's four boys came dashing in the kitchen. They stopped just short of Kate. Marty and Matthew took hold of her hands. "Kate! You gotta come with us and see the turkeys we made yesterday!" Max exclaimed.

Michael nodded seriously. "Grandma wrote names on all of them, and they're all on the table! To tell us where to sit!"

Mitzy smiled in agreement. "The Thanksgiving place cards are a sight to behold."

Claire's triplets appeared. Fellow artists Oliver, Andrew and Isabella all urging the same.

Kate looked at Mitzy, not wanting to bail on the cooking any more than she wanted to disappoint the kids. "Go," the older woman shooed her in the direction of the great room where the tables for thirty had been set up. Her smile widened. "The rest of us have already seen them, and I have a feeling Alex and Zach would appreciate the kiddo-wrangling assistance."

As it happened, the kids had not exaggerated. The artwork was incredible. As was the holiday meal. The company. And the feeling of deep familial love and camaraderie.

So much so that Kate was a little reluctant to have to call it a night at just 7:00 p.m. But the kids were fading fast, and it didn't take an experienced parent to see that Alex was anxious to get them home and in bed, before they reached the meltdown stage that always came when kids were vastly overtired.

"Thank you so much for having me," Kate told Mitzy and Chase, who accompanied them to the door. She received hugs from them both.

"You're welcome anytime," Mitzy said.

Alex's dad winked. "And maybe next time you won't have to help do quite so many dishes."

She knew Chase was exaggerating, since literally every adult had pitched in to help with the cleanup, which had made it go very quickly.

Kate smiled back. "My pleasure. And thanks again." She couldn't remember when she had ever felt so much like family. Even with her own small clan.

She and Alex escorted the boys down the drive to his SUV.

Together, they helped the kids climb into their safety seats and get securely buckled in.

Once that was accomplished, she and Alex settled into their seats in the front. He waggled his brows. "Your mission, should you choose to accept it," he teased, with a telltale glance in the rearview mirror behind them, is to keep our little kiddos from falling asleep during the drive home."

Our little kiddos.

He was speaking collectively. She knew that. Still, it made her think what it would be like if they were a happy family of six. Heading home after a wonderful holiday meal with his big loving clan.

Wouldn't that be a lot to be thankful for?

Alex's gaze narrowed on her. Seeming surprised she hadn't answered automatically, the way she usually did. "You up for it?" he asked cheerfully.

"Of course." She turned to look at the boys, who were already on the cusp of sleep, yawning and rubbing their eyes. "Who wants to play the *My Favorite Thanksgiving Memories* game, with me…?"

That one question was all it took to ignite their competitive spirit. By the time Alex parked in front of the Rocking M's ranch house, they had pretty much covered everything important from the day. From their perspective, anyway.

"What was your favorite kind of pie, Kate?" Michael asked as Kate hopped out to help the boys get out of the SUV, leaving her bag in the floor well.

"Pecan, I think."

"Daddy, what is yours?" Max inquired.

Alex made a comically greedy face. "Every kind!" he said, in a way that made his boys all laugh uproariously.

Kate's phone rang.

She pulled it out of her pocket and looked at the screen, stunned by what she saw.

"Everything okay?" Alex asked.

Honestly, she had no idea.

"It's my parents," Kate said, still staring at the caller ID in disbelief. They rarely called her, never mind early on the eve of the biggest retail day of the year…when their attention was always focused solely on business.

Her festive mood fading, she looked back at Alex. Abruptly feeling anything but carefree. Which was a shame because he and his boys, and the entire McCabe clan, had made her feel so darn good today… Frowning, she said, "I'm sorry. I have to take this call."

Chapter Five

Kate wasn't sure what she expected her parents to say when she rushed down the porch steps to take their FaceTime call, but definitely *not* this.

"Katherine, please, listen to us," her father said.

He and her mother were in the executive suite in downtown Houston. Both dressed in stylish business clothing.

"I know what you're thinking, but it's not too late!" her mom implored. "Thaddeus is still very interested in you!"

So everyone kept telling her. *All their mutual friends*. Who weren't really her friends anymore, but his, ever since she had ended their engagement and struck out on a non-corporate business path. *His parents. Hers*. "And the merger?" Kate retorted wearily as she unlocked the door to her chef's trailer, switched on the light and climbed inside.

"Are you working tonight, too?" her dad asked as she settled onto the leather banquette near the front, where she wrote out menus and bills and took her breaks.

"No. I had dinner with friends and just got back."

"Perfect," her mother murmured, and then without missing a beat, continued to push for what they wanted. By the time the call ended fifteen minutes later, Kate was exhausted.

She slid her phone back in her pocket and stepped out of her silver stream. Just in time to see Alex walk out the front door, Reckless by his side, his own cell pressed to his ear. He had a grim expression on his face that matched her own mood.

Not wanting to disturb him, she went toward his SUV. Finding the passenger door unlocked, she opened it up and removed her bag from the front floor well of his silver Lincoln Navigator.

Seconds later, he ended his call and strode down the front steps toward her while Reckless trotted happily over to greet her as well. As she knelt to pet the cheerful sheepdog, Alex went to the rear of the vehicle, his expression still unusually harried, and opened up the cargo hatch. She saw him move a blanket aside and lift the plastic superstore sack that had been underneath.

Purchase in hand, he headed back toward her.

"Everything okay?" Kate asked.

Alex shrugged, his emotions still under wraps. "That was Gabe. He wanted to know if anything else had happened with Tiffany since she was here on Monday."

A whisper of unease ran through Kate. She had known the silence from her old nemesis was too good to be true. "Has it?" she asked warily.

He shook his head, keeping a watchful eye on Reckless as he headed off into the far corner of the yard, sniffing. "No."

Alex walked up to sit on the comfortable porch furniture. He dropped the sack on the table beside him. "Is that a good sign or a bad sign?" she asked as she joined him. Aware there was still much she didn't know about the situation and his former marriage.

He flexed his broad shoulders. "Hopefully good, if she got a better offer for the upcoming holidays. Say a month with friends in a yacht on the French Riviera or a villa on Lake Como."

Kate could picture that. It was the woman's MO after all. Tiffany would definitely opt for luxury for as long as it lasted.

She took a seat on the other end of the glider, feeling herself begin to relax, yet still had to ask, "Then why did she come here last Monday and make such a scene?"

Alex ran a hand over his face. "Who knows?" He emitted a weary sigh. "Maybe she was trying to make a point with Paolo. Show him why they shouldn't have kids. Or get him to do something—like spend a week skiing in the Swiss Alps—that he has been reluctant to do."

"I can see her using you and the kids as leverage."

"My ex is something, all right."

Curious, Kate asked, "You didn't realize that when the two of you first got involved?"

He shook his head. "She can be incredibly charming, when it suits her purpose."

And manipulative, doing whatever it took to get her way. Kate shifted toward Alex, her body tingling with awareness as she took in his handsome profile. She still had trouble seeing Alex and Tiffany together for even a short period of time, never mind married with children! "Her entitled attitude didn't bother you?"

He shrugged. "I knew she was spoiled. That wasn't surprising. Most heiresses of her immense wealth are. But I also knew her parents had never really given her much attention, and that she didn't have any siblings, either." He paused, suppressing what seemed to be pity, or maybe just a need to rescue someone in distress. "I thought if she had a husband who loved her instead of the money she could pony up, and a family who supported her—"

"Meaning yours?"

He nodded. "—that everything would change. She'd realize people and relationships mattered, not things."

"But that didn't happen," Kate guessed.

He shook his head again.

"Which taught me that you can't love someone hoping to change them into what you want, you have to love them for who they are."

He was so right.

"Too bad we both had to learn that lesson the hard way," Kate quipped.

His mouth twisted ruefully. "No kidding."

With a weary sigh, he turned to her, his gaze gently roving her face. "How about you?" he asked kindly. "Everything all right with your folks?"

"Yes," she fibbed, figuring he had enough on his agenda without listening to her familial woes.

He took in the abrupt return of her unabashedly glum mood. Lifted a brow. "Then…?"

Kate watched Reckless come back toward them, sniffing diligently around the yard. As if on the scent of something yet to be found.

She twisted her hands together in her lap, then turned her glance to the starlit sky over head. Aware it was starting to get a little chilly, she fought off a shiver. "They want me to drive to Houston first thing tomorrow to meet up with my ex-fiancé Thaddeus Northam and his parents."

Alex paused. Standing, he offered her his hand. "Are you going?"

Luxuriating in the chivalrous warmth of his grip, she rose. "No."

He signaled for the canine to come inside with them, and opened the front door. "Any particular reason why not?"

She caught a whiff of his masculine scent as she passed. She set her bag on the foyer table and shrugged out of her lightweight down jacket with his help. "Both our parents, and apparently Thaddeus as well, want us to give it another go."

He took off the tie he had worn during dinner and laid it overtop the sport coat he had obviously taken off the moment he came in the door with the boys.

"And you're not interested."

She watched him unbutton the first two buttons on his olive dress shirt. "No."

Was that relief she saw on Alex's face?

"Then why are your parents pushing it?" he asked, rolling up his sleeves to just below his elbows.

He guided her into the kitchen.

She moved her gaze away from the brawny muscles of his forearms. Deciding she should tell him everything she had purposefully omitted the night before, about her most recent relationship. "Because there is a very big, very lucrative merger at stake," she admitted with a disappointment that encompassed her heart and soul. "Thaddeus and I met at business school. Our families hit it off as strongly as we did. The Northams have owned a chain of outdoor gear stores in the northeast, for generations."

Meaning they were Old Money—the frugal, hardworking kind.

Alex poured kibble into a bowl and refilled Reckless's water dish as well. He set them on the mat bearing his name, then smiled as the sheepdog ambled over to get his dinner. Still listening intently, Alex straightened. His gaze roved Kate's face as he guessed what kind of inventory the Northam's sold. "Things for camping, fishing, hiking and so on…?"

Kate nodded. "Whereas, my parents had bought a failing sporting goods store in Houston and turned it around to make it really prosperous. And then expanded on that, acquiring more stores all over Texas, building their business from the ground up."

Which made them New Money.

And had allowed them to become very financially successful in the process. Which is why she usually didn't mention it. Because she wanted to be liked and accepted for who she was, and what she did, instead of for how much money her parents now had.

Money that hadn't really been there during her childhood, since they had always poured every bit of profit they made right back into the current business they were expanding.

Alex kept his eyes on hers. Absorbing what she'd told him. "Wait. Taylor's Sporting Goods is owned and run by your parents?"

Kate nodded. Hoping he didn't have the same ideas about New Money versus Old Money that some had. "And Northam's is run by Thaddeus's family. Anyway, Thaddeus was a marketing and branding guy who wanted to take some of the things my folks had done with their business and use his family's Old Money capital to merge the two stores into one much bigger entity that would eventually go nationwide. And also have a significant on-line presence."

Which was why, she had realized belatedly, he had started chasing her. And ultimately managed to sweep her off her feet.

Because he had seen the potential in the merger of their two families.

Pursing his lips, he gave her a leisurely once-over. "And where did you come in? Besides as Thaddeus Northam's fiancée?"

Kate sighed and sat on one of the padded leather stools at the island. "I have a talent for dealing with employee issues and improving customer service."

Alex smiled, as if able to see that.

"The idea was that Thaddeus and I would marry and eventually run the new generation of merged stores upon our parents' retirements."

Alex took two Shiner Boch beers out of the fridge and uncapped them both. Their hands touched as he passed her one. Then he turned and got two frosted mugs out of the freezer. "And you were excited about that?"

"Yes." Kate poured her beer slowly into the glass. Finished, she forced herself to meet Alex's probing gaze, and picked up her glass. "Until I realized that Thaddeus was a lot more interested in the merger than he was in building a life with me."

"When you read the terms of the prenup he presented you with." He recalled what she had told him the other evening.

"Right."

He shook his head as if he could hardly believe anyone would treat her that way. Which made two of them, Kate thought wryly.

Alex tipped his mug forward, toasting her silently, then slanted her an assessing glance. "And your parents know all that and *still* want you to reconcile with your ex?" he asked as if in disbelief.

Still holding his level gaze, Kate fought back a flush of embarrassment. "They think romance fades and a couple needs a solid foundation of shared interest and values to really have a union that lasts. And that if I gave myself half a chance, I could have that with my ex."

Alex fell silent, not sure what to say to that, especially given his own life experiences.

She sipped her beer. "Please tell me you don't agree with my folks."

Alex motioned for her to follow him into the living room. He set his beer on the coffee table in front of the sofa, then went to the hall closet in the foyer, and got out the card table and four folding chairs. He carried them to the living room and set them next to the windows overlooking the backyard in two short trips. Answering casually as he worked, "As far as Thaddeus Northam goes, I don't think he is the right guy for you. Not if a mutually advantageous business deal was more important to him than your relationship."

Kate settled on the U-shaped sectional sofa, the frosted beer mug resting mid-thigh of her tailored wool slacks. Despite the long day, her tousled honey-blond hair, minimal makeup and bare lips, she still looked incredibly beautiful. Desire coursed through him as he paused to meet her eyes.

"And as for marriage in general…?" She sipped delicately from her glass again.

Alex finished setting up the chairs for the kids, then returned to the sofa and settled beside Kate. He took another drink, too.

Aware he usually didn't talk about this with anyone, he confided to Kate, wanting her to know more about his past, too. Reluctantly, he admitted, "I had a hot romance with Tiffany. When the passion fizzled, and the kids came along, our marriage crashed and burned. Spectacularly." It hurt just thinking about how unnecessarily ugly their divorce had been.

He got up again and went to get the bag he had brought in from the SUV. Taking out all four boxes, he set them on the card table and folded the bag for repurposing later as a trash sack.

Kate slipped off her shoes and tucked her legs beneath her. "Because ultimately you didn't share the same values or have enough in common."

"Right." Alex went into the kitchen and returned with a

pair of utility scissors. "I know there are some couples, like my parents, who are the loves of each other's lives and have it all. But I'm not sure I'll ever get that." He ran the scissor blade along all four sides, cutting the paper that held it closed. "And that's problematic because I'm beginning to see my boys need a mom as well as a dad." He worked the top off and dumped the puzzle pieces onto the center of the table.

Kate came over to join him. Inundating him with her soft feminine scent, she sat down on one of the folding chairs and began turning the pieces over so the colored side showed. "So you'd settle for less than what you want to get them a mom?" she asked in a too-casual tone.

He noted she didn't look exactly happy about that prospect.

Any more than he was happy about her parents trying to get her reunited with her ex.

Separating out all the edge pieces, he said honestly, "If I were ever to marry again, I'd be pragmatic from the start. And create a satisfying family life…" *With someone like you, Kate. Someone warm and kind and innately loving.*

Someone who thought about others more than she ever thought about herself.

Kate turned the top of the one hundred piece puzzle box over, smiling as she saw the cute picture of the iconic red sleigh parked in front of the North Pole workshop. Santa Claus was loading up to leave, presents spilling out of the bags. Rudolph the reindeer was ready to go, his big nose glowing red. While Mrs. Claus smiled, seeing her husband off.

Kate kept working, turning the pieces over so all the vibrant colors could be seen. Her cheeks registered a pretty pink flush. "What do you want in a wife?"

Such an innocent question. And yet… Was there real interest behind it? As genuine as his?

Hoping that was the case, Alex reached over to snag a few

pieces from the ones in front of her, his forearm brushing her wrist in the process, causing a surge of heat and awareness inside him.

Realizing she was still waiting for his answer, he said, "I'd want someone who shared my values and would love my kids, rowdiness and all. Someone who liked life on the ranch and who wasn't afraid of hard work. And didn't care that much about money. Except, of course, to have enough to live comfortably on, put the kids through college or trade school and so on."

Her lips bloomed in a soft smile. "That sounds reasonable."

"And yet," he sighed, beginning to put the puzzle edge together to give the kids a head start on what would be a challenging but doable assembly for them. He paused to gaze into her long-lashed amber eyes. "The thing is, even without a wild, romantic love…finding the right person is not a simple process. And I don't want to end up like Sadie," he admitted ruefully, "waiting for someone or something that may never materialize."

Kate went over to the coffee table and returned with their drinks. "She's in love with Will, isn't she?"

Alex nodded, his heart going out to his little sister. "I think Will's in love with her, too."

Kate blinked. "Then what is the problem?"

"Two things, actually. They started out as friends."

She looked at him for a long, thoughtful moment. "So if one of them admits they feel more and the other doesn't…"

Alex nodded. "It could ruin everything. Second, Will is in the Special Forces." Alex let out a frustrated huff. "And last I heard, anyway, not the least bit interested in getting married or having kids."

A quizzical, concerned look adorned Kate's pretty face. "And Sadie wants those things."

"I think so, yes, although she downplays it and is instead focusing on getting her lavender ranch up and running. Meanwhile, time is passing them by. And she could be giving up her chance to have a family of her own while she waits around for Will to realize he wants to be with her—as much as she secretly wants to be with him."

Kate pushed a hand through her hair, giving him a winsome smile, and he had to shove aside the sudden desire to kiss her.

"That's sad," she said softly. "Although I completely understand where she is coming from."

He quirked a teasing brow. "You've got the hots for someone who doesn't know how you feel?"

Someone like...me?

Apparently oblivious to his growing interest in her, Kate hesitated. "More like..." She lifted her slender shoulders in an artless shrug that drew the fabric of her ivory sweater snugly across the feminine curves of her breasts. "...wondering if my parents are right and I'm waiting around for a fairy-tale life that may never materialize."

He ignored the twinge of something tightening inside him.

She shook her head, as if suddenly wondering if maybe her folks were right, and that she was wasting every day that passed. That, like his sister, Sadie, she would likely never get the loving husband and kids she wanted.

And that would make him unbearably sad for her.

Kate straightened, inhaling sharply. "What I do know—" she met his eyes and told him frankly "—is that being around the boys has made me realize how much I do want a home and family of my own. Sooner rather than later..."

Alex feigned an ease he could not begin to feel. "You're talking kids?"

"Oh yes." Her eyes shone with hope that she would one day

get what she wanted. And maybe she would. It was Christmas time, after all. A holiday when wishes miraculously came true. "At least four, if not more," she continued happily.

He could see her achieving just that. She was so kind and loving and patient with his kids. So inherently maternal.

The urge to take her in his arms and kiss her, the way he had always wanted to, grew even stronger. It took all his willpower to tamp down that desire but somehow he managed. Releasing a breath, he relaxed in his chair, his knees shifting beneath the card table, nudging hers. "What about a husband? Do you want one of those, too?" he asked, lightly teasing.

Kate stayed where she was, making no move to ease away from him. "If I'm truthful, yes." A wistful look crossed her expression. "But," she said, finally shifting so their knees were no longer touching and creating tingles of awareness, "I'm not into the dating apps, so…"

Which was something else they had in common. "Neither am I."

He put together the bottom edge of the puzzle, while she worked on the top.

Their fingers touched as they both reached for the same corner piece. He let her have it.

She snapped it in place and then added several more edge pieces, down the side. "Being a chuck wagon chef is fulfilling and challenging, but the constant traveling doesn't allow me to develop a serious relationship or even find someone I wanted to date more than once or twice."

That was understandable. "Sounds a little lonely."

Their progress quickened. Kate nodded, still studying the board.

Realizing how lucky he was to have his boys, and all his family nearby as well, he asked, "Do you have a lot of friends in Fort Worth?"

"Not really. Not yet, anyway. I moved there because I like the Western vibe of the city, and because of the proximity to so many ranches, and other places where I could pick up gigs. But I'm not in town enough to form anything but casual acquaintances, and all my friends from my previous business school grad life have pretty much cut ties with me."

"Because of the breakup with Thaddeus?" Alex guessed.

She finished one side. He completed the other.

Shrugging, she stood. "More like they don't understand why I got out of the corporate world any more than my parents do, to cook for ranchers and cowboys and be my own boss."

His heart went out to her for the way she'd been ditched by her former friends and colleagues. "That sucks."

"Yeah, well—" She gave one last glance at the completed puzzle frame, then swung away from the table. Walking over to the unadorned floor to ceiling windows, she looked out at the dark, starry night. "That's the way life is. Then again," she laughed in soft resignation, turning to face him as he joined her. "Maybe it's not really the demands of my job that are keeping me from finding someone to date." Sadness filled her eyes, and the corners of her lips turned down. "Maybe my expectations are just too high."

Like hell they are.

The silence thickening, Alex moved closer. Gently, he surveyed her face. "In my opinion, they aren't high enough," he told her gruffly, thinking about all she had done for him in four short days. He cupped her shoulders lightly between his palms. "You deserve it all, Kate."

She swayed toward him, smiling and drawing in a slow breath. "I could say the same about you, cowboy," she teased sweetly.

His desire for her growing by leaps and bounds, he regarded her intently. "Could you, now?"

Her eyes sparkled with invitation. "Oh yes..."

Alex had promised himself he wouldn't put a move on her until after her catering company was no longer under contract with the ranch. That he would use this time to get to know her, the way he hadn't gotten to know his ex, before jumping into a relationship with her.

He'd thought he was wiser now. No longer too quick to judge and trust someone.

But darned if Kate didn't make him want to toss every reservation he had.

And why not?

He had seen her at her best and worst during the brief yet incredibly challenging time they had spent together during Hurricane Inga. And he had been with her the past four days. Seen her with his kids and his entire family.

She was the same incredibly giving, selfless person now that she had been then.

Beautiful. Sexy, in that adorable girl-next-door way.

And he was tired of waiting to find out how she would feel, snug against him, her lips pressed to his.

She leaned toward him, her soft mouth tipped up, and then at long last their lips met. As passion soared through him, and he got his first taste of her sweet, lovely mouth, he knew this kiss, their friendship, was going somewhere. Somewhere fantastic.

And sure, the future was uncertain. But for now, having her in his arms was more than enough.

Kate could hardly believe this was happening. He'd just said he didn't want wildly romantic love. Not again. He wanted the kind of pragmatic relationship she had declined to pursue with her ex.

But somehow, this kiss didn't feel like her disappointingly unromantic past.

It felt wild.

Enticing.

And full of promise.

There was just something so dangerously compelling about Alex's embrace. She had never been kissed with such fierce possessiveness. Had never felt such need or desire welling up inside her. He was so deliberate and determined. So fiercely masculine. Making her want to succumb to the pent-up lust she had been feeling ever since they had reconnected.

So what if he wasn't offering the kind of traditional love she had always thought she wanted, she thought, as she reveled in the continued sensual demand of his mouth on hers, the masterful way he held her.

But instead, something a lot more reasonable.

Something to build on.

All she knew for sure was that anyone who could kiss like this, in a way that made her feel all woman to his man, was worth her consideration for more than just a past, present and future friend.

Even if it was all happening a little too fast.

Aware she was as reluctant to trust in someone as ever, she broke off the kiss. Still trembling with reaction, from head to toe. Wanting him. Yet...afraid to surrender to it...

Afraid in the end she would be hurt. *Again*.

Alex seemed to have no such reservations. "Wow," he whispered, looking just as stunned as she felt by the kiss that had rocked her entire world. He flashed a satisfied grin. "*That* should have happened a long time ago."

And it would have...during Inga...

She splayed her hands across his strong chest, cautiously

wedging distance between them. Softly, she reminded him, "Except we were both pledged to others back then."

And would never have acted unethically.

A complex array of emotions crossed his handsome face. He lifted her hand to his lips, kissed the back of it, still as determined as ever. "Lucky for us," he rasped, giving her a long, measuring look and another soft, seductive kiss, "we're *both* free now."

Chapter Six

Friday morning, Kate woke, still thinking about her intimate conversation with Alex the evening before, and the passionate kiss that had ended it. He knew so much more about her now. But he wasn't aware of her disturbing connection with his ex-wife. A connection that Tiffany McCabe DeLuca luckily did not seem to remember. And probably wouldn't, Kate assured herself, given how little stock the heiress had put into her bullying way back then.

Kate was just another "annoying" New Money student who had gotten in the pampered Old Money princess's path. And once gone was promptly forgotten, as they both went on with their lives.

And now she was here on the Rocking M, with Alex McCabe and his cute sons, Kate thought, heading over to the ranch kitchen and dining hall.

She had just settled down with her laptop, notebook and pen when the door to the breezeway swung open with a bang. All four boys raced in to see her. "Hey, Kate, whatcha doing?" Max asked.

She paused to exchange fist bumps and exploding palms with him. "Working on the menus for next week's meals," she replied.

Alex ambled in after his sons, flashing her a sexy smile.

Trying not to think of the steamy kisses they had shared,

she returned his smile with a casual one of her own. But, in truth, her heart was fluttering with excitement as she turned back to his boys. Cheerfully exchanging fist bump greetings with the other three, too.

"You can't work on a holiday," Michael explained seriously while Marty ran circles around the long wooden plank table.

"Yeah," Matthew chimed in, hopping on one foot. "You gotta come with us to get two Christmas trees!"

"Two?" Kate echoed in surprise.

Marty skidded to a halt next to her. Breathing hard, he said, "One for in here for the cowboys and one for our house—so Santa can come!"

"Oh," Kate said, taking that in.

She wondered what it would be like to be around all of this male energy, continually. Fantastic, maybe?

Alex took a seat next to her, his back to the table so he was facing her. "So will you come with us?" he asked in that low, charmingly gruff voice she loved. "We're headed out to the fairgrounds now, where all the charities sell their trees. The fire department is putting on a pancake breakfast. So we can all eat there."

Kate smiled, already rising. She might only be here for the next month, but darned if she didn't want to enjoy Alex's company and that of his sons while she could. "Sounds fun!"

The pancakes and bacon were as delicious as the guys had all promised. By the time they stood in line and finished eating, most of the morning was gone.

Alex doled out the wet wipes provided by the firefighters and left Kate to supervise the removal of syrup from four cute faces while he dispensed of their trash in the appropriate bins.

"Ready to go find the trees?" he asked the boys.

They cheered yes in unison.

He handed out glow-in-the-dark, lime green knit caps to all of them. "Keep your hats on," he said sternly. "It'll make it easier for me to keep track of you."

The kids promised they would.

"How about you take Michael and Matthew, and I'll take Max and Marty," he said to Kate.

She noticed he had assigned her the two easiest children to handle. "Sure." She held out her palms, and they eagerly latched on to her hands.

The Christmas tree lots were set up in an organized fashion, one after another. Each charity had a different type pine—Scotch, Afghan, Fraser fir...and so on.

The boys had to inspect all of them, of course. Mulling over the types of needles and hues of green.

Alex seemed content to let them explore as much as they wanted. Kate followed suit.

The only problem was the inquiring glances they were getting. Seemed like everyone there knew Alex and the boys, and when they stopped by to say hi, they wanted to know who Kate was.

"A family friend," he said, over and over.

Which was absolutely true, as far as it went.

Only deep down, Kate wished it was more...

"Daddy, I'm ready to pick out our two trees now!" Michael said, when they reached the end of the lot.

"The ones just like we had last year!" Max chimed in.

Alex bobbed his head eagerly. "Which would be the blue spruce."

And they set off toward the middle of the fairgrounds once again.

More than once, Kate felt uncomfortable. Like everyone was watching them with unusual interest. But when she glanced around to see, it seemed like everyone there was as involved in their task of selecting a tree as she was supposed to be.

Which meant no one was actually watching them. Not really. Even if it was a rural community, where everyone seemed to know everyone else.

"Everything okay?" Alex asked, after she had turned completely around for the second time. He looked puzzled.

She moved closer to him. Tipping her face up and meeting his protective gaze. "Ah, yeah. I was just marveling at the enormity of the crowd here today."

He nodded, agreeing, as he briefly wrapped his arm around her shoulders and gave them a gentle squeeze. "I love this event. I bring the boys every year."

They reached the blue spruces being sold by the high school athletic association. The boys grew excited, dashing from one to another. Glad for the lime green hats that kept them easily visible, Kate followed, along with Alex. Twenty minutes and much arguing later, the boys picked out the two eight foot trees they wanted. Kate stayed next to the two evergreens, to make sure no one else claimed them, while Alex went to get a cart that would carry them to the register. Promising it would only take a moment, he set off, leaving the boys with her.

Again, Kate had that weird sensation that she was being watched. But when she turned around to look behind her? Nothing.

With a shake of her head, she turned back to guarding the trees. Alex was coming toward her, bringing the metal cart. It took less than a second to realize all four boys were gone!

He looked as panicked as she felt. "Where are they?" he demanded, brows furrowing.

"I d-d-don't know. They were right here." Kate did a full spin. Searching.

Again. Nothing.

"Stay right here in case they come back!" he ordered.

He scanned the area, calling for his boys. Moving farther and farther away. Kate yelled their names, too. And now people really *were* looking at her.

One after another, they asked if they could help.

Fighting back tears, she told them all what had happened.

That the four boys were wearing matching lime green hats and were nowhere to be seen. Others began shouting, too. While an announcement came on the fairground PA system, letting the boys know their family was looking for them. And to stay in one place.

And that was when Kate heard it. The first irrepressible giggle.

OMG.

Followed by another and another and another.

The sounds were near the ground.

She dropped to her knees, then went flat on her stomach to be able to see beneath the trees. And there they were, all four of them playing hide and seek, merry as could be.

"Guys, you scared us to death!" Kate chided. "Get out of there now, please, before a tree falls on top of one of you!"

She ushered them out, one by one, and then helped them up, just as Alex returned.

He would have been within his rights to be furious with them. As well as her! To give all five of them the scolding of their lives.

Instead, he looked as if this were just another day in the life of the single dad of quadruplets. And her heart went out to him.

The boys were quiet during the ride back to the ranch.

"Dad, are we going to have a time-out?" Michael asked nervously.

"Yes." Alex parked his Navigator in front of the house.

Max unbuckled his seat belt. "How long?"

Alex turned to look each of his sons in the eye. "Fifteen minutes."

A mixture of guilt and regret rushed through Kate as she and Alex got out and opened the rear passenger doors. All four boys came tumbling out. Frowning as they hit the ground.

"That's a long time! Longer than usual," Marty piped up.

Alex nodded, leading the way up the steps and into the house. "I want you all to think about what could have happened had you gotten separated from us and gotten lost," he said. "How scary it would have been."

The boys fell silent, looking as rueful as Kate felt.

Once inside, the kids took off their hats and jackets and trudged slowly into the family room. Then they took a place on the U-shaped sectional, roughly six feet apart. They were calm and prepared to do what their dad asked. Reckless curled up in front of them on the floor. Their pet seemed to sense the boys had done something wrong, but was going to be there for them, nevertheless.

Alex hadn't said much to Kate since the incident. It was hard to tell if he was ticked off at her, too.

Not that she didn't feel guilty as hell for what had happened. She should have been more watchful! "I'm going to bring both the trees in," Alex told her.

Determined to make it up to him in some way, Kate asked, "Want some help?"

Still not looking at her, he grabbed a pair of scissors out of the kitchen drawer. "Sure."

Tension simmered between them as they headed for the foyer. He held the door for her, and they headed back outdoors, walking side by side down the wide front steps. "You know you don't need to blame yourself for what happened at the fairgrounds," he said gruffly, "'cause I don't."

Kate had known they needed to talk about this. These were his boys, after all, the most precious thing in his life. And quickly beginning to mean so much to her, too. As she thought for about the hundredth time what could have happened to them had the boys not stayed as close as they had, a lump rose in her throat. "Come on, Alex. Don't let me off the hook!" she choked out. "I was in charge of them."

Setting the scissors on the roof of his SUV, he caught her hand and reeled her in to his side. This time he *did* look at her—with those mesmerizing ocean blue eyes of his. "And I know how quickly and quietly they can start up a game of hide and seek," he retorted.

The chilly late November wind blew across their bodies, wafting through their hair. Awareness shot through her, weakening her knees. Her heart did a funny little twist inside her chest. "Still, like you said, if anything had happened to them…"

He took her by the shoulders, holding her gently, then gave her a sensual once-over. His gaze lingered on her lips before returning to her eyes. "It didn't."

Tears suddenly blurred her vision. Wishing she didn't want to kiss him as much as she did, she said thickly, "I just want you to know—I'm sorry."

"Kate," he reprimanded softly, "it's okay." He put a hand around her waist and tugged her against him. Then he leaned over and whispered in her ear, "Their misbehaving on your watch was an anomaly. It's not going to happen again."

"How do you know?" she whispered back, wanting so badly to believe him.

Nothing of real import would be possible between them if he thought she was incompetent with kids.

Especially *his* kids.

"Because—" the corners of his lips quirked, as he promised her with his trademark good humor "—99.9 percent of the time they save all their naughty antics for me..."

Kate grinned, as he meant her to. "Thanks for saying that," she managed.

He sobered. "It's true, Kate. Today really was just fun and games for them. I'm pretty sure, even without the time-out, they learned their lesson and won't be scaring us like that again. At least not anytime soon..."

"Never say never...?"

Amusement filled his voice. "Exactly."

He brought her closer with the palm of his hand, a wickedly sexy gleam in his eyes. Their bodies aligned as perfectly as if they had been made for each other. The unyielding imprint of his strong, hard body had her nipples tingling and pressing against the soft fabric of her cashmere sweater. The next thing she knew, he was holding her even closer and kissing her tenderly.

Unable to help herself, she kissed him back with all her heart and soul.

Alex hadn't meant to put the moves on Kate. Not with the boys just inside, albeit out of view.

Reluctantly, he ended the kiss and let her go. Promising himself they would pursue this at the right time.

She stepped away, as if realizing the very same thing. He gave her the physical space she craved and said, "We better get a move on with these trees." He glanced at his watch, seeing the kids only had six minutes left on their time-out.

"Absolutely right about that," Kate agreed, all business once again.

He moved around, cutting the heavy twine holding the

trees to his luggage rack, while Kate stood clear, giving him room to work. Together, they eased the two spruce trees off the top of the Navigator and onto the ground. They carried one to the ranch dining hall and the other inside the ranch house, to the family room.

Relaxed as ever, Kate grinned at what they found.

All four boys were fast asleep on the big sectional. She sent Alex a playful glance. "Do the time-out minutes count if they sleep through them?"

Glad she wasn't holding the impulsive kiss against him, he grinned back at her. "In this case, yes." He set the tree down next to the mantel. "Not that I'm surprised they dozed off practically the moment they sat still. It's been a busy few days for them."

Kate reflected affectionately. "That it has."

Unable to help but think what a good mother she would make, he continued telling her the plan. "The good news is we'll be able to get this tree in the stand and the lights on before they wake up. Then they'll be able to go straight into decorating it."

Which meant they would be too busy to kiss again. And that was probably a good—if somewhat disappointing—thing, Alex thought.

Because he had the sense that whatever was happening between the two of them, was moving way too fast for Kate. And maybe him as well.

"What do you think, Kate?" Matthew asked her, hours later, when the six of them had put all the decorations on the family room blue spruce. "Is our Christmas tree pretty or what?"

She smiled down at their beaming faces, tenderness flowing through her. She might not be sure how she felt about their dad yet, but she knew how quickly she had grown attached to them.

Affection welled in her heart. "I think it is the most gorgeous tree I have ever seen in my life. And it smells wonderful, too." Like pine air freshener times ten.

Brows furrowing, the boys approached the branches in unison and took a deep sniff. "It does smell pretty good," Max agreed. His brothers nodded.

"Can we go outside with Reckless and kick our soccer ball around?" Marty asked.

Alex nodded. "Stay in the backyard where I can see you, okay?"

"'Kay!" they shouted. Then, grabbing their jackets and ball, they took off out the door.

Kate watched them from the windows. "I'm always hearing parents talk about how their little children run them ragged." She remembered feeling envious and, up to now, a little skeptical. She watched the boys race up and down the grass, kicking the soccer ball between them. "But it's amazing how much energy they have."

Alex moved next to her. He gave her an admiring glance. "You're very good with them, you know. Very patient."

His praise warmed her through and through. Even as she took note of the wonder in his low, sexy voice. She turned to face him. "That surprises you?"

The grooves on either side of his mouth deepened. His gaze roved her lips. "It's not a talent everyone has."

She had the sense he wanted to kiss her again. She wanted that as well.

Kate supposed it was the season making her so acutely aware of her own loneliness. How much she wished for a family of her own. A family just like Alex's.

But that wasn't likely to happen.

Not unless she met the love of her life.

And though Alex McCabe might seem to fit the bill, in so many ways, he was still lacking the most important trait. A wish to find the love of his life, too, instead of just a reasonably compatible companion.

The rest of Friday was equally busy. The boys started work on the Christmas puzzle Alex had set up for them while he went out to the barn to take care of the horses.

Kate rustled up a spaghetti and meatball dinner for all of them. Then she went back to the Rocking M Ranch's kitchen and dining hall, to continue working on her menu plan for the next week while Alex took his kids through their bath and bedtime routines.

Around 8:00 p.m., he came into the dining hall, monitor in hand. As always, Reckless was by his side. He set the monitor down on the table. "Since I'm not in the house, I want to be able to hear if the boys wake up. Which I doubt they will…"

Kate had seen how physically and emotionally exhausted his little ones were, too. But… "Better safe than sorry."

"Right." He inclined his head at her laptop and the handwritten lists spread out next to her. "Now, how can I help you?"

His calm, businesslike attitude was the last thing she had expected. She'd thought he came in here to flirt. Suppressing her disappointment, she asked in surprise, "You really want to do that?"

Still holding her gaze, he nodded slowly. "The way I see it, I owe you after all you did to help me today."

His thoughtfulness touched her to the core. When she had known him before, he had always been so nice to everyone. It was good to see that had not changed. Despite the curveballs life had thrown his way. "Well, then." She straightened, and with cheerful practicality, explained, "Since I'm going to be here for a month, I'm trying to do a complete inventory of what you have in the freezer, and pantry and fridge. So I can figure out what I'll need. As well as where would be the best place to shop."

He flashed her a grin. "I get my meat from the butcher shop in town. He gives you a discount if you buy in bulk."

"Sounds good." Kate made a note of that. "What about dry goods like flour and cornmeal?"

"Grocery store in town. Or the superstore, depending on what you are looking for. They have more specialty flours, for instance."

"I wouldn't have thought you would be into that."

"I'm not." He shrugged affably. "The sacks just get in the way when I'm trying to find the regular AP flour."

Kate laughed and shook her head as she jotted that down, too. "Produce?"

"Ah. Now that's a place you're really going to like. The Buy Local food co-op at Rose Hill Farm. I'll take you there tomorrow. While the kids are at my folks' house in town for the day."

A thrill went through Kate at just the thought. She loved shopping for her ingredients!

It had been her experience that most men who weren't into cooking hated it, though. She peered at him closely. "You sure you don't mind?"

And why was he suddenly looking at her like they'd just made a date? Albeit a platonic one.

He shook his head, promising in the gruff, sexy voice she loved, "It'll be my pleasure."

Chapter Seven

"You look like a kid in a candy store."

Kate sure felt that way. The high-ceilinged, cement-floored barn at Rose Hill Farm was filled with a bounty of fresh fruits and vegetables that would put the best farmer's markets in the state to shame.

She turned to Alex. Marveling at how handsome he looked in the bright lights of the co-op. He had showered that morning, but hadn't shaved, and his jaw was covered with a light scruff of beard, his short dark hair was shiny and clean, though slightly rumpled. She bit her lip, trying not to betray how affected she was by his presence. But how could she not? He smelled of an intoxicating mix of soap and wintergreen. Unable to help herself, she continued her perusal. His blue and gray plaid flannel shirt emphasized the width of his shoulders and brought out the ocean blue of his eyes. Dark rinse jeans snugly cloaked his sturdy lower half.

"I had no idea this was here," she said, gesturing around her. "The butcher shop and grocery were incredible, too." Thus far, she had cooked with what was already in the Rocking M Ranch's kitchen and dining hall. Now, she would be able to do an even better job providing meals for the cowboys—and Alex and his boys, too.

He smiled down at her. "Glad you like it." Their gazes met and held long enough for her pulse to kick up yet again.

Aware they had attracted more than a few interested glances and casual hellos—and she could still feel eyes upon her—Kate stepped back.

He'd been introducing her as a chef friend who was temporarily helping him out, cooking for the cowboys, via an ongoing contract between their two businesses, until he could find someone to take the job permanently.

Not that Alex seemed to be working all that hard on finding a replacement. Although she was aware that he could be and she just didn't know...

What she did realize was that every day she stayed in Laramie was making it harder for her to ever want to leave...

"Listen, there are wreaths over there." He leaned forward to whisper conspiratorially, inclining his head toward the far corner. "Mind if I mosey on over and get one, while you continue to hand select brussels sprouts?"

"Take your time." She still had sweet potatoes, green beans and peas to select. And she might add a few more items to her array of mandarins, apples, peppers, russets and melons that she'd already chosen.

By the time she had finished, Alex was back with a wreath to put beneath the cart. As they headed for the checkout line, the aisle grew congested. He stepped close to her to give another shopper room to pass. Putting his arm around her back in the process.

His touch was light. Gently guiding, masculine and protective. She felt a shiver of awareness go through her. Then, yet another sensation that she was being carefully surveilled. Although every time she glanced around, all she saw was shoppers filling their own carts with nature's bounty.

Alex sent her a quizzical look. "Anything else you want?"

"No. This is plenty." Out of the corner of her eye, she saw a woman gazing appreciatively at Alex. Then another. This must be what she had been feeling—surreptitious glances from other interested single women. Not that she had any reason to feel jealous. Alex was very attractive. Very successful. And generous. Not to mention *very* available...

She smiled up at him, giving him her full attention once again and admitting, "Though I'll probably come back next weekend, just to see what else they have."

"Sounds good. If you want, I'll come with you."

Kate knew she would like that, even as she warned herself not to get used to it.

An hour later, they were back at the Rocking M, putting everything away in the ranch kitchen, when Alex's cell buzzed.

He glanced at his watch with a perplexed frown. "My mom."

Kate knew he wasn't supposed to pick up his kids from his parents' place in town for another hour.

She put down the sacks of flour that she'd been about to take into the pantry. "Want me to leave so you can have some privacy?"

"No." He put out a hand, imploring her to stay and continue what she was doing. "What's going on?" he asked, a moment after answering.

Then listened.

Finally, he said, "You're sure?"

He listened again. "Okay, but if you change your mind..." He grinned. "Of course I think you and Dad can handle that. Yes. A break would be fantastic, actually. Right. See you then. Thanks again, Mom. Bye."

"Everything okay?"

"Claire and Zach are both on call at the hospital until six tomorrow morning. Their triplets are staying with Mom and Dad tonight for a sleepover. The boys want to stay, too. So

I said they could. I'll go over for brunch and pick them up then. You're invited, too."

Kate was tempted but—aware she was already getting way too attached to him—forced herself to dial it down. "Thank you, and thank your parents, but I probably will have to work. I have a lot to do to get ready for the week."

A hint of disappointment came and went in his eyes. "Okay." His attitude was as casual as she needed it to be. His smile widened. "Just know that the invitation is open."

She appreciated that he didn't pressure her.

Alex picked up the wreath and the holder meant to go over the top of the door, and they walked outside. Reckless met them in the breezeway and followed them down the cement sidewalk, then around to the front entrance of the house.

Alex opened the front door and slid the gold metal holder over the top with the hook facing outward. Kate watched as he positioned the wreath, then stepped back. "Is it straight?"

She surveyed his handiwork. "Maybe a little to the right." He adjusted.

"Mmm…" She tilted her head, squinting. "To the left…?" He adjusted again.

She squinted harder. "…the right?"

With a huff of exasperation, he turned in time to see her grin. Eyes glimmering with humor, he strolled back to her side at the edge of the porch. His husky laughter flowed between them as he tugged a lock of her hair playfully before dropping his hand again. "Should have known."

"Sorry." She stood, letting the brisk wind flow over them. It felt so good to just hang out with him. So right, somehow. She returned his affable look with an amiable shrug. "Couldn't help myself…"

"Just so you know." He tapped her nose with his index

finger, in that moment reminding her of his oft mischievous sons. "What comes around eventually goes around, too."

She sized him up with mock solemnity. "I'll be on the lookout for a yuletide prank."

He seemed up to the challenge of playing a joke on her, too. "Speaking of the future... Since I'm suddenly kid-free tonight, would you like to go out? Have dinner with me?"

Kate paused to consider. Thinking how first-date or overly romantic that might feel, she suggested instead, "Or we could stay in. Rustle up some dinner together."

He seemed puzzled by the suggestion. Maybe, oddly, hurt.

"Cooking is fun for me." Although he was right in his assessment. She didn't mind a reprieve now and again.

"Then...?"

She chose what she could comfortably discuss. "You and I are already the object of a lot of speculation, Alex. First from your family, and yesterday and today, the people in town."

"And that bothers you?"

She recalled the feeling of being watched. Judged, somehow. The way she had been back in high school when she hadn't ever seemed to measure up—socially anyway. "Yeah. I wouldn't want them to assume anything just because you're being, well, charitable to me. You know, helping me with errands and learning my way around Laramie County and keeping me from spending a holiday weekend alone."

Was that all she thought this had been? Alex wondered, jaw tightening. Because from his perspective, it seemed like a whole hell of a lot more. But maybe that's what he got for trying to keep what he really wanted from her a secret.

He took her by the hand and led her over to the cushioned glider on the left side of the porch. Then sat down beside her, so close their legs were pressed up against each other.

On the horizon, the dark clouds of a blue norther were rolling in.

"You think I feel obligated to do all that?" he asked gruffly, a little insulted. "Because we knew each other, briefly, years ago?"

She bit her lip as color flooded her pretty cheeks. "Well, no. Maybe. I don't know. You are a pretty gallant guy after all."

Saying to hell with holding back, he picked her up and shifted her onto his lap. "I'm selfish, too."

She drew in a quick breath of surprise, at his unexpected maneuver, then smiled, seeming not to mind his desire to be a lot closer to her. Relaxing even more, she settled against him. Perplexed, she asked, "Selfish in what way?"

He sifted a hand through the silky strands of her hair. "I want time alone with you, darlin'. Time to get to know each other—the way we couldn't during Inga."

The memory of that time hung between them. Eventually, she sighed. "I want that, too. I just don't know if it is wise." She stood again and walked to the other end of the porch before she swung back to him, hands planted adamantly on her hips. "Given that I'm leaving in a few weeks."

"Three and a half," he corrected, walking over to join her. He looked down at her, this time keeping his hands to himself. "And you don't need to remind me. I think of it every day."

"You're worried about finding a permanent ranch chef."

He shook his head and closed the distance between them even more. This time he did take her hands in his. He gazed down at her, letting everything he felt show. "I'm worried about losing track of you again."

Staring into his eyes, she let out a wistful breath. "Oh, Alex..."

Giving her no chance to argue further, he said, "We missed our chance once, Kate. I don't want to do it again."

***

Kate hadn't expected him to kiss her, right here and right now. But now that he was, she wasn't about to let him stop.

She needed him to take this step with her. Had to find out once and for all if there was something really special developing between them.

Or not.

But in any case, maybe if she got the urge to make hot, wild, tempestuous love to him out of her system, she could go back to her everyday life.

And stop wanting the impossible with him. Because the once-in-a-lifetime love she craved wasn't going to happen. At least not with Alex. Not when he had already told her that if he ever married again, it would pretty much be just to give his boys the maternal care they needed.

He had tried wild romance and passion once, in his first marriage, and failed. He clearly had no interest in doing that again.

Whereas she still wanted the real and abiding, deeply romantic love she had never yet actually experienced.

The question was, with whom?

She was thirty years old.

Single.

And romantically unattached. *Again.*

The only thing that felt real to her was this.

She moaned as he deepened his kiss even more. Letting her tongue play with his, fighting and losing the battle with desire that had been haunting her since they had first met. "Sure you don't want to get dressed up and go out to dinner?" Eyes turbulent, he swept his hands down to cup her hips.

"Uh-huh. Want to stay here." She went up on tiptoe, kissing him again, even more ardently this time, molding her curves to his hard muscular planes. This felt so good. *He* felt so good. Her hands slid over his pecs. Even as her lips discovered the U of his collarbone.

Yearning washed over her.

He caught her face between his hands as he bent down and reclaimed her lips with his own. Making her feel sexy, vibrant, alive. As if it was okay, when she was with him, to let down her guard, savor the moment…and the pleasure they brought each other.

He savored her, too. Their mouths melded and their tongues tangled as he kissed her, again and again. She loved the way he tasted, how he encouraged her to open herself up to passion in a way she hadn't ever really felt before.

Hungry for more of him, she pressed against him, wanting to feel connected to him, not just body to body, but heart and soul.

"Let's go inside," she whispered.

He paused to cup her face in his big hands. "I want you. But we don't have to do this…"

Kate arched against him in abject surrender. "I think we do…" Feeling the pulsing heat of his lower body, she wreathed her arms around his neck and smiled up at him. Then, planting kisses on his jaw, she said, "We can consider it an early Christmas present…"

"Well, then, all right." He took her by the hand, led her inside, and straight up the stairs to his bedroom on the second floor…

Alex knew what was going on here. Kate wanted to forget even attempting to date, and instead was choosing to rush into something physical so she would feel justified in calling it quits before they had a chance to see where things led. He had the feeling she would regret this, at least in the short term. But he hoped in the long term, she would see it as the beginning of something that should have happened a long time ago. Had fate been on their side.

Body aching with need, he watched her turn and lean up against the wall. She looked so beautiful and sexy. So full of want and need.

He stepped in and fit her against him. Moving in until her soft breasts nestled against his chest. She swayed slightly, knees wobbling. They began to kiss. Her mouth opened, softening to allow him greater access. And just that quickly, they were on the path to the fulfillment they both sought.

Enjoying the rush of adrenaline, he danced her toward his bed. She reached for his clothes. He reached for hers. They unwrapped each other simultaneously, then paused to enjoy the view.

His body hard, he ran his hands over her taut nipples and the insides of her thighs, seeking out the feminine heart of her. She caressed him, too. Her touch wild in a way he never could have imagined. Sultry…seductive. Giving him exquisite pleasure, yet also letting him adore her completely, too.

He found a condom. She trembled as they rolled it on. Then he was stretching out beside her. Stopping to lick and caress every pleasure point.

And then they were kissing again, even more passionately. Lower still, she was wet and open. He was hot and hard. He made her his. Amazed at how perfectly they fit—as if they were made for each other.

He slid his hands beneath her, lifting her, going deeper. She arched her back and wrapped her legs around him. And then there was nothing but pleasure. The rise to fulfillment and the sweet, hot, melting bliss.

Kate hadn't expected any of this. Not the shopping expedition, and all the time spent together. Nor the emotional intimacy that had returned between them from the very first moment they reconnected.

She hadn't been close to anyone in so long, or wanted anyone so freely and so much. Even now that they had almost caught their breaths, she didn't want to extricate herself from him.

Alex seemed to feel the same.

His arms wrapped around her and he rolled onto his back and tenderly stroked her hair.

Luxuriating in their sensual closeness, Kate lay with her head on his chest for a long moment. She realized that if they kept this up, it would be all too easy for her to fall in love with another man who wasn't going to love her back.

And she knew her heart couldn't take another disappointment like that.

Which meant, like it or not, it was time to come back to reality. To face what this meant—and especially what it didn't.

He paused. "Tell me what you're thinking."

Glad he had given her the opening she—*they*—needed, she eased away and gazed deeply into his eyes. "Like you said before…" she inhaled a bolstering breath and held the sheet against her like a shield "…this was a long time coming."

He sat up against the headboard, as relaxed and confident as she was tense and nervous. "As well as inevitable," he said, his voice low and sexy.

Emotions in turmoil, she reached for her clothes and began to dress. "That doesn't change our circumstances."

Listening, he began to dress, too. His expression patient but grim.

"I'm leaving in a few weeks. Your life is here, with your boys who, by the way, are your main priority. As they should be. My life is either in Fort Worth or on the road. So—" she forced herself to go on "—for that reason, I think we should accept this was going to happen, once, and leave it at that."

Chapter Eight

"I didn't realize this was out here." Kate set a tray down on the edge of the fire pit an hour later.

Alex followed with a bottle of wine and two glasses. He prodded her with a lift of his dark brow. "Not surprising, since you haven't actually been in the backyard, have you?"

"Not until this evening. No."

The fire exuded warmth against the chill of the evening, as well as the wintry scent of wood smoke. The ranch house's exterior lights provided just the right amount of illumination. Six Adirondack chairs and small side tables rimmed the large round fire pit, which was covered by a fitted iron safety grate.

Kate set the food on a table.

She sent Alex a teasing glance, glad he had not bailed on their plans to spend the evening together after she had told him she wanted their relationship to go back to being platonic. "Had I known how nice it was, I might have wanted to cook out here sooner."

Kate laid the half-dozen kabobs on the grate, side by side. Soon the smell of searing steak, onions, peppers, squash and potatoes filled the air.

He continued to treat her cautiously. Studying her kindly one minute, but regarding her with reverent tenderness the next. "Nice to know. Although this is a little fancier than anything the boys and I have fixed."

Trying not to wonder if he felt the same confused mix of feelings she did—wanting to revisit their lovemaking one minute, wishing it had never happened the next—she said, "Let me guess what's been on the menu to date." She widened her eyes at him. "Hot dogs and s'mores."

Amusement filled his smile. "Correct."

Still keeping an eye on their dinner, she settled in the Adirondack chair beside him. "What else?"

He stretched his legs out lazily in front of him and continued sipping his wine. "That's it."

She laughed. "We'll have to expand your repertoire so you can do better after I leave."

"Speaking of that..." His gaze roamed over her languorously, head to toe, before returning to settle on her eyes. "How important is it for you to reside in Fort Worth?"

Kate tried unsuccessfully to fight a blush. "Not that necessary, I guess, given how much I travel. Though I don't know where else I would live."

He nodded, his expression maddeningly indecipherable. "How about here? In Laramie County?" He continued his pitch with an enticing grin. "Just think, you'd be able to buy your produce at Rose Hill Farm, your proteins at the butcher shop here."

She saw where this was going. "And see you and the boys whenever I was in town."

He nodded thoughtfully. "Works for me."

She could see that.

"When is your lease up?"

She tried not to feel too thrilled that he was already arranging the next "date" before the current one ended, the way all guys did when they were really interested in a woman. But he was thinking beyond that, too. To how they could see each other after her temporary gig at the Rocking M ended.

Although it was a little early for this kind of talk, wasn't it?

He didn't seem to think so.

Aware he was still waiting for her reply, she answered, "My lease ends the first of February."

"Plenty of time to put in your notice, then. And get moved in January, before work gets really busy for you in the spring."

She reminded herself that she had a business to run, a future to build. She didn't want to worry she was jumping into a hot love affair that could leave her emotionally devastated and ripped apart if it ended. "I didn't see a lot of apartments around here," she pointed out casually.

"There aren't that many." He moved his knee next to hers and gave it a nudge. "But if you're willing to live outside of town, I do know of a place."

Ignoring the tingles the brief touch had engendered, she tilted her head and said, "I'm listening."

"My sister, Sadie, has a caretaker's cottage at her lavender farm. She's been fixing it up in hopes of renting it. It's only got one bedroom and bath, but it's private, and there would be plenty of room for you to park your trailer and your truck."

Kate liked Sadie. If her farm were half as nice as Alex's ranch, she would love living there. Instead of an apartment complex in the city. "Hmm."

He frowned at the caution in her tone. "Does that mean you'll think about it?"

Kate sure wanted to.

She wanted to dive headfirst into whatever this was with him, with her whole heart and soul, and never look back.

But she had done that before—with her college boyfriend and then with Thaddeus. Neither relationship had worked out. Was she doing the same thing here? She didn't want to think so. But…she had just made love with him a few hours ago, and already she wanted to be intimate again. Even though the practical side of her knew this was all happening way too fast.

Forcing herself to put on the brakes, she eased her knee away from his and asked, "You don't think that could be uncomfortable?"

He sat up straighter. "In what sense?"

"Your little sister is pretty protective of you. Whereas your mom seems to be doing a little matchmaking—if her offer of babysitting the boys tonight is any indication."

Alex lifted a staying hand. "As far as Mom goes, that happens all the time," he corrected. "She and Dad like hosting the grandkids for sleepovers on the weekend."

Still not convinced the offer was as innocent as he thought, Kate exhaled. "Good to know."

"And Sadie's probably just projecting because her own situation with Will is so convoluted."

Kate thought about the disappointment and sadness his sister had shown every time she checked her phone on Thanksgiving Day. "That makes sense." More to the point, she knew Alex was just as worried about Sadie as his sister was about him. "But I still think I would need to get to know Sadie a lot better before leasing the cottage on her property." Landlord-tenant relationships could be tricky. Even when your boyfriend's family was involved.

Not that Alex was her boyfriend, of course.

Oblivious to the wayward nature of her thoughts, he narrowed his eyes and inquired, "But you'll think about making Laramie your home base?"

Kate nodded. Doubting she'd be able to think about much of anything else now that he had brought it up. Even if it was way too soon to be considering such a leap of faith.

"That's the third time you've looked at your watch in the last ten minutes. Somewhere you have to be?" Kate asked while they worked together on dinner cleanup.

At eight thirty on a Saturday night, there were plenty of places in town—like the Lone Star Dance Hall—that were still open. As well as holiday parties Alex might have been invited to attend…

Which, come to think of it, might be why his mom had wanted him to be kid-free tonight. So he could go to one of those. And mingle with the local single women who'd been eyeing him while they had been out yesterday and today.

"No." Alex dried the skewers he had just scrubbed clean with a dish towel. "Just a chore I forgot. I promised the boys that I would get their Christmas stockings out of the attic so they could hang them up as soon as they come home tomorrow."

"Sounds simple." Kate slid their plates and utensils into the dishwasher.

He fit the cork in the half-full wine bottle, since neither of them wanted another glass. His expression turned rueful. "It would be if I knew where they were."

Kate turned to him in surprise, her shoulder brushing the solid heat of his arm in the process. "What do you mean?"

"The boys helped me put the decorations away last year. And they aren't that great about following directions when they're excited. And they are always excited when they get to go up in the attic. So I could be up there an hour or more, hunting for them."

She wondered, "How much stuff is up there?"

His eyes lingered on her form, as if he were already mentally ending the evening by making love to her again. "You don't want to know," he told her with a wry twist of his lips.

She put her hands on her hips. "Now I have to know!"

"Seriously, you don't want to sift through that mess."

She put a pod in the dispenser, shut the dishwasher door and turned it on. "Like I have anything better to do? You helped me with the shopping today. Let me help you with this."

* * *

The third floor attic was accessed by a set of stairs at the end of the hall outside the master bedroom.

Kate tried not to look at the rumpled covers on his king-size bed, where they had impetuously made love just hours before.

Looking relaxed, happy and powerfully masculine, he switched on the light switch just inside the door and led the way. Kate followed, appreciating yet again the way he filled out his dark jeans and flannel shirt. Especially now that she knew firsthand what lay under them...

Gallant as ever, he was there to give her a hand when she reached the top. "So what do you think?" he asked, glancing around.

Technically, it was super nice and modern as far as attics went. There were big windows on either end of the large rectangular space. Lots of calm lighting overhead that gave it a bright and cozy aura. The floor was covered with a sturdy, industrial dark gray carpet, the walls painted a neutral ivory. Built-in shelving lined one long wall, from top to bottom, and the space seemed to be climate controlled.

But otherwise, it was a mess. He had not been exaggerating about that. There were clear plastic storage containers everywhere, filled with all sorts of things. Some with lids on, some off. Closest to her were pool toys and some camping gear, including a pup tent that had been set up.

"Looks like your little rascals have been rifling through just about everything."

"I bring them up here every now and again. Especially on rainy days during the weekend. They think it's a giant treasure chest."

"Or a museum," Kate noted wryly. She paused by a shelf, impressed. "Are these athletic trophies all yours?"

He sent her an admiring glance. Letting her know he was focused on her, not some former fame. "Ah…yeah."

Baseball, soccer, football. And right beneath it…more boxes, all with his name on them. Nursery school. Pre-K. Kindergarten… First grade. All the way to senior year of high school. She swung back to him. "You kept all this?" she asked in shock.

He exhaled, admitting reluctantly, "Not by choice. But my mom had kept it, and she insisted I would want it all someday, as sort of an archive of my life."

Kate peered into one of the elementary school boxes. Saw report cards, art work, test papers with big red A pluses and "Nice work, Alexander!" scrawled across the top. A little down the row, there were more clear plastic storage boxes full of papers. These with the names of his four sons and the time periods.

"I guess the tradition continues, hmm?" she couldn't help but tease.

He folded his arms. Staying close, but not too close. A mixture of amusement and affection in his gaze, he said, "You'd be surprised how hard it is to toss one of your kids' treasures."

Not for some parents, Kate thought. Reminded how much her own parents had hated "clutter."

Alex walked to the other end of the attic, to an old rocking glider chair and footstool, surrounded by open boxes of yuletide decorations. Hands on his hips, he gazed around with a frown. As if he honestly did not know where to begin. "Back to looking for Christmas stockings," he said with an overwhelmed sigh.

"Right."

Kate located a few more boxes, and after rifling through them for a few minutes, she waved him over. "This what you're searching for?"

Looking through them, he smiled in relief. "Yep."

Kate had found a heaping box of ornaments that hadn't made it onto the tree. Each bore the name of Alex or one of his sons. There were also stockings for the mantel, and their silver holders, in the second box. He grabbed it and began to sort. "Let's take all the stockings and the boys' ornaments downstairs."

"What about the ones you made?" Kate asked, thinking how cute those were, too.

"Nah."

"Seriously?" She glanced back at the rough-hewn ornaments. "You should put at least one of your artistic creations on the tree. The boys would love it."

He gave a mild grimace. "I'll think about it."

And then probably say no, she figured. Again.

"Where is all your stuff?" Without warning, he turned the tables on her. "At your apartment in Fort Worth or with your folks?"

She knew he hadn't meant to upset her, but he had, as painful memories returned in a flood. Long moments passed before she finally answered him, as matter-of-factly as she could. "My grandmother kept the ornaments I made in school, and she let me put them on her tree until she passed away when I was seven."

"And after that?"

Now, something she didn't want to discuss. "My parents don't like things that are tacky," she admitted. "So they didn't want the ornaments from school on the tree the interior decorator set up for us. The same went for the stocking I made with stuff from the craft store."

He paused to take that in. "So what happened to them?"

Having met his family, this part was even harder for her to reveal. "For a few years, they let me keep the decorations in a box in my room, but eventually it all got thrown away with the rest of my old papers and art projects."

Alex's voice dropped another notch. "I'm guessing you were upset."

Trying to hide her embarrassment, Kate looked away. She had wanted those decorations to mean as much to her parents as they did to her.

It hadn't worked out that way.

Although she couldn't really say she had been surprised. Only that they let her keep them as long as they had. She shrugged and sighed. "Yeah, I was sad about it. But my parents were never ones for 'clutter' so I didn't have a choice."

He came close enough that she could feel his body heat. He looked down at her compassionately. "Suddenly my mom's traditions don't seem quite as crazily sentimental..."

Unable to resist, she teased lightly, "And yet you don't seem to want your handmade creations on your Christmas tree, either, cowboy."

Alex walked over to stand in front of the big window, looking out at the darkness of the December night. He wreathed his arm around her.

"Although, who knows," Kate mused, wondering if she had made too much of this all these years. She felt herself floundering. "Maybe if I'd kept my decorations and could look at them now and see how corny they actually were, I would feel the same way you do. About wanting to turn my back on that part of my past..."

When her grandmother was there for every holiday. Always making it special. And even more important? Making her feel *loved*. Reminding her of the importance of family and that life didn't always have to revolve around business.

"Hey..." Alex tugged her close, bringing her all the way into his arms. Brushing the back of his hand across her cheek, he bent to kiss the top of her head. "I'm sorry," he whispered in her ear. He seemed serious now, in the way that meant he wanted the two of them to get closer. The heck of it was, she wanted that, too—so much...in spite of the walls she'd put around her heart.

"This stuff means a lot to a kid..."

She realized she could fall for him. Hopelessly. Irrevocably.

And then where would that leave her?

Empathetic tears blurred her eyes. "And sometimes an adult, too..."

He brought up a hand to the nape of her neck, sliding his fingers beneath the silky fall of hair. He looked into her eyes for a long, breath-stealing moment, before slowly shifting her lips to his for a sweet, seductive, oh-so-tender kiss.

She curled into his body as snugly as she could, wrapping her arms around him. And he groaned—the sound very male and hungry.

"Kate..." his voice was low and thrillingly rough. He inhaled deeply and kissed her again, even more ravenously this time, his blue eyes shuttering to half-mast. "I thought we weren't going to do this..." His body moved against her, one hard thigh sliding between hers.

She moaned softly, too. Swept up in the moment, in *him*. In the intoxicating feeling of wanting and being wanted in return. So much so that she let herself be immersed in the wonder of his mouth claiming hers again. Forgetting time and place. Concentrating only on the touch and feel and scent of him. Of the possessive yet protective sweep of his hands down her back, over her hips, then back up, past her ribs, to the aching tips of her breasts.

Desire pooled low in her belly.

And still they kissed, again and again, hot waves of lust

flowing through her, consuming her. Until sensation spiraled through her, unlike anything she had ever known. Or wanted.

"Tell me," he implored gently, cupping her shoulders, "if we do this again, there will be no regrets this time..."

He was so strong and virile, she noted, her heart hammering in her chest. She pressed up against the burgeoning arousal beneath his jeans and kissed him deeply. The two of them taking kissing to a whole new level. One created specifically for the most wonderful time of the year.

He brought her closer still, claiming her as his. "I know what I said," she whispered when he lifted his head and locked eyes with her. "I changed my mind," she told him wistfully. *And for very good reason.* "It's Christmastime..."

Which, for her, had always been the loneliest time of the year. Until now, anyway...

"There is that," he whispered back. Kissing her ear, her temple, the sensitive spot behind her ear. Until she quivered and his tall body hardened even more. He let out a low, pleasured growl of anticipation. His compliance as blissful as his touch.

"And though this is only temporary..." Her voice trailed off as she opened up one button, then another and another. She slid her hands beneath the fabric of his shirt. Across his warm, hard chest, with its sexy mat of dark hair that spread across his nipples, before arrowing down past his navel, into the waistband of his jeans.

He met her smile indulgently. And she wrapped herself against him again, aware that was just the beginning of something oh so wonderful. "Please let me have my merry way with you," she breathed.

When Kate put it like that, there was no refusing. "Whatever you want, darlin'..."

He took her by the hand and led her toward the exit, then

down the stairs to his bedroom below. Hitting the lights of the attic as they left.

This time, Kate was the initiator.

And he let her do whatever she wanted. Which meant kissing him. Languidly exploring every inch of his body. Then stripping down so he could enjoy hers. Both of them caught up in something too primal to fight, she cupped him in her hands. Then bent to kiss and caress the most masculine part of him.

He groaned, on the verge of losing control.

Flipping positions with her, shifting her onto her back, she gasped as he took total control. Spreading her thighs wide and finding her with lips and mouth—in the most intimate way possible. Exploring. Adoring. Until she too groaned and made a sexy little sound in the back of her throat. "*Now*, Alex…" She arched her back impatiently, "I want you inside of me when I…"

"Just savor it," he commanded softly. "I'm not going anywhere, darlin'." And just that suddenly, her release came, her entire body surrendering against him in boneless pleasure.

He stroked the insides of her thighs. Kissed the dampness. "Worth it?" he murmured, satisfaction roaring through him.

"Oh yes…"

He reached for a condom. "Ready for round two?" He palmed her breasts and took her taut nipple into his mouth.

"Yes, again."

Grinning, he sheathed himself, then slid up her body and once again captured her mouth with his.

She opened up her thighs, beckoning him to bring his whole body into contact with hers. Desire welled. He slid inside, delving deep. They took their time. Drawing out the inevitable pleasure. And then she was raising her knees and wrapping her arms around his back, pulling him deeper, until he was awash with sensation. She was trembling. Urging him on. Until they were both close, *so close*. And together at last, they found the blissful release they sought.

To his mounting satisfaction, this time Kate didn't ease away like before. Instead, she clung to him. Eyes shut. Relishing their closeness.

Fulfillment ripping through him, he brought her nearer still, holding her close as they both fell asleep.

Chapter Nine

"Last chance to go to brunch..." Alex said, shortly after nine the next morning.

Kate looked up from her laptop to see Alex standing in the doorway of the ranch kitchen and dining hall. She had slipped out of his bed before he had woken up, then padded soundlessly downstairs to shower in the guest suite.

As her gaze drifted over him, she was inundated with memories of their lovemaking the night before. He was such a tender, passionate lover. So kind and protective. Seeing things about her no one else ever had or would. She wanted him to fill her up and end the aching loneliness deep inside her. Even if leaping into this with him was the last thing she should be doing. If she wanted to avoid another broken heart...

"Thanks, but I have to figure out the menus for the week ahead. Make sure I have everything I need."

To her relief, he didn't push. He came toward her, looking even better than he had when she'd left him—clean shaven, showered, in a cerulean blue corduroy shirt and jeans. "Do you want Reckless to stay here with you, or go with me?" he asked.

Kate reached over to pet the gray and white sheepdog's silky head. "He can stay with me. Can't you, buddy?" He had been following her around all morning, tail wagging.

"Okay." Alex flashed an easy smile. "The boys and I will be back around noon."

Which meant she would have the ranch to herself, since the cowboys weren't due to be back until late that evening.

Happy not to have the scrutiny of Alex's family, Kate went back to work. Comparing needed ingredients to what was in the pantry, fridge and freezer. Then figuring out which recipes she needed to double or triple to satisfy the cowboys' hearty appetites.

She was just about done when she heard the sound of Alex's Lincoln Navigator in the driveway. Reckless, who had been curled at her feet, jumped up and rushed toward the door. Seconds later, the boys barreled in from the breezeway on a burst of icy air that had come in with the cold front the night before. They ran toward her, giggling mischievously.

Alex was right behind them. Looking every bit as merry as his four sons.

"You have to take Reckless outside and stay there until we tell you that you can come back in!" Matthew announced.

His three brothers nodded.

Kate tilted her head to Alex in silent inquiry. His eyes twinkling, he merely shrugged. "Just know," he said mysteriously, "it wasn't my idea."

"But it *is* a Christmas surprise!" Max shouted.

Alex cut the rambunctious quadruplets off with the sign for silence. He handed Kate Reckless's leash. "If you wouldn't mind…"

She grabbed her jacket from the hook next to the door and walked outside. The hilarity continued for the next fifteen or so minutes. She kept her back turned away from the house as Reckless sniffed the yard, so she couldn't see anything, but she could hear them dashing from one end of the first floor to the other. Giggling. Shouting. Then eventually... they grew quiet.

The front door opened and Alex walked out onto the porch. Two boys flanked him on each side.

"You can come in now," Michael announced, trying hard to squash his glee.

Alex met Kate at the top of the porch steps. He took Reckless's leash, unhooked it from his collar and waved the sheepdog inside.

"Keep going!" Marty urged Kate. He jumped up and down, beside himself with excitement.

Completely caught up in the holiday revelry, Kate followed the family pet into the foyer.

"Now, Dad!" Matthew said.

"Do it!" Max ordered.

"Do what?" Kate couldn't help but ask.

Michael pointed up toward the chandelier. And then she saw what the ruckus was all about.

The next thing she knew, Alex was taking her in his arms, guiding her beneath the mistletoe. His head slanted down. She caught her breath and then his lips brushed hers softly and tenderly.

And in that instant, she knew that this was no fleeting holiday love affair. This was something much more special. Something that was already involving them all.

"I wouldn't have figured you for a mistletoe guy," Kate murmured the moment they were alone.

Ever the gentleman, Alex helped her with her coat and hung it up for her, next to his, in the foyer closet. His eyes sparkled with devilry. "I'm not really."

She inhaled the brisk masculine scent of him. "Then...?"

"Mom was giving out sprigs to Joe and Ellie, and Claire

and Zach, and the boys insisted you and I and Sadie and Gabe all needed mistletoe, too. They said to be fair, all the adults had to have mistletoe for the holidays. Or nobody should get it."

Kate couldn't help but admire the boys' logic. And sense of equality. Another legendary Texas McCabe trait. "What did your parents think about that?"

Grinning, Alex shook his head. "Oh, Mom and Dad were quite amused. As were all the other adults. Anyway, on the way home, the boys started arguing about where we should put it, and when we should surprise you. Given how excited they were, I thought the sooner it was up, the better. Otherwise, your surprise would have been spoiled."

She glanced back at the mistletoe. "Are you going to leave it there?" So every time they came in or out of the door... he'd kiss her?

He shrugged, as if thinking the same thing she was and not minding one bit. "Probably going to have to..." He waggled his brows at her.

The boys came running back to the foyer, their Christmas stockings and homemade ornaments in hand. "Dad! Can we put these up?" Marty asked.

"Sure." Alex went along to assist.

Soon, the tree was decorated with school art projects and all five of the stockings were up on the mantel. Including Alex's.

It was a heartwarming and homey sight, and Kate couldn't help but think how lucky she was to be here with Alex and his family, enjoying all this.

Perplexed, Michael turned to Kate. "Where is your stocking? Is it at home?"

"Actually," she answered reluctantly, "I don't have a Christmas stocking." It was yet another yuletide tradition her family did not honor.

Well, that wasn't fair, the kids complained. They insisted they had to get her one to put on the mantel. "Good idea," Alex said, to one and all. He put his hand on Kate's spine, already ushering her toward the door. "Let's hop in the Navigator and go to town. And make it happen."

"Everybody got their hats?" Alex asked, as he parked down the street from the craft and fabric store.

Looking cute as could be, in their matching green knit caps, all four boys shouted "Yes!" in unison, as Kate and Alex helped them out of the SUV, and onto the sidewalk. The downtown area of Laramie was bustling with shoppers and tourists alike, there to take in the festivities. Wreaths and trees decorated every business, and holiday music played on the loudspeakers. In the town park, food trucks offered both seasonal and traditional fare.

To Kate's surprise, this time they didn't have to ask. The boys all latched on to her and Alex's hands, staying close by their sides.

Once inside the store, they made their way to the back, where lots of different style stockings hung on the wall.

"You gotta get one just like ours," Michael declared.

His brothers nodded.

Kate wasn't sure that would happen. The ones they had were made of quilted red-fabric and snowy white cuffs. The displayed variety were quite different. With all colors and fabrics, various sizes and designs.

She looked at Alex, wondering what he thought. Was this the time to differentiate her from him and the boys, via her choice of stocking, or bring her all the way into the clan?

He was already reaching high, to the red quilted ones with the snowy white cuffs, and bringing one down.

The boys let out a delighted cheer.

Alex turned to Kate. "What do you think?" he asked. "This good?"

Unexpected emotion welling in her throat, she nodded. "It's perfect," she said.

The boys wanted to make more decorations to put on the tree, so they picked out what they needed for that activity, too.

As they stood in line to pay, Max looked out the storefront windows, at the people passing by with insulated cups, and asked, "Dad, can we get hot chocolate?"

"Sounds good to me." He smiled.

Minutes later, they were all in the park, sitting at a picnic table, with the treats in hand. It didn't take long for the kids to get chocolate and whipped cream mustaches. Alex facetiously imitated his sons, while giving Kate a look daring her to do the same.

Figuring what the heck, why not, she took a sip, making sure to let the whipped cream touch her upper lip, too.

The boys hooted with glee, then giggled uproariously. Alex laughed, too.

Another customer passing by, murmured to Kate, "Cute family!"

Except they weren't really her family, Kate thought, even as Alex nodded at the woman, and thanked her for the compliment.

Was this what he wanted?

It seemed so, Kate thought. Even as she warned herself not to let the joy of the holidays alter her perspective about what was really possible, in the long run, and what was not.

A couple of hours later, Kate, Alex and the boys had returned to the Rocking M and were gathered around the kitchen table. Homemade Christmas tree ornaments were spread out in front of them.

All were precut and sewn and made out of the felt they had purchased at the craft and fabric store in town. Ribbon ties served as hooks, which made them extra safe for the kids.

Glitter, glue, and all manner of additional felt or cloth "details" finished the reindeer, Santas, snowmen and gingerbread houses.

"These are awesome!" Michael declared, looking them over.

His brothers agreed. Even Reckless, who had been curled up at their feet beneath the table, thumped his tail in happy agreement.

"What do you think? Should we hang them on the tree?" Alex asked, rising.

"We'll do ours. Kate can do hers," Matthew said.

"And Dad, you do the ones you made for Reckless!" Marty suggested. Which was how Alex had avoided doing any of his own, Kate thought drolly.

The boys hadn't noticed that yet.

They would eventually.

And then he would either have to get his old ones out of the attic or pony up and make some new ones, the way she had been forced to do.

Not that she minded.

It had been fun to shop with them and then sit together, working on decorations they would cherish for years to come. And eventually likely be a little embarrassed by, too.

Alex met Kate's eyes, the way most married parents of children did. "Sounds like a plan," he told his boys as they went off to start round three of tree decorating.

For the next half an hour, the quadruplets arranged—and then rearranged—their new family-made ornaments, using the ones they had made at school in previous years, as well as the store-bought ones they'd already had.

Kate and Alex let them cover the branches they could reach, and put the ones they had made up near the top of the tree. Alex nudged Kate's shoulder with his. "The stockings look nice, too."

All six of them were hung side by side. Although Kate still wasn't sure they should have purchased an identical one for her, too, and put her name on it with the same black fabric paint and stencil kit they had used on theirs. It sort of made her feel like a member of their family, and she really wasn't.

Not yet.

Even though she was secretly starting to hope that would eventually be the case. This afternoon had just been so much fun! Heartwarming, too... "I just don't want the boys to be disappointed," she murmured in return, trying to be realistic once again.

He followed her back to the kitchen. "Why would they be unhappy?"

She was reminded yet again of how, when she had been a child, spending the holidays with her grandmother had always been a magical time for her. Which was what made them so hard for her since, given that her parents, and even her ex-fiancé, did not feel the same way. For them, it was all retail sales numbers and bottom lines and profit margins for the calendar year.

Out here in Laramie County with Alex, however, Thanksgiving and Christmas were about tradition and family, giving and love. All the things she wanted in her life.

It would be hard to celebrate it so joyously this year. And then, presumably, have to go back to the norm, next year.

Aware Alex was still waiting for her answer, she forced herself to answer him honestly. "I can't help but wonder how the boys are going to feel when I leave here in three weeks." Her contract with the ranch only went to December 23. She swallowed around the tightness of her throat. "And I'm not actually here for Christmas. Especially after all the trouble they have taken to try and include me today."

Looking as if that hadn't occurred to him, Alex went very still. He locked eyes with her and held her gaze so intently that she couldn't look away. "You're thinking it will be like the scene in *A Christmas Carol*? When Tiny Tim's crutch is still there, and he's not?"

What the hell! He was comparing her to *Tiny Tim*?

Crinkles appeared at the corners of his eyes. She realized he was teasing. Even though he was also very clearly making a point.

"Probably not that dramatic," she muttered.

"Although there would be an empty place on the mantel." A notion that made her feel even grumpier.

"Unless I left the stocking and ornaments, which might make it even worse for the kids…"

"And me," he corrected archly. "And you're right, that would be a heart-wrenching reminder of the incredibly beautiful woman we have so enjoyed having with us. Luckily, there's an easy solution for that," Alex said, his expression turning both serious and hopeful. "Stay here on the Rocking M. And celebrate with us."

He meant it. Kate could see it in his eyes. A thrill swept through her. Matched by the worry he was acting impulsively again. As was she. Darn it! What was it about the two of them that made it so hard to stay away from each other? She sucked in a breath. "I don't want to intrude…"

He made a face like that was the silliest thing he had ever heard. "Are you *kidding*? You're making this holiday season the best ever for all of us! I've never seen the boys look so happy." He reached up and picked a clump of silver glitter and school glue out of her hair. Opening his palm, he showed it to her. "And the same goes for me."

She went into the kitchen to get a wet wipe from the plastic container. Figuring fair was fair, she cleaned some glue from the side of his jaw. Grinning, she showed it to him. "What about Reckless? Does he get a say?"

Alex's eyes sparkled as he laughed. With his hand against her back, he guided her farther out of earshot of the boys. "I think our canine buddy has already weighed in. Haven't you seen the way he perks up whenever you come in the room?"

She had.

Kate had also seen the way Alex looked at her. The way he had during Inga, times one hundred. She knew she was looking at him the same way, too.

As if he were the key to her happiness right now. That being the case, did she really need to worry about anything besides the holiday season they were in? Wouldn't reality come crashing back down on them soon enough? Why ruin their current happiness?

"So what do you say? Will you stay on the Rocking M and celebrate Christmas with us?"

It was quite a gift he was giving her. More than she had ever hoped to receive.

"You make it awfully hard to say no," she whispered to him, as Reckless went in to watch over the boys.

He cupped her face with the side of his hand. "Then don't."

She knew he wanted to kiss her. She wanted to feel his lips on hers, too.

Aware of drawing the boys even further into something that very well might not last, she stepped back and turned her attention to the chore they had been neglecting. Looking down at the kitchen table, she wrinkled her nose. "We really made a mess, didn't we?"

Shrugging, he went to get the kitchen waste can. Set it between them. Then, together, they dropped the scraps of paper and ribbon and little felt pieces into the trash. The sides of their hands bumped as they cleared the last of it, sending an enticing tingle of heat and need speeding through her.

He inhaled, but made no move to step away. "Yeah," he said softly, "but we had fun doing it, so..."

And she knew, in that instant, he was looking forward to more fun in the future.

Not just in bed with her.

But with his kids. As a family.

Without warning, all four boys were back. Before she knew it, she was wrapped in a heartfelt group hug. "Thank you, Kate!" the four boys shouted enthusiastically and in unison.

"Yeah, we love you!" they said.

And although she had heard them say the same to everyone else in the McCabe clan, she knew they meant it. And that was a lot. Because the truth was, Kate loved them, too.

Alex knew his boys were emotionally attached to Kate. And it was no surprise.

She had filled the space left by Tiffany's abandonment.

A hurt, he had never been able to ease on his own.

Even with the continual help of his extended family.

There was always something missing. A mother's touch, he supposed. A woman's gentleness.

Kate.

He could tell by the touched but wary look on her face that as much as she appreciated the affection and admiration of his kids, she was also worried.

About what would happen if this all fell apart.

If he were honest, he was a little worried, too. He had always been too quick to judge and trust someone.

It was why his first marriage had failed.

As for Kate, she didn't seem to really trust anything on a personal level. The only thing she had faith in was a business arrangement.

So maybe, he thought, this was why he should slow down a little. Hope she took him up on his offer and stayed to have Christmas with them. And then go from there.

Chapter Ten

"Can I give you a hand with that?" Alex asked on Monday morning. The holiday weekend was over, and it was back to business as usual.

Kate finished unhitching her cooking trailer from her pickup truck. She dropped the tools back in the box. "No. I've got it. Thanks for offering, though. Boys get dropped off at school okay?"

"Yeah. Although they did mention they'd much rather stay at the ranch and hang out with the two of us about one hundred times."

Realizing they had to tamp down the sexual intensity between them, now that they were no longer alone on the ranch—as they had been for part of the weekend—Kate ignored the heat in his eyes. "That sounds about as exciting as being asked, 'Are we there yet…?'"

Hooking his thumbs through his belt loops, he rocked forward on the toes of his boots. "You do know my boys."

She pushed away her desire, smiled and stepped to one side. "I do."

He folded his arms, seemingly in no hurry to go. "Thanks for giving them something special for their lunch boxes today."

She lifted a playful hand, aware it was awfully hard not to flirt with him. Especially when he kept looking at her as if she were the most beautiful woman he had ever encountered. "Pretzel sticks and yogurt covered raisins work every time."

He caught her eyes and flashed that grin she loved. "That they do."

Behind them, an unfamiliar car came up the drive. It was a Mini Cooper. Not the kind of vehicle you usually saw in cattle country. "Expecting anyone?" Kate said.

"No." Alex frowned, perplexed. "You?"

Kate shook her head.

He turned back to her, an inscrutable look on his face. "But you were planning to go somewhere this morning?"

"I thought I'd get to know the area a little better, do a little shopping…" She had figured whether she stayed for the holiday or not…and she was leaning heavily toward doing just that…that she needed to buy some Christmas presents for Alex and the boys—and the cowboys, too—since everyone had been so nice to her and made her feel so welcome.

The little car came to a halt. A guy in a jacket and jeans got out. He had a big envelope in hand. "Alex McCabe?" he asked, taking out the sheaf of papers inside.

Alex nodded.

He handed them over with one hand and snapped a photo on his phone with the other.

"You've been served."

A litany of swear words went through Alex's mind. He should have known Tiffany wasn't done. That she wouldn't give up on whatever it was she wanted.

He watched the process server drive hurriedly away.

Kate looked at him, as mindful of the circumstances—and his feelings—as ever. Unlike him, she did not make any assumptions about who the legal papers were from.

"If you want me to give you space..." She was already backing up, ready to depart.

Tension coiled inside him. He looked her in the eye. "Actually, if you have a few minutes, I'd like you to stay."

She hesitated, still seeming to think she was intruding, then said, "Sure."

Frowning, he continued, "I have to make a call..."

She waved an airy hand. "Take your time."

Before he could punch in the number, his phone rang. He looked at the screen. It was his brother Gabe.

"Talk about good timing," Alex muttered, putting the phone to his ear. "Hey," he said.

"You're about to get served..." Gabe warned.

Alex blew out a breath. "Just did."

"I got some information delivered to me, too," his brother said.

Great. That meant Tiffany was really serious about making his life hell again. At least until she got what she was aiming for.

"How soon can we talk about it?" Alex asked.

"Can you come in to my office now?"

His gut twisting, he promised, "I'll be there in twenty."

"And bring Kate with you, too."

"Why does Gabe want to see me?" she asked, short minutes later, as they both climbed into his Navigator.

"He didn't say."

She huffed out an exasperated breath. Beginning to look as tense as he felt. "What's your guess?"

Alex grimaced. "Probably that you're somehow involved in whatever is going on with Tiffany."

Kate turned toward him. "And what *is* going on exactly?"

Alex had only scanned the first page or two, but it was enough to let him know. "She wants an immediate modification to our custody arrangement," he bit out. "And she has hired an attorney to help her get it."

Kate fell silent after that. Alex was quiet, too.

The papers he had received hadn't said a lot; it seemed to be just a request for a family court hearing regarding the care of the boys.

They soon found out Gabe had received a lot more.

Not one bit of it good.

Gabe ushered Kate and Alex into his office conference room and motioned for them both to have a seat. "I'm going to make a call to Tamara Marshall, Tiffany's lawyer, while you look at the packet that was delivered to me this morning. When you've had a chance to absorb it, and I get a little more info, we'll talk. And Alex, have your car checked for a tracking device. There must be one on it somewhere."

He slipped out.

Kate stared at the folder as if it were kryptonite. Alex knew exactly how she felt. He didn't want any part of this, either, but if his brother had insisted he and Kate both come in and view this, then it was imperative they did.

Inhaling deeply, he reached over and flipped the file open.

"OMG," Kate whispered. It was a photo of them standing in the window of the attic, kissing passionately.

More, with the boys watching and cheering them on when they'd hung the mistletoe. Pictures of them flirting while they'd visited Rose Hill Farm to buy produce. And last but not least, their panic when they'd visited the Christmas tree lots at the fairgrounds and the boys had briefly disappeared.

"I kept feeling like we were being watched on Friday and Saturday," Kate whispered, her face pale. "I thought it was just because I was new to town, and I was with you…and people were curious."

"They were. But it looks like Tiffany hired someone to spy on us, too."

"Why would she do that?" Kate whispered.

So many reasons, Alex thought bitterly as there was a brief knock on the door. Then Gabe reentered the conference room, expression solemn.

"What did you find out?" he demanded.

Gabe sat down opposite them. "Tiffany has decided she wants joint custody."

Alex felt like he'd been sucker punched. He leaned forward, both hands flat on the conference table. "Well, she can't have it, can she? Not after all this time! Especially when her only true connection to them is via a legal agreement!"

"It's still a binding contract," Gabe reminded.

Kate stared at them, looking completely lost. "What are you talking about?"

Gabe left it up to Alex to explain. "Tiffany told me she couldn't have children, that if we were going to have a family it would be by surrogate."

"So that's what you did," Kate surmised slowly, looking even more stunned.

"Yes. We used my sperm and donor eggs." Alex ran a hand over his eyes, remembering. He looked back at Kate, figuring she should know this, too. "The only trouble was, it was a lie. She could have children, she just didn't want to physically go through a pregnancy or ruin her figure."

Kate took a moment to absorb that, her heart seeming to go out to him. Finally, she asked compassionately, "When did you find out?"

"During our divorce. We were arguing, and it just slipped out, and then she owned it. Insinuating the issue was mine, of course, not hers."

"Because if you had been more open-minded...?" Kate guessed.

"She could have been honest with me, all along, about what she wanted to do," Alex finished. "She wouldn't have had to hide her distaste for the physical aspects of pregnancy, and her unwillingness to personally go through it."

Kate's brow wrinkled. "Is that why she isn't interested in them, because there is no biological connection between her and the children?"

Alex shrugged. "Maybe. Although there was a point where she was on board with having a family. And like Gabe said, she is still their legal mother and has been since they were born. The fact she hasn't seen them for the last four and a half years doesn't alter that fact in the eyes of the court."

"It should," Kate muttered.

"And maybe it will, in the long run," Gabe said, still in lawyer mode. "But right now all we need to know is that her attorney says she's had a change of heart, now that she has seen the kids again. Her position is going to be that the boys are out of control and suffering from neglect."

Neglect! "In what sense?" Alex gritted out.

"That you're more interested in an affair with a new contractor at the ranch, than you are in taking care of them. Which is why you lost track of them at the fairgrounds during the Christmas tree sale on Black Friday."

"Wait a minute!" Kate interrupted, leaning forward, too. "Alex had nothing to do with that. That was my fault," she insisted. "I had them with me when that happened."

Gabe glanced at his notes. "According to the petition her attorney filed, you were also at the Rocking M when the boys rudely attacked Tiffany with their toy water pistols."

Alex let out a growl of dissent. "That is on Tiffany."

"Not according to her and Paolo." Gabe shook his head.

"Bottom line, they say the boys need to be in a two-parent home. In Houston. With them."

Was Alex about to lose his sons? Because of *her*? Guilt rushed through Kate like a roaring river. She got unsteadily to her feet. "Obviously, me working for you is creating problems. I should just quit. Now. Leave the area."

"I definitely wouldn't advise it," Gabe countered.

Alex gently encircled her wrist, then guided her back down into her seat next to him. "I agree," he said, giving her a look that said he had her back.

"You bolting will make it look like there was something to be regretful about," Gabe pointed out.

And maybe there was, Kate thought, recalling their impulsive lovemaking. Alex closed the file of incriminating pictures. "How did they get those photos anyway?"

"Telephoto lens. Tiffany's attorney hired a private investigator to dig up dirt on you, to strengthen her case. And this is all they've come up with. At least so far."

"But it's damning," Alex guessed flatly.

Gabe sighed. "Depends on the judge. But yeah, it could be a big problem if there is anything controversial in your background, Kate."

A cold chill of fear went down her spine. "Like what?" she asked, doing her best to hide her anxiety.

"Like you tell me," Gabe returned with a steady look.

Was this the time to tell Alex she had known his ex, once upon a time? Even if Tiffany didn't seem to remember her? And that it hadn't exactly been a pleasant experience?

Kate swallowed. Pushed on carefully, "The only time I ever got in trouble was high school."

Alex cocked his head. Gave her a thoughtful squint. "Hard to imagine," Alex murmured.

And yet for a few miserable years, her behavior had been as out of control as the situation she had found herself in. Her gut knotting with the memories of that stressful time, she continued her explanation with difficulty. "I...acted out."

"Why?" Gabe asked.

Avoiding Alex's careful survey, Kate told his brother, "My parents put me in a ritzy all-girls prep school for high school, because they thought it would help me get into a top college." She ran a hand over her eyes. "And let's just say... I wasn't happy."

Gabe listened as intently as Alex, his legal pad and pen in front of him. Both men seemed to think she was personable to a fault. And these days, she pretty much was. "Why not?" Gabe prodded.

Kate drew a quavering breath. Looked both men in the eye, and finally said, "Because I didn't fit in. I had the wrong car, the wrong clothes." The wrong *everything*, she remembered. "Almost all the girls there were Old Money. My parents could barely afford the steep tuition. Things like that."

It was hard to tell which of the brothers was frowning more deeply. "So you were being bullied," Alex growled, as fiercely protective as ever.

Kate nodded slowly. "Yes." *By none other than your ex, and the circle of exceedingly popular girls she ran with.*

Gabe continued taking notes.

"Did your parents know?" Alex demanded softly. As always, his ultramasculine presence and the crisp scent of his soap made her feel sheltered and intensely aware.

Kate swallowed to ease her parched throat. "I told them."

"And...?" Gabe got up to get them all a bottle of water from the small office fridge in the corner.

Kate took hers. Sighing, she untwisted the lid and took a

grateful sip. She realized it wasn't just Alex and his parents who were giving and kind—it was all the McCabes.

She and Alex were lucky to have Gabe on their side in this.

"My parents just expected me to figure out how to make friends at my new school, and if not, then *at least* blend in—because getting along with others no matter what was a skill I would need in the business world."

Alex moved a little closer to her.

She thought about the kisses they had shared, and how quickly he had rocked her entire world. Enticing her to give even more than she ever thought she would want to give.

"But you didn't agree with your folks," Alex guessed.

On so many things. Then and now.

Her heartbeat quickening at the compassion in his low tone, Kate took another sip of water. "I wanted to go to culinary school but they wouldn't listen to me. So I started acting out—skipping class, getting detention, deliberately misinterpreting assignments, disrespecting all the prep's esteemed rite of passage traditions. Stuff like that."

Alex's gaze skimmed her intently, as both he and his brother continued to listen closely to everything she said.

"But...luckily...none of this is on my high school transcripts because my parents made a hefty donation to the school to have my record wiped clean, prior to graduation. And last I heard, the headmaster and top administration has all changed, too..."

"I don't think you have to worry about that," Gabe said firmly. "The court isn't going to go back that far...when it comes to character...unless you had an arrest or something of that nature."

"No, there is nothing like that!" Kate assured him. She would never break the law. Or hurt anyone else. "Just stuff that, when I look back, I find juvenile and embarrassing."

Alex reached over and gave her hand a reassuring squeeze. The kind that said he would support her, no matter what.

The warmth and strength of his fingers encircled hers. She let out a slow breath and began to relax, but did not remove her hand from his.

Gabe looked up from his notepad. "What about your college years?" he probed.

Kate looked down at her and Alex's entwined hands. Noticed how perfectly they fit together, despite the variance in size and strength.

She returned her attention to the interview in progress. And tried not to think about the emotionally painful end to her high school years. And how responsible she had been for all the drama.

"College was good," she admitted softly. Even though she wasn't studying what she wanted, she loved the independence of living on campus and felt more in control of her situation. "I had learned my lesson about making life harder than it had to be, just to prove a point. And had stopped rebelling and making unnecessary problems for myself. I just wanted to start fresh and make my parents proud of me again."

Aware she and Alex had been holding hands way too long, she eased her palm from his. Sat back in her chair.

"I lived in the library. Made the dean's list. And was all about making a positive impact and achieving excellence in everything I did. So I could get into a top business school. And I did."

Gabe nodded, still writing. "And after?"

"I went to work for my family's retail company. Got engaged. When that didn't work out because Thaddeus and I realized we wanted different things, I decided to reset my life again, and left to start my own traveling chef business, and here we are."

"Any drama with your ex or your parents about all that? Loud arguments? Clothes thrown on the lawn? Cars keyed? Restraining orders?"

Kate couldn't help but laugh as she shook her head. "No. It was all very civilized…"

Neither her parents nor Thaddeus had been happy with her, but they had let her go.

Gabe put down his pen. "Tiffany's attorney will have you investigated, too. To see if there is anything that would make you unfit to be around the kids."

"There isn't," she said firmly.

"I can vouch for that," Alex agreed. "She's the most wonderful woman I've ever met."

Gabe scoffed. "I wouldn't let Tiffany hear you say that, either."

"I'm well beyond caring what she thinks," Alex muttered.

"I'm aware. I also know you don't go poking a filthy rich oil heiress," his brother reminded him. "Especially one with an agenda."

Which was why she had made sure they saw all those incriminating photos, Kate thought angrily. It had been a warning shot to let them all know how ugly this was likely to be. Unless, of course, Alex's ex got whatever she wanted. "You think she is out to get Alex, then? By starting all this?" Kate asked.

"Yeah, she's definitely up to something," Alex interjected.

Kate silently agreed.

"Who knows what her true agenda is. The important thing is for us not to be surprised in court by anything," Gabe told them.

Would the social media ruckus she had briefly stirred up in her senior year qualify? Kate wondered. Especially since Tiffany didn't seem to recognize her?

Alex looked so tense and worried by the turn of events, Kate decided not to tell him about the havoc she had caused. There was no way he would find out about how immature and disrespectful she had been before she nearly got expelled. The incident wasn't on her school records. And the internet had been scrubbed clean at the time, shortly after the incident occurred. So there was no way anyone would find out about that. She needed to do now what she had done then. Let it go. Move on. And most of all, she needed to keep Alex out of it. So if the worst happened, and Tiffany did remember and bring it up... Then Alex could truthfully claim no knowledge of her past mistakes.

As his brother had said, as long as no laws were broken, and they hadn't been, it was not going to be relevant.

"In the meantime, we're going to have to figure out how you want to handle this," Gabe continued. "Today is December 1. We have twenty days to file a response with the court."

Which would be right before Christmas, Kate thought. She just hoped and prayed the boys would be safe from more upheaval in their life. At least for this holiday season...

"That's kind of hard to do," Alex said gruffly, standing and beginning to pace the conference room, "when we don't know what is behind all this."

His brother nodded, still talking about the needed legal response to Tiffany's petition for a change in custody. "Which is exactly why we need to hire an investigator to look into Tiffany, Paolo and her parents. See what is going on with all of them that might be prompting her to move against you after all this time."

Alex grimaced. "Do it."

Gabe stood, too. "It'll probably take a week or two, depending on what we find. In the meantime, we will file a civil restraining order against the PI who was following you and the kids around. So there shouldn't be any more photos. At least not from him." He cleared his throat. "That doesn't mean there won't be any more defamatory information presented. Because they will likely present anything else they can scrounge up legally. Without violating any stalking laws."

Alex turned away from the window overlooking the street. "You really think Tiffany has a chance?" He spoke as if he had been hoping she didn't.

Just like Kate.

Because she could not think of a woman *less* suited to be in a supervisory position of Alex's four delightful sons, never mind placed in the mother role she'd already summarily rejected.

Gabe picked up his notepad and pen. His tone was as earnest and straightforward as his gaze. "As I said earlier, it will depend on the judge. Tiffany's argument is going to be that you've embarked on a reckless love affair in full view of her children. And say that the boys need to be in a two-parent home. With more structure and safety than you are currently providing."

"So, bottom line...this is all going to be about the fact I'm not married, and Tiffany is," Alex said. "'Cause if I were..."

"And if there was no affair. If it were instead a legally sanctioned marriage, that would definitely level the playing field," Gabe said, understanding—like Kate—where this was all heading. To a full, ugly custody battle.

He continued in full attorney mode. "But you're not married, bro, so we're going to have to go with the situation as it is. And make sure there is nothing objectionable going forward between you and Kate."

"Meaning?" Alex looked ready to do whatever he had to do to save his kids.

His brother shrugged. "Get that tracking device off your truck. And no more PDA. Especially not in front of the boys."

"So you're saying we can't date?" Alex asked. "Even after Kate's contract with the Rocking M is up?"

"I'm saying you either have to go public and make this a serious relationship that is good and beneficial to the boys, or declare it all a terrible mistake—one you won't repeat—and never see each other again."

Silence fell.

As the bleak reality of the situation sank in, Kate couldn't help but ask, "Which one would go over better with the court?" And help Alex maintain full custody of his boys?

This was Christmas, the season of giving, after all.

"Whichever one of those options is true," Gabe said.

Chapter Eleven

The ride back to the ranch was as silent as the one into town had been. Kate didn't mind the silence. It gave her time to think.

By the time Alex parked in front of the Rocking M's ranch house, she knew what she had to do.

For all their sakes.

And that was make it as easy on him and the boys as possible. Even if she was breaking her own heart in the process.

"You don't have to worry about the contract between our two companies," she said when she got out of the Navigator and walked around the front to come face to face with him. "I'm not going to hold you to it." Already mentally hitching her silver stream back up to her pickup truck, she promised quietly, "I'll quit and be out of here today."

Alex slanted her a look. "You really think that's what I want?"

Kate raked her teeth across her lower lip. Pushing aside the memories of their tender kisses and heated lovemaking, she attempted a tranquil attitude she couldn't begin to feel, and responded with the levelheaded approach to the problem he needed to hear.

"To be bullied by Tiffany to make big changes to your life? Again? No. I don't. But..." she admitted miserably. "I also can't see any other way forward."

Sensing he needed comforting, as any friend would, she reached out to lightly stroke the back of his hand. He leaned into her easy touch, the warmth of his skin contrasting against the chilly December air. Alex sighed. "Gabe said if we made our relationship public, and knocked off all the PDA and so on that the court might ignore all the innuendo my ex's lawyer intends to present."

Kate thought about the damning photos that had not been part of the initial petition, but would be included if they went to trial. Guilt and regret soared through her once again. She hated the fact that she had fallen into the trap and helped put him in this untenable position. The notion that their reckless affair could cause him to lose full custody of his kids was unimaginable.

"Or the judge could decide a two-parent home is still better than one with only a single parent," she countered.

He turned his hand over so their palms were pressed together. The feel of that was oddly intimate. The contact reminded her of the kisses they had shared, and the physical longing that welled inside her whenever they were alone.

Still looking into her eyes, he made no effort to release her hand. "Which is exactly why we need to level the playing field ASAP," Alex said.

Kate's heart skittered in her chest. "What are you saying?" she asked, already afraid she knew.

"That we should take the overall situation into account and skip a few steps. Go ahead and admit what we feel about each other is serious. And get married now."

Alex had planned to use a lot more finesse when he broached the possibility of tying the knot. To already have a ring in his pocket when he popped the question. He never predicted that he'd be trying to make this all happen in just a few days—so that they could include their marriage, the secure home and the satisfying family life they were building for the boys in his response to the change in custody petition Tiffany had filed.

But seeing Kate ready to sacrifice her own happiness and leave them all behind had changed all that.

She stiffened. "You're serious."

He nodded. Wishing that fate wasn't rushing what, in an ideal situation, could have taken months to nurture and develop. But it was what it was. And the only other choice had them walking away from each other again, this time forever.

Giving her back the same reasoned approach she had just given him, he escorted her up the steps and into the house. "You've been here exactly one week, Kate." He shut the door and took her coat. Removed his. Hung them both up.

"In that time, our life has changed substantially. The boys are happier and more content than I've ever seen them. The cowboys, too."

She flashed a wan smile and met his gaze once again. "What about you?"

He took her elbow and led her into the kitchen. Thinking she looked a little pale, he decided to pour them both some orange juice. "I think you know how I feel about you."

She stood next to the stool, refusing to sit. "I think you need to tell me," she said firmly. "Not just infer."

Alex wished he could give Kate the complication-free courtship she deserved. Unfortunately, circumstances were forcing him to cut to the chase.

"Okay." He handed her the tumbler of juice, and this time she did sit. He joined her at the other side of the island and took the stool next to hers, facing her. Looking into her eyes, he confessed, "I didn't tell you this when we met up again, because I worried it would sound like the kind of line a loser gives a girl in a bar, when he wants to take her home with him under false pretenses."

Silence fell as he let that sink in.

"I know you're not that kind of guy," she said.

"Good. Because here is the God's honest truth. When we met, years ago, during Inga, I felt an immediate kinetic connection to you that never really went away. I was also extremely physically attracted to you."

She sipped her juice, remembering, "But we were both involved with other people at the time."

He nodded, glad to see some of the healthy color coming back into her face. "So we walked away without dishonoring those vows."

Sorrow came and went in her eyes. "Right."

He inhaled. Shifting closer, so their knees were touching. "I figured you were always going to be the one who got away."

Sadness touched her soft smile. "Also, same."

Alex took both her hands in his. "But when you walked back into my life…and I found out you were single, too, now… I couldn't help but wonder if maybe we hadn't been given a second chance."

For a moment she hesitated, then whispered shyly, "I felt that way, too."

"In case you haven't noticed, I have pursued this opportunity with all my might. With the intention of getting you to stay on. Permanently."

To his pleasure, she seemed happy about that.

Frowning, he continued, "I was a fool to think my ex would just show up once out of the blue and then go away. I apologize for my naivete about that. And of course I'm ticked off that Tiffany has waltzed back in, as selfishly disruptive as always."

"That's not your fault," Kate returned.

"And though, after Tiffany abandoned the boys, I had always imagined I would raise them as a single dad, now I realize that inviting you into our lives, to help me give them all the love and nurturing they need while growing up, is a much better option. Which is why I think we should consider moving on to the finish line and getting married ASAP."

Even as he spoke, Alex knew it was a lame proposal.

Luckily, Kate seemed more thoughtful than offended. Which just confirmed his high opinion of her.

"You really think a practical marriage between us would work?" Her brow furrowed as she studied him intently. "That we would grow to love each other?" she continued uncertainly.

Which meant what? he wondered. That she wasn't falling in love with him now the way he was already falling for her?

He had no way to discern that. Yet, anyway. Although his gut instinct told him she was leaning that way.

What she *did* love, however, were contracts. Solid business arrangements that spelled everything out. And that gave him a way to proceed. To convince her he was sincere.

"My first marriage was all passion and heartache." Honestly, he confided, "This time around, I want something more practical. Something I can *trust*. With someone I can depend on."

She nodded at him, in a way that indicated she was really listening. Considering...

Lifting their joined hands to brush a reverent kiss across her knuckles, he continued persuasively, "A marriage between us seems doable. We get along really well—have from the very first moment we met years ago, even in really stressful situations. Plus we have the same values." He winked.

"And let's not forget that we also have proved we have great physical chemistry."

Mischief tinged her smile. "We do. No denying that."

Knowing how much hinged on her answer, Alex continued making his case. "The boys love you."

Affection came and stayed in her pretty amber eyes. "I love them, too," she said tenderly.

Realizing all over again what a fantastic wife and mother she would make, he rasped, "The season is only just beginning. You've already brought such joy to all of us. Easily making it the best Christmas ever."

Her expression grew abruptly troubled. She locked eyes with him. "I thought you didn't want to get married again?"

He acknowledged this with a small dip of his head. "You're right. When we reconnected again a week ago, I didn't. But our time together has changed my perspective. Now, I see that giving up my single status is a small price to pay for such a great gift. But you're right," he admitted with regret. "I've only been thinking about the big picture, what this would all mean for me and the boys. I haven't considered the sacrifice that marrying me would require you to make." *And what kind of selfish idiot did that make him?*

She slid off the stool and began to pace. Circling the island so it was between them. She put her hands out flat on the granite in front of her. "You're right." She took a deep breath and seemed to force herself to go on. "My engagement to Thaddeus ended because I realized he didn't love me in the way I needed to be loved. And that, at the end of the day, we didn't want the same things."

Was she about to tell him no? Alex wondered anxiously.

Funny, he had been so sure about her, how he assumed she felt, he hadn't even considered that as an option.

"But…" She lifted her chin. "I am also tired of waiting for

the love of my life to magically appear." Her determination seemed to grow. "I'm not getting any younger. The fact is, I might never get the big, happy family life I have wanted, as far back as I can recall."

Now, he was the one who wasn't sure what she was leading up to. All he knew for sure was that she seemed to momentarily need her space. He stayed where he was with effort. "What are you saying?"

She shrugged her shoulders. And just like that, the sunshine was back in her resolute expression. "I love it here. Life on the ranch, cooking for the cowboys, stepping into the role of Bonus Mom for the boys, being with you… It has all felt so *right*. From the very beginning." She shook her head, smiled. "And you're correct." She came back to him again. "We have fantastic chemistry. And get along great, even in the midst of turmoil, which is a big test of any relationship."

He loosely encircled her waist with his hands, a surge of hope beginning to bubble up inside him. "So you'll consider it?" He got to his feet.

"More than that, cowboy." She wreathed her arms about his neck. "This is my chance to make my deepest Christmas wish a reality. So I'm saying yes!"

Kate and Alex both knew it was a huge decision. One that would impact not just their lives, but his sons as well.

So they decided to give it twenty-four hours for the idea to marinate. If they were both still on board with the idea of getting married after that point in time, then they would make plans.

Meanwhile, both of them had work to do.

She was putting the finishing touches on dinner for the cowboys when the door to the breezeway shot open. The quadruplets stormed in, their expressions mutinous.

Alex—and Reckless—were right behind them.

Wondering what in the world had happened, Kate wiped her hands on a towel and moved toward them. "Hey, guys," she said hesitantly.

Within seconds, she was engulfed in a four-kid hug.

They weren't crying, but they were near tears.

She stroked the tops of their heads, letting the gentleness of her touch transmit the love she felt. "What's going on?" she murmured.

"Dad won't let us ask you to make cookies!" Matthew cried.

Alex met Kate's glance. "That's because Kate is busy cooking for the cowboys, and I already called Aunt Ellie and asked her to make them for us at her bakery. We can pick them up on the way to school tomorrow, and you can take them into class."

Max huffed. Stepping back, he slammed his hands on his hips. "Dad," he said with a great deal of aggravation. "You don't *buy* the cookies somewhere. *The mom* has to make them!"

And they didn't have a mom.

Kate's heart went out to them.

"What kind of cookies do you need?" she asked.

"Kate…" Alex started to intervene.

She lifted a staying hand.

"Christmas ones," Matthew went on to explain.

"I think I can do that, but it will have to wait until after I feed the cowboys their dinner."

"Yay!" The boys danced around her, so exuberant it made her smile.

"Can we eat in the dining hall tonight?" Marty wanted to know, looking immensely relieved that the near catastrophe had been averted.

Kate looked at Alex, waiting for him to decide.

"Sure," he said.

He did not, however, look all that happy about the way she had countermanded him on the baked goods, she noted with a whisper of unease. Was this what it would be like if they were to marry and take on the task of co-parenting the boys together? She had to wonder.

Three hours later, all was quiet. The cowboys had invited some friends from a nearby ranch to play poker in the dining hall, so Kate was baking in the main house, in Alex's kitchen.

He walked into the kitchen, looking simultaneously worn out and all wound up. In a tone that reminded her who the boss was at the Rocking M, he said, "You really didn't have to do that." He inclined his head at the stand mixer.

"Yeah, I did. Because I know exactly how they feel," she admitted. He lounged against the counter, close enough so they could talk really quietly, yet far enough to be out of her way.

She tamped down the welling hurt as she added eggs, one at a time, to the mix of butter and sugar. "My parents never wanted to participate in anything at school when I was growing up. So they were never there for the holiday parties, or track-and-field day, or even the choral programs each grade did every year." Her voice thickening with emotion, she continued, "My grandmother would come, of course, and happily cheered me on…"

"But she died when you were seven." Alex remembered what she had told him.

Kate nodded, blinking back the tears. "So I had this divide. There was the way I felt when things were normal and my grandmother was there to make sure I felt loved and cared for—when she ensured I had whatever I needed to bring to school functions and holiday celebrations. And then after she passed..."

He continued listening intently, wordlessly prodding her to continue.

She swallowed a lump in her throat, forcing herself to go on. "M-my parents made time for me whenever they could, which honestly wasn't very often. And just grabbed anything they could find in the grocery store and sent me in with that when it was our turn to supply the treats."

His gaze drifted over her, igniting wildfires wherever it landed. "Did the other kids make fun of you?"

Wishing they could just shove everything troublesome aside and go upstairs and make love, Kate shrugged. "Some did. It was the kids who felt sorry for me, for showing up with a smooshed bag of sandwich cookies, that really hurt."

He put an easy hand on her shoulder and caressed it lightly. Her heart raced at the casual contact. "You know how much I care about the boys," he said thickly.

Tingling everywhere he had touched, and everywhere he *hadn't*, Kate stepped away. "Then you should know that if something is this important to them, it's got to be this important to you, too."

The blue of his eyes darkened. He continued to regard her steadily. "Got it."

Her breath hitched. "If I take this on...if I become their mom...you have to know I'm going to give it my all. I will also tell you if I think you're in the wrong."

"Beginning to see that," Alex mumbled.

Without warning, Reckless jumped up from his place on the kitchen floor. Ears cocked, he stood still, as if listening for something. Then he moved off toward the stairs.

Figuring the family pet was going upstairs to sleep between the boys bunks, as per usual, Kate went back to mixing up the dough.

Stubbornly, she went back to making herself clear to him. He had to know if they were going to do this, she wasn't going to be some sort of Stepford wife. She was going to be a full-fledged partner and mother, with equal say about what went on in their new family!

"I want them to have the kind of Christmas they deserve, Alex. I want every aspect of their holiday to be wonderful."

"Seeing that, too."

"So..." She sighed, relieved to be able to talk about what had been bothering her all day. "There is really no reason for me to delay making a decision until tomorrow. I already know what I want to do."

His brow lifted hopefully. "Marry me, and become their mom?"

"Yes." *The sooner the better.*

As eager to get the ball rolling as she was, he told her, "Texas has a three day waiting period. If we get our license tomorrow, we can get married on Friday."

Suddenly things were moving fast again. Maybe not too fast, though, Kate decided. Given what they were facing with his ex. Turning back to her baking task, she added dry mix to wet ingredients. "We'll need to tell Gabe what our plans are."

Alex nodded. "We will, once we set everything in motion. Hopefully, he'll agree to be my best man. Sadie your maid of honor. Unless you have someone else in mind who could help us out on such short notice?"

No one who wouldn't call her crazy.

"I'd love it if Sadie would agree to stand up for us."

Without warning, footsteps clomped noisily down the stairs. The boys charged into the kitchen, all in their pj's, still smelling of baby shampoo and soap. "What are you all doing down here?" Alex chastised. "You're supposed to be asleep."

Michael explained, "We waked up. We needed to know if the cookies were getting done."

Kate grinned. She imagined the smell of sugar and vanilla was wafting through the house. And since she had already made one batch... "Not only that, but I have a few you can taste test for me, along with glasses of milk."

"And then you're going to bed so you can get some sleep," Alex said gently but firmly. "'Cause tomorrow is Tuesday and it is a school day."

"Okay, Dad," the boys said, smiling dreamily.

Matthew sat down at the kitchen island. "But tomorrow, we got to write our letters to Santa!"

"Do you think we will get any surprises this year?" Max asked, his eyes twinkling like he knew something.

Kate thought about the Shetland pony Alex was buying for them. Couldn't help but wonder if they hadn't picked up on that somehow. Overheard something...

She exchanged smiles with their dad, able to see he was contemplating the same. "I imagine there will be a surprise, or two, or three or four," he said with a playful wink.

The most astonishing of which was not the new ranch pet but a new wife for him, a new mom for them and a new husband for her, Kate thought.

Chapter Twelve

"So we're in agreement," Alex conferred with Kate on Tuesday morning, after he'd sent the boys upstairs to brush their teeth and finish getting ready for kindergarten. "We'll both drive into town, meet up at the courthouse, get our marriage license and then go our separate ways. You can do the errands you were planning to do yesterday while I go to the Knotty Pine Ranch and help the cowboys with the herd of cattle we have over there."

"Sounds good." She tried not to be nervous. "Have you given any thought to how we're going to manage the actual wedding?"

"There's a bait and tackle shop on the outskirts of town that also does weddings, among other things. Joe and Ellie actually got married there when he was still in the military. And on leave."

Sounded crazy. Although possibly romantic in a wildly unconventional way if people were actually getting hitched there.

Then again, how easy was it to find a place to elope without going to Mexico or Vegas? Kate wondered nervously.

"But I don't want to go there," Alex continued.

Kate breathed a sigh of relief. "Me, either."

His expression remained impassive. "It's got to be more dignified."

"Serious," Kate added.

He leaned closer, keeping his voice low to make sure they would not be overheard. His mesmerizing eyes met hers. "I'd also rather our parents not be involved until after the vows are said. Rings on."

No kidding! Kate leaned in, too. "Agree." She had an idea of how their idea would be received. At least on her side of the family. Not well.

Alex exhaled and rocked forward on the toes of his boots. "Otherwise, we might get advice we don't want to hear," he said, his gaze roving her upturned face.

"Or resistance to our plans," Kate put in

He folded his arms across his broad chest. "Which we definitely don't need."

Silence stretched between them. Kate drew a breath, aware this situation with his ex was going to force her to be stronger, more pragmatic and selfless, than she had ever been.

But that was what Christmas—and family—was all about, wasn't it? Giving?

Reality descended. "Once we're married on Friday evening, though, we are going to have to tell them," she warned. After all, she couldn't have either of their parents finding out from anyone else.

"And we *will* tell our families," Alex promised. "Starting with the boys."

Another wrinkle. One she hadn't thought much about until now.

"They'll probably be disappointed we didn't include them."

"I know." His eyes softened in the way she was beginning to know so well. Alex traced her cheekbone with the pad of his thumb.

He shook his head, brooding over that aspect, same as she. "Unfortunately, I don't see that we have a choice."

Probably not, since they would never be able to keep a secret as big as this one.

"We'll be able to take them to the party we have later, though," Alex assured her. "And they can be part of the reception. Just not the wedding ceremony."

Footsteps pounded down the stairs along with the sounds of jostling and racing. Seconds later, the boys hit the first floor with more energetic thuds and barreled into the kitchen, their faces lit with the usual pre-kindergarten excitement.

Kate held up the four plastic boxes, containing the home-baked treats. "Got your cookies, guys!"

"Awesome!" Matthew said.

His three brothers agreed.

"Thank Kate for staying up late to do that for you all," Alex instructed his sons.

The boys complied. Their thanks were followed by enthusiastic hugs. Affection flowed through Kate as she embraced them back. And, just like that, any reservations she had disappeared.

The boys needed her help as much as Alex did. And she needed them, too. More and more with each moment that passed.

Already her life felt so much fuller and happier. As if the future were going to feel like Christmas every day.

Alex looked at Kate. "Ready to go?" he said.

Another wave of emotion went through her. Reminding herself that both their lives were about to change irrevocably, she nodded. "Let's do it."

Kate got to the county courthouse first, parking her pickup truck in the lot next to the historic limestone building.

Alex arrived ten minutes later.

"Sorry," he said, when he met her halfway between their two vehicles. "The drop-off line at school was unusually long this morning."

"No worries." Kate fell into step beside him, glad they had a moment alone before they had to deal with the paperwork. She shifted her bag over her shoulder. "How long do you think this will take?"

His steps meshing perfectly with hers, he flashed her a sexy grin. "No idea. Guess we'll find out."

They mounted the steps. Alex held the door for her, protecting her the way a man protected a woman he loved and intended to wed, and they walked in.

Only to come face to face with the last person they expected to see.

Gabe McCabe headed toward them, in a suit and tie and with a briefcase in hand, looking professional.

"Tell me what is going on," Gabe said after he had ushered them into an empty attorney-client conference room.

"Exactly what you probably think," Alex returned, taking a seat next to Kate, opposite his brother. "We are here to get a marriage license."

Gabe frowned. "It has been less than twenty-four hours since you were served with the petition for change in custody."

"We're aware," Alex shot back.

"I was thinking *at most* that you would publicly declare yourself a couple," Gabe said. "Maybe eventually get engaged to be married...if it seemed right..."

Kate could tell Gabe thought she and Alex were being as reckless as they both had been in their last relationships, hooking up with mates who did not share the same values.

When the truth was that Tiffany—and Thaddeus—had never coveted a satisfying home life and children. Not the way she and Alex had.

Their exes may have wanted a mix of passion and excitement and financial success, but they'd never sought a relationship that could grow and develop and deepen...even when the initial infatuation faded. And neither of them would ever understand the concept of a marriage where they always put each other and their children first.

Alex was a man who her grandmother would have called "a real keeper." She knew Alex saw her that way, too. That he had as far back as hurricane Inga. It was why he had been trying to figure out how to get her to stay in Laramie County, so they could be close to each other, even before the legal firestorm with his ex-wife had occurred.

Kate took his hand. Looking Gabe in the eyes, she said, "Alex and I have talked about it and think forming a traditional family is best for all of us, especially the boys."

It was the only way they would be able to level the playing field and effectively fight Tiffany. Keep her from using the boys as pawns. Not just ruining this holiday season but disrupting the rest of their childhoods as well.

"And you are okay marrying for practical reasons?" Gabe asked Kate bluntly.

The indecision she had suffered initially was completely gone. Vanquished by hours to think on it, and a good night's sleep. "More than okay. I'm *completely* on board," Kate said. She needed Alex and the kids in her life, as much as they needed her in theirs.

Gabe looked at his brother, brow lifted.

"I wouldn't have asked Kate to marry me if I didn't think we could make a go of it, over the long haul," Alex replied evenly.

Gabe sat back, evaluating them silently, then finally threw up his hands and said, "Okay, then. What can I do to help?"

By the time they left the courthouse, dark blue clouds were rolling in. The second blue norther in a couple of days was predicted to bring a lot of cold rain with it.

Hoping it wasn't a sign of anything to come, Kate said

goodbye to Alex and then went to Main Street to explore the stores and boutiques, perusing potential holiday gifts for everyone on her list.

The cowboys were easy. All had been bemoaning the lack of warm wool work socks. Ones not thin from constant wear, that was. Fortunately, there were plenty of them in the Western wear store.

Alex and the boys were not so easy to shop for. She couldn't pick out toys for the kids when she didn't have a clear idea of what they liked, or already had.

As for Alex…he had been her friend turned lover. Now he was going to be that plus her husband.

And his family would be paying attention to what she did or did *not* do in the gift-giving department.

So, bagged socks in hand, she headed back to the ranch to fire up her computer and give it more thought. She got there just as a hard rain started.

She stowed the gifts and marriage license safely out of sight in the guest suite. Reckless was by the door so she took him out briefly, then brought him in and toweled him off. He curled up on his cushion and she went into the dining hall to start that evening's dinner.

She had just put a big pot of chicken tortilla soup on the stove to simmer when Alex's Navigator pulled up in the driveway, hours before she expected him home.

To her surprise, Alex was not in the SUV.

Sadie got out of the driver's side instead and helped the boys rush inside, rain jackets on, school backpacks slung over their shoulders.

Rather than heading for the house, they raced up onto the connecting breezeway and charged into the dining hall. All four ran over to give her a hug.

She hugged them back.

"Everything okay?" Kate asked Sadie. Usually the kids didn't get home until around 4:00 p.m. It was only 2:00 p.m.

Nodding, the other woman took off her jacket. "School let out early—due to weather."

"Ah." Which begged the question. "Any word from Alex?" She checked her phone for messages, surprised she hadn't heard from him.

His sister nodded. "They're still moving cattle over at the Knotty Pine. He said he and the cowboys would be late getting back here. So you should figure dinner around six o'clock tonight. Meantime, I'll keep an eye on the boys."

Who were now, Kate noted, busy taking off their damp jackets and wrestling the empty plastic containers from their backpacks. "Everybody loved your cookies!" Max told her. "They said they were the best mom cookies of all!" His brothers nodded emphatically.

"Well, that's nice. I'm glad they were a hit." She remembered all too well how important it was to fit in. She was glad she had helped them in that regard.

The boys walked over to look out the windows. Rain was sluicing down. Puddles were forming everywhere. Kate imagined some of the low water crossings and bridges in the area were already starting to flood. "Can we go outside and look for bugs?" they asked, their expressions hopeful.

Sadie shook her head. "Your dad would not want you out playing in this. It's too cold and wet. That's why you got sent home from school early today, remember?"

"But bugs *like* to come out when there is water!" Marty pointed out.

"Tell you what, you can go the next time it is either warm and wet or just warm," Sadie retorted.

They looked at Kate for confirmation. "I promise, too,"

she said, glad the other woman had taken it upon herself to be the bad guy in this situation.

Although she supposed with her and Alex getting married, and her stepping into the mom role, her turn would come soon enough. "In the meantime, why don't you go get your favorite bugs, to show me and Kate," Sadie suggested. "While we go into the kitchen to fix you a snack."

With a shout of glee, they raced off. Reckless came to the door to greet them, then followed them back into the house, tail wagging. "You handled that really well," Kate said.

Sadie laughed as they crossed the frigid breezeway to the ranch house and stepped into the warmth. "It's what comes from growing up with four brothers. You learn how guys think."

Upstairs they could hear the boys racing around, shouting. Apparently the happy chaos was too much for him, because Reckless came back down and set up sentry at the entrance to the kitchen. He kept an eye on both Kate and Sadie, and the direction the boys would come from upon their return to the first floor.

Kate turned on the lights in the kitchen and, thinking Sadie might appreciate some tea, put the kettle on to boil, too. Watching, Sadie sobered. "Speaking of guy-think, Alex told me the plan when I went over to pick up his vehicle."

Kate tensed. Her future husband was close to his family. For this to work, they all needed to welcome her, too. And she had sensed how protective his baby sister was of him from the first time she met her.

She got out four juice boxes and graham crackers shaped like tiny animals, then set them on the island in front of the stools. "You're on board with it?"

Abruptly, Sadie looked as concerned about the threat from Alex's ex as Kate felt.

She leaned across the island, lowering her voice even more. "We all have to do whatever necessary to fight Tiffany on this. Plus—" without warning, her expression turned as dreamily contemplative as her voice "—I also know how he feels about you."

Kate paused, curious.

Sadie continued, "When he came back from helping out during Hurricane Inga, you were all he talked about—how great you were, how kind and patient and giving. Had he not been engaged to Tiffany..."

But he was.

"Anyway." Sadie grimaced. "We all saw how that worked out. And now here she is, wreaking havoc again, probably wanting more money from him."

That was exactly what Kate had privately concluded. Tiffany would certainly be unhappy if she was low on funds. And when Tiffany was displeased, she was especially mean!

"Thanks for being so understanding, and supportive," she told Alex's baby sister sincerely.

"No problem. I really do want to see things work out well for everyone. Even Tiffany, if it makes her go away..."

Kate grimaced, and went on honestly, "I'm with you there, too..." Alex and the boys needed to be protected from further hurt and disruption. That would only happen if Tiffany were happy elsewhere.

Sadie sighed and shook her head. Then, as if feeling exactly the way Kate did, went on to say, with McCabe-level resolve, "Anyway, I want to do my part to help bolster his chances of maintaining full custody with, at most, supervised visitation for her and Paolo.

"So I told Alex you could get married at my ranch house Friday evening. I'm still renovating the second floor of the house, but the downstairs is done, and the property is quiet and private. Gabe got a friend who is also a justice of the peace to perform the ceremony.

"Now all we have to do is get Mom and Dad to babysit the boys. Alex said he would call them and ask tonight," Sadie said as youthful footsteps once again pounded down the stairs. She whispered the rest. "And the two of you should be all set."

That evening, after the boys were in bed, Kate sought Alex out. He was in his study, working on his computer.

"Can I talk with you for a minute?"

He rocked back in his chair, clearly as happy to see her as she was to see him. "Come on in."

She hesitated. He had seemed awful busy just now. "You sure?"

"I'm just calculating year-end bonuses for the guys to add to mid-month payroll checks. Have until midnight to get all the numbers in."

Speaking of money... She stood on the opposite side of his desk, facing him. Feeling a little like an employee tasked with talking to the boss, she hitched in a breath and said, "Well, that is actually one of the things I wanted to talk to you about. I want us to have a prenup agreement."

Briefly, he looked surprised that she was bringing it up. She imagined he thought he would have to be the one to do it.

"Something simple," she rushed on. "That says we plan to keep our finances separate. My business is mine. The cattle operation is yours. As is the ranch and everything on it. If either of us leave the marriage, for any reason, we take what we came in with. Nothing more, nothing less."

He regarded her contemplatively, his expression maddeningly inscrutable. Finally, he said, "I could do that."

Needing to know more about what he was thinking and

feeling right now, she came around the desk to better see into his eyes. "Why didn't you ask me?"

"Honestly? I didn't think I needed to go there with you. But now that you've brought it up, I think it is a good idea. It cements the notion that we are of the same mind and entering this union as serious-minded adults."

Relief poured through her. Next question. "Do you think Gabe can get a prenup drawn up?"

He caught her wrist and tugged her crossways onto his lap. The softness of her bottom hit the hardness of his thighs. He regarded her, promising gently, "I'll talk to him. See what he can do. But probably the answer is yes."

"Good." Kate traced an idle pattern on his chest and released the breath she hadn't even been aware she was holding. She looked at him solemnly. "Because I don't want money ever coming between us."

"I don't, either."

She eased off his lap. Wanting to go back to business, she moved a short distance away. "We didn't discuss this, either, but...in addition to stepping into the mother role for the kids... I'm going to want to keep working as a chef, too. I mean, I'd like to keep the contract between our two businesses going and supply the meals for the guys, as long as you want my chuck wagon catering service to do that."

He flashed an enticing grin. "Ah...how about forever?"

She answered his flirtatious grin with one of her own, then continued matter-of-factly, "Of course I'll cook for you and the boys, too, if that's okay with you. That would not be under contract because as their mom and your wife, it's just something I would *want* to do."

Kate had the feeling he wanted to argue with her about that, but didn't. Probably because he knew how it would look if he paid her for anything marriage related. Finally, he shrugged. "That all sounds good. As long as you let me foot the grocery bill in its entirety, so it will feel like a fifty-fifty proposition."

She liked how he was willing to meet her halfway. Come up with solutions that seemed fair to both of them.

Kate continued, not sure how he was going to feel about this next part. "Just so you know, there are jobs at other ranches I am already under contract for in February, March and April."

"I figured as much."

"And...?"

"We'll work it out, however we need to, so you can keep your business going."

"Thank you." Noticing his face was windburned from the cold, she moved closer and said, "I was worried about you guys being out in the weather." They had all been drenched and chilled to the bone when they got home.

"You don't need to be, darlin'. We're used to it."

She could see that.

Which begged the question. How far would he go to let her take care of him? Where exactly would the boundaries between them be set?

"What's on your mind?" He stood and came closer.

"I was just wondering, how do you think the boys are going to react when they found out we've gotten hitched without telling them first?" Would there be meltdowns? Joy? A combination of the two? Or something else she couldn't even imagine yet?

Alex drew her into his arms. He looked like he wanted to kiss her again. And she wanted it, too. So, so much. Sifting his hands through her hair, he said, "I think they'll be really happy. They need a *real* mom. Someone who will be there for them, day in and day out. And when we get married, and are officially husband and wife, that's what you'll be for them..."

Without warning, there was the muted sound of something in the hallway. Maybe the boys coming down the stairs? Panicked, Kate slid out of Alex's arms and quickly moved away from him.

Seconds later, there was more noise. Reckless bounded in. The boys came in after him, clad in their pj's, looking resentful and...something else she couldn't quite identify.

"Dad!" Michael propped his hands on his hips. "We *forgot* to write our letters to Santa Claus!"

"Yeah," Max said, indignant. "We were *supposed* to do that tonight!" Marty and Matthew nodded in support.

Alex moved to greet them with a mixture of apology and kindness. "You're right. We were," he agreed gently, taking his angry little ones in for a group hug they weren't ready to receive. Not until they had forgiven him for the misstep.

"Can we do it now?" Max asked.

It was already past nine o'clock, Kate noted. The wintry rain was still pounding against the glass. Although the news had said there would be school tomorrow, even if it was on a one-hour delay.

"It's pretty late. How about tomorrow?" Alex said.

Marty glared at their dad, suspicious. "You *promise* we'll do it then?"

Firmly, Alex replied, "First thing. Before school."

He had them say good night to Kate, then ushered them upstairs.

"All good?" she asked when he returned ten minutes later, unable to help the underlying tension in her voice.

He nodded, coming closer. Taking her by the hand, he led her toward the sofa and sat down beside her. "Why do you ask?"

"I was just thinking about what we were talking about before they came into the study." She swallowed around the parched feeling in her throat. "The fact they nearly caught me sitting on your lap, or us about to kiss." She turned to face him more fully and drew a quavering breath. "You don't think they overheard or saw anything, do you?"

"No." Alex draped his arm along the back of the sofa and drew her closer. Leaning over, he pressed a kiss in her hair.

"How can you be sure?" Kate straightened, unable to push aside her niggling doubt.

He turned her wrist over, letting it rest on his thigh. Idly tracing the lifelines on her palm with the pad of his thumb, he exhaled and said, "Because they would have asked questions or made some sort of comment to test the waters if they had."

Appreciating how ruggedly handsome he looked in the soothing light of the study, Kate carefully mulled over what he'd said. Considering how inquisitive and outspoken the quadruplets were, he had a point. She sank back against the cushions and acknowledged that. "I suppose you're right."

Alex rubbed his fingers through the mussed ends of her hair, in a way that reminded her how skillfully he made love to her. "What's really going on?" He took a moment to search her eyes.

She rested her head against his shoulder, breathing in the evergreen soap he used when he showered, and the woodsy scent of his cologne. "I guess I'm still just nervous about how the boys are going to take us getting hitched. I mean—" she lifted her head again, feeling uneasy " what if they react badly?"

She'd seen how they had treated Tiffany and Paolo.

If that happened with her, too, when the overall situation changed, it could ruin Alex's custody case.

And like it or not, she would be responsible.

A conflicted expression crossed his handsome face, then disappeared just as swiftly, before he declared, "They won't."

Kate studied him, not sure whether she was relieved or worried that he seemed to be having the same flashes of ambivalence she was having.

In her heart of hearts, she knew protecting the boys and helping Alex was the right thing to do. And marrying him and creating a solid family foundation for his children was the best way to keep Tiffany from triumphing in her wish to hurt or bully Alex. Plus, marrying him and becoming a permanent part of his family would be good for her, too. It would give her the husband and children she had always wanted. And wonderful in-laws, too.

But it was still a very complex situation, with twists and turns likely to arise.

"You're sure?" She shifted to better face him, splaying her hands across Alex's chest. "I mean, we go back a ways, but they've only known me for a little over a week now..."

"Listen to me, Kate." Alex cupped her cheeks in his big, strong hands and lifted her face to his. He kissed her tenderly. "The boys are quick to decide whether they like someone or not, and they adore you as much as I do. And *that*," he promised her sincerely, "is not going to change."

Chapter Thirteen

"We want to go with you," Marty declared Friday evening.

"Even if it's somewhere fancy," Matthew agreed.

The two of them were dressed up, as if for a very special date. With Kate looking gorgeous in a red cashmere sweater dress and he in the dark suit he had worn to his brother Zach's wedding to Claire, several months before.

"Now, boys," Mitzy said with grandmotherly authority. "Your dad deserves a grownup night out on the town, and so does Kate."

"It's not like you all are going to be suffering," Chase continued drolly. "Your grandmother and I are going to be here with you. And we promised we would play Go Fish or Old Maid." Their favorite card games.

"We can even make some popcorn if you want," Mitzy added.

The boys looked at each other. Silently communicating the way they had since they were infants.

Whatever they were thinking, they were in complete agreement.

"We're going to bed."

Michael spoke for the group. He sounded as petulant and grumpy as the rest of his brothers looked.

"I'll tuck you in." With an apologetic look at Kate, and another at his parents, Alex followed them up the stairs. They climbed into their beds. Immediately turning their faces away and shutting their eyes. Figuring they would get over their pride eventually, Alex kissed them good night, one by one, then turned out the light and shut the door.

"Long week?" his mom asked when he joined the other adults.

Alex got their coats out of the front closet and helped Kate into hers. "Very," he said.

It had been cold and raining for three days straight. He'd been busy helping the hired hands with the cattle and horses and preparing for the wedding, which included meeting with Gabe again—this time about their prenup. Kate didn't have anything but jeans and work clothes with her, and she wasn't sure anything she had in her apartment in Fort Worth would work, either, so she'd had to go into San Angelo with Sadie and find a dress and heels and pick up the wedding bands they'd ordered over the phone.

On top of all that, the boys'd had two after-school birthday parties to attend. Which always left them overtired and cranky. And they still hadn't gotten their letters to Santa written because whenever he had time to do it, they weren't in the mood, and when they were up for it, he was busy with ranch work.

"I think they will cheer up when we get their letters written and sent to the North Pole tomorrow." He looked at Kate, aware they hadn't actually talked about this, but pretty sure she'd be on board. "We'll probably take them to see Santa Claus, too."

Chase petted Reckless. "Yeah, I'm sure they'll be fine after a good night's sleep."

Upstairs, the sounds of little feet moving around could be heard.

So the kids weren't in bed, Alex thought, wondering how much more difficult this night was going to get before he and Kate could even get out the door.

Mitzy lifted a staying hand. "I'll give them a little space to work out their feelings, then check on them in fifteen minutes or so. You two get going so you don't miss your reservations."

Or the secret wedding, before that, Alex thought.

The only problem was, he couldn't find the key fob to his Navigator. It should have been on the hook in the kitchen, next to the phone charger.

It wasn't.

He went to his study.

The spare was not in the center desk drawer, either.

He had only to look at her to know that Kate understood as well as he did where both had likely gone. And how difficult it was going to be to retrieve them from four uncooperative children who were ticked off not to be included in the fancy night out.

With an amused grin and a shake of her head, she fished in her bag, being careful not to pull out their marriage license. "We'll find them tomorrow. In the meantime, we can take my pickup truck." She handed over her keys.

Grateful for her calm demeanor, no matter what the situation, Alex exhaled. "Good idea." He wrapped his arm around her waist, loving the way she felt nestled against him, so soft and willing. So much like the wife he had always wanted. So much like *Kate*. "Let's go."

To their mutual relief, Gabe was already at Sadie's farm when they got there. Kate and Alex had time to read and then approve the prenuptial agreement he had prepared for them before Gabe's friend, justice of the peace, Roy Shepherd, and his wife arrived.

To be official, the signing of the prenup document had to be witnessed by two people other than Gabe, Kate, and or Alex. So Roy Shepherd's wife and Sadie were able to do that, and Roy was also able to notarize it, making it official.

Money wouldn't come between them, Kate thought in relief. She and Alex would never have to argue about that.

They each had their own businesses.

Own incomes.

And if they ever did decide to leave the marriage, which was something she could hardly imagine even now, then they could do so freely and easily.

Without any ugly divorce...or battle over finances.

In the meantime, it was time to make everything else official, too. Sadie had put up a wedding arbor threaded with red and white poinsettias in front of the fireplace in her living room. Gabe took charge of the plain gold wedding rings they had bought.

They were ready to get started, when a vehicle pulled up outside the cottage-style farmhouse.

"Expecting someone?" Alex asked his younger sister.

Her brow wrinkling, Sadie said, "No." She went to the window and opened the blinds enough to peer out, then groaned.

Kate soon found out why.

They had six visitors.

Alex's parents, and all four of his sons.

Alex didn't need a magic ball to see how their visitors were feeling as they stormed into Sadie's farmhouse en masse. Although the fact his sons were in their suits and bow ties, instead of the pajamas he had last seen them in, was a definite clue as to what was going on in their little minds. No wonder they had wanted to come with him and Kate so badly tonight. They had hoped something special was going to happen and wanted to be part of it.

"So it's true?" his mom asked, in raging disbelief. "You're *eloping* tonight?"

Alex winced at Mitzy's tone. "I don't know," he tried teasing her out of her shock and resentment. "Is it an elopement if you've been planning it all week?" He turned to his dad for help and got none. "Or just a really quiet wedding?"

Mitzy harrumphed and aimed a lecturing finger in his direction. "Do *not* sass me, Alexander Robert McCabe! Do you *know* what your secrecy nearly caused? Well, I'll tell you! The boys nearly drove over here tonight in your Navigator! Would have if they had been able to figure out how to get it started."

With a huff of dismay, Michael blurted out. "We pushed the button next to the steering wheel, just like you do, Dad, when you drive. Only it didn't work!"

"Probably because they didn't know a necessary component to turning the engine on," Chase said grimly.

Like putting your foot on the brake, before you pushed the button, Alex thought.

Mitzy continued, incensed. "When we caught them red-handed, they told us they knew you were getting married tonight. They've known it all week!"

Alex swore inwardly. "How?" he asked.

It was Michael's turn to throw up his hands. "'Cause you've all been talking about it, Dad! Aunt Sadie. Kate. You... Even Uncle Gabe when he called you one time on the phone."

Mitzy gave that a second to sink in, then turned back to look at Alex, then all the boys and then back at him and Kate again. "Of course," she said one hundred times more calmly, now that the confrontation had been had, "I told the boys, that this *had* to be some sort of mix-up, and now I can see tonight must be some sort of *rehearsal* for the actual ceremony, which for so many very important reasons, you would not want your children to be excluded from." She arched a brow. "Am I correct?"

"Yes," Kate stepped in, apparently willing to help Mitzy smooth over this situation in any way she could. "That is *exactly* what this is. A practice run for the real thing..."

"Then how come we didn't get to go to this?" Max demanded. "Everybody got to go to Uncle Zach and Aunt Claire's rehearsal, including us and the cousins!"

Yes, they had, Alex remembered. And if he had thought about it much, he would have realized how much they loved being part of a family wedding, and he would not have excluded them, even if it meant hearing his parents feelings on whether he and Kate should be doing this or not.

"We were going to make our marriage a Christmas surprise for everyone," he said. "With just one announcement to the family and one reception...er...party...to celebrate it."

"Were we going to get to go to *that*?" Marty demanded.

"Yes," Alex assured him, knowing that part was absolutely correct. "You were."

"So when is the wedding gonna be?" Matthew asked, clearly recalling how it had been for Claire and Zach, and their wedding weekend. "Tomorrow?"

Alex looked at the justice of the peace, hoping he could still help them out. "I can do it at four p.m.," he said.

Kate and Alex locked eyes, in new agreement. "Then four o'clock tomorrow it is," Alex said.

Everyone went back to the Rocking M. Kate and Alex took the kids upstairs and got them back in their pj's, then stayed with them until they really were sound asleep.

Mitzy and Chase called the rest of the family and arranged for everyone else to be there for the wedding the following afternoon.

"Have you told your parents you're getting married to Alex?" his mom asked, once Alex and Kate came back downstairs.

Embarrassed, Kate shook her head.

"Don't you think you should? I know they live in Houston, but they have plenty of time to drive up if you call them tonight."

She sighed. "I don't think they'll be able to make the trip, but you're right, I should at least tell them."

Kate went to the guest suite to make the call. When she came out fifteen minutes later, Mitzy and Chase had left. Only Alex remained.

Interest simmered in his ocean blue eyes as she walked back over to him. "How did it go?"

Kate tried not to thrill at the possessiveness in his voice. "Exactly as I thought. The only person they can see me married to is Thaddeus Northam. Anything else is a mistake. They think I should call it off. Come back to Houston immediately. And get involved with the family company again."

"I'm sorry."

Kate sighed and sent him a wry look. "I'm not." All too aware of the heated glance he sent her every time she turned her back, and sometimes even when she didn't, she said, "It would have haunted me if I had waited to tell them."

He frowned and leaned down, so his face was next to hers, his lips close enough to kiss. "Still, my mother shouldn't have interfered," he countered in a husky voice that sent shivers up and down Kate's spine, and brought to mind all the passionate kisses they had shared the previous weekend.

Knowing they wouldn't be making love again until they were actually married, Kate twisted her hands in front of her and moved away. "Your mom was right. Just because my parents aren't doing the right thing in this situation, doesn't mean I shouldn't behave appropriately. I'm their daughter. They had a right to know, and the option to be here to witness it. Especially because your whole family is going to be there."

He nodded, a mixture of pity and compassion in his expression. "Are you going to be okay?" he asked, closing the distance between them to draw her into his arms. He ran his palm up and down her spine. Seeming to know how much her parents had disappointed her without her saying. *Again*.

Kate relaxed into his comforting embrace, reminding herself that she had him, his sons, and the entire McCabe clan on their side now.

And somewhere up in heaven, her grandmother was watching over her, too.

"None of this is new to me. Families are the way they are. All different. Flawed in some way." She let out a shaky breath, curved her hands around his biceps and forged on determinedly. "What matters is that we are getting support from your family." She paused to look into his eyes. "I think that is going to be important as we go forward. Tiffany will have a hard time wreaking havoc if the McCabes show a united front."

He began to relax, as did she. "I like the way you think, darlin'."

The feeling was mutual. "And I like the way our family is already shaping up," she returned softly.

As Kate expected, Saturday was incredibly busy. Alex took the boys with him, and they all got haircuts as well as some more flowers for the ceremony.

Meanwhile, Sadie and Ellie went to her family bakery, Sugar Love, and made a wedding cake. Claire and Zach picked up finger foods to be eaten after the ceremony. And Joe and Gabe bought champagne for the adults and sparkling grape juice for the kids. Then, finally, by three o'clock, they were all ready to head for Sadie's lavender ranch.

The boys met her at the door of the guest suite. All were dressed in the same suits as the evening before, their bow ties straight and their hair combed this time. They held their hands behind their back, and excitement shone on their adorable little faces.

"What's up, guys?" Kate asked, wondering how she had ever lived without such bliss.

"We got wedding presents for you," Michael announced.

Kate pressed a hand to her heart. "Oh wow! How nice. You want to show them to me?"

"Yes, but you got to sit down because you might be scared," Marty warned soberly.

Kate crossed back to sit on the reading chair in the corner. One by one, they showed her what they'd brought her. Marty had a dragonfly, in a lightweight acrylic case. Max had a butterfly. Michael, a praying mantis. And Matthew had brought her a rose chafer.

"Oh, these are beautiful," she said, touched by the generosity they showed. "But are you sure you want to part with them?"

Max ventured, "If you put them on a shelf, then we can still look at them."

Kate smiled. "That is true."

She thanked each of them, one by one, then drew them all into a big group hug. "I love you guys," she whispered, meaning it with all her heart.

They squeezed her tighter and responded in unison, "We love you, too."

A moment later, Alex appeared in the doorway. He looked incredibly handsome in a dark suit, and a festive red tie that matched her cashmere dress. "Hey, guys," he said in that low, gravelly voice she loved. "Time to go…"

The drive to Sadie's ranch was both quiet and blissful. The kids seemed to realize what an important day this was.

And, as Kate swiftly found out, romantic, too.

The evening before she and Alex had been focused on the legal issues surrounding their union. Today, with the prenup out of the way, and his whole family in attendance, the atmosphere was sweet and sentimental.

White folding chairs had been set up, in front of the wedding arbor, and soft music played. His parents had sprung for a professional photographer and videographer. The beautiful cake and buffet set up...

As Kate started down the aisle, toward Alex, simple bouquet in hand, she couldn't help but think how real this all felt.

And was.

And it became even more so as they clasped hands and recited their vows.

She looked solemnly into his eyes. "I, Kate, take you, Alex, to be my lawfully wedded husband...to have and to hold from this day forward...for better for worse..."

When Alex had promised the same, the officiant smiled and told them, "You may exchange rings."

Still looking tenderly down at her, Alex slipped the gold band on Kate's left ring finger.

Kate put the matching band on Alex's.

The boys, who had been perfectly behaved all this time, could contain themselves no longer. "And you may kiss the bride!" they shouted merrily, making everyone laugh.

"What they said," the justice quipped, pointing at the boys.

Grinning, Alex took Kate into his arms, holding her close. Their laughter faded, replaced by something much more passionate and tender, as he pressed his lips to hers. She wreathed her arms about his neck and kissed him back, the same way he was kissing her, with all his heart and soul.

It was official, she thought, as joy spiraled through her.

They were husband and wife.

About to share a home and four adorable boys.

In that instant, Kate knew her life had just taken a magnificent turn for the better.

Chapter Fourteen

Alex and Kate set down their overnight bags and walked through their suite in the lodge. Still marveling at the generosity and support of his family, and a gift they didn't expect to have—a wedding night in the bridal suite at the Lake Laramie Lodge

The view of the lake, shimmering in the moonlight, was absolutely stunning. As were the twinkling Christmas lights decorating the shoreline, and the homes and boats situated there.

"Wow," she said. A room service table had already been set up for them. Complete with a tempting array of fresh fruit and pastry, a charcuterie board and champagne on ice.

He wrapped an arm about her shoulders and kissed her temple. "Feels a little like Christmas came early, doesn't it?"

She turned to face him, pressing her hands across the warm, solid musculature of his chest. "I can't believe all your family has done for us in the last twenty-four hours." The McCabes were a shining example of everything a family should be. Strong, loyal, accepting.

Whereas her parents' affection had always been conditional.

She either did what they wanted or was shunned.

That had always devastated her.

But now, with Alex and his big extended family, she was beginning to see it didn't have to be that way.

That there were those who would accept her as she was.

She'd never felt more valued. Or wanted to belong more.

Kate stared up at him, noting how devastatingly handsome he looked in the dark suit and white shirt, his bright red tie and boutonniere perfectly matching her sweater dress and the wreath still in her hair. She crossed the distance between them, her stiletto heels sinking into the plush carpet. Annoyed, she steadied herself with a grip on his arm, then bent down to take off her shoes, one by one.

He watched her, eyelids falling to half-mast, the way they did when he was about to kiss her.

Finished, she straightened and pushed on resolutely. "We have to do something to thank them."

An affirming smile tugged at the corners of his lips. "We will."

"Like…?" She waited, suddenly feeling unutterably fragile. What if, after all this, she went on to fail Alex and his boys? And the McCabes didn't accept her in the end?

She'd be right back where she started.

Alone. During the holidays and after.

His expression gentling, Alex put a protective hand on her shoulder. "We could invite them for a big family dinner at the Rocking M Ranch," he told her huskily, turning her around. "Maybe during the week between Christmas and New Year's, which is always a little dull. Holiday themed, of course."

She watched as he poured them both a glass of champagne. "I'd love to cook for them."

He handed her a flute of the bubbly golden wine, then toasted her reverently. If she didn't know better, she'd think it was pure love for her filling his gaze. "And I'd love to help," he promised.

Glass in hand, Kate stepped away to curl up on the sofa, her legs to one side and tucked beneath her.

In turn, Alex shrugged off his jacket and loosened his tie and the first two buttons on his shirt. Gaze still roving her languidly, he settled beside her.

The champagne was as exquisite as his company. Happiness wove through her and she noted he looked relaxed and content, too. "I wasn't expecting today to be so romantic," she admitted softly.

"Same here." He paused, his expression turning reflective. "Although I can't say I mind all the traditional wedding festivities since it made it easier and more real for everyone, especially the kids."

"True. But do you think it's a mistake to start out feeling so…" she struggled to find the right word, finally settling on, "…starry-eyed?" She let her hand settle on the rolled cuff of his dress shirt, just beneath his elbow. "When we had planned to forego all that and embark on a practical union?" What if she disappointed him? What if they disappointed *each other*?

From the reciting of their vows, to the private party afterward, to now, it all felt so genuine.

Like they had gotten married the conventional way, for the usual reasons.

Love. Passion. And lifelong commitment.

Instead of friendship, and a need to provide a complete family for themselves and the boys.

He put aside both their drinks and shifted her onto his lap, the way he had the other night in his study before common sense had prevailed. Gently, he removed the bridal wreath from her hair. Set it aside, too.

Alex lifted her hand and kissed the inside of her wrist. Looking deep into her eyes, with an expression that reminded her they didn't have to worry about being interrupted tonight, he said, "What I think is that we need to take it moment by moment. Day by day."

The next thing she knew, instinct was taking over. She was straddling him, her dress hiked high on her thighs. Wreathing her arms about his neck, she was all the way against him, her chest pressed into his. Wrapped in his strong, steady warmth. His head slanted. His lips captured hers. She opened her mouth to his invading tongue. And then everything she wanted, everything she needed, was right there, in the feel of him, in his intoxicating kiss.

Alex hadn't known what to expect when his family had gifted them an actual wedding night at the Lake Laramie Lodge.

Although amenable to getting along well with others, Kate still wasn't a woman who liked to be told what to do. That had to include making love with her new husband, just because it was expected.

Hence, he had promised himself he wouldn't do more than test the waters with one kiss, or let things get out of hand. Unless that was what she *wanted* to happen, of course.

But the moment she launched herself against him, all bets were off. She made a lusty little sound in the back of her throat that drove him wild, and as her mouth softened beneath his, opening to allow him deeper access, his desire for her reached a fever pitch.

Then her hands were coming up to cup his head, and he felt the need pouring out of her, matching his own. Felt the barriers around her heart lower, just a little bit. In a way that made him wonder if getting married hadn't changed things between them after all.

For the better.

Succumbing to the moment, he pulled her closer, tighter,

feeling the dampness between her thighs as she settled even more intimately against his hardness. He enjoyed the adrenaline-fueled rush of their tryst.

The end to what had been a very long, very emotional few days.

For now, she was all about the moment.

As was he.

So he went with it.

Refusing to think about the fact they were now officially husband and wife, and how or if that might change things, he shifted her again. Long enough so he could stand, sweep her up into his arms and carry her across the living room, to the threshold of the bridal bedroom.

"Mrs. McCabe..." he said as he set her down ever so gently next to the bed.

She gazed up at him. "Yes, Mr. McCabe?"

He sifted his hand through the honey-blond silk of her hair that tumbled down onto her shoulders. "I want to make love to you."

"I want to make love to you, too," she admitted softly, while she kissed his jaw, his throat and ear, with playful abandon.

"We'll be consummating the marriage." Which in his view, was a very good thing. Because no matter what she claimed, she wasn't anywhere near a sex-without-real-love kind of woman. He knew that because every time they had made love, without any kind of real future ahead of them, she exhibited some small regret after. Would the vows they had taken this afternoon change that? He sure hoped so. He wanted her to feel secure in their relationship, and her place in their family.

She spread her hands across his chest. Then gazed up at him with a look that was both playful and solemn. "Consummation is probably a good thing if we want to be taken seriously as a couple." She undid the buttons on his shirt and spread the fabric wide, her fingertips tantalizing him even more.

Unable to hide the outline of his male anatomy pushing against his pants, he chuckled, "Ah… Well, then…"

He undid the back zipper of her clinging cashmere wedding dress, slipped it down over her hips and helped her step out of it.

Her undies were red, too.

Satin and smooth, with lace around the edges.

And hot as hell.

She watched as he unlaced the front of her bustier and the luscious mounds of her breasts fell free. Relishing the sight of her partially undressed, he smiled before returning his attention to her bikini panties and eased those right off.

Her amber eyes glowed. "You're going to ravish me tonight, aren't you?"

"Oh yeah…" He backed her to the wall, his hands and lips making a leisurely tour of her body.

She let out a soft, acquiescent sigh. "Works for me." She trembled when he found the sensitive place between her thighs. "Although be warned, cowboy, I plan to do my part, pleasuring you, too."

Desire soared through him. He loved the way she insisted on giving back, even as she responded to his tender ministrations by removing his shirt, pants and boxer briefs. Sucking in a breath, he shuddered as she smoothed her hands over his shoulders, down his spine, to his buttocks.

Reciprocating, he moved his mouth to her breasts, laving and sucking, making sure there was nothing he missed. Her nipples tautened even more, and her skin grew as hot as the fire burning inside him.

He loved her like this.

So soft and womanly as she rocked against him, wanting more.

Determined not to let it go by too fast, however, he wedged his knee between her legs, shifting farther against her so she could ride his thigh as they kissed. She moaned into his body, just as he wanted her to, rubbing, seeking. He deepened their kiss, and her tongue tangled with his, until he was as lost in their embrace as she was. Her breath caught even more as he lowered his hand and stroked her, finding her center, the hot, wet, velvety heat.

"Alex...?"

"Hmm..." He kept right on going.

"I don't think I can wait..."

Grinning, he went to get a condom. He returned to where she stood, weak-kneed and restless, still waiting for him. "Me, either..."

She climbed his body and, still resting against the wall, wrapped both her legs around his waist. One sexy move on her part, and he was inside, pushing deeper.

He moaned as she clamped around him even tighter, bringing him home. And this time when they climaxed, they did it together, catapulting into oblivion.

Kate and Alex made love several more times throughout the night. Taking breaks to enjoy the delicious spread the hotel staff had wisely left for them.

Talking some, about everything and nothing.

They fell asleep after one more sensual round, wrapped in each other's arms.

She woke the next morning, feeling very married.

And a little worried about feeling that way.

Kate knew full well that wasn't the deal they had made. This was supposed to be a practical union. They were friends, lovers, co-parents to the boys, and that was all. It was just being in the lodge's bridal suite that was making her feel otherwise.

So she was glad when they realized checkout was set for eleven o'clock, and it was time to pack up and head back to reality.

Upon returning to the Rocking M, of course, everything swiftly went back to normal. Leaving Kate very relieved, as she warned herself not to let her romantic fantasies get ahead of her, even if it was the most spectacular time of the year.

"So what do you think?" Alex asked his four boys, after they greeted each other and answered about a zillion questions about their one-night honeymoon. Clearly ready to change the subject, he continued, "Since we're all here, and we finally have the time, do you want to write your letters to Santa Claus?"

"Yes!" The children let out a unanimous cheer. "But Kate has to help!"

"I'd be honored." Smiling affectionately at the boys, Kate got out a pack of colored construction paper and the kids' art kit they had used to finish the tree ornaments.

They all sat down at the kitchen table.

Alex let the kids dictate what they wanted Santa to bring for Christmas. Michael coveted more bug catching paraphernalia. Containers to put them in.

Max asked for toy construction trucks with working parts that they could use to build stuff outside.

Marty wanted a pony for them all to ride, and the stuff they would need for that, like a blanket and saddle and reins...

Matthew was stumped.

"I was gonna ask for our dad to get a mom for us, but now we got one. So...maybe a baby sister?"

"You still look shell-shocked, by that last letter to Santa Claus," Alex commented as they got ready for bed that night, in what was now going to be their master bedroom with en suite bath.

Kate sent him a provoking look, unable to help but tease. "You laugh now. I thought you were going to faint. You probably would have, too, if you hadn't been sitting at the table."

He shook his head. "Where do they *get* these ideas?"

Trying not to think how comfortable it already felt to be sharing the master bedroom with him, Kate shrugged in reply. Finally offering, "I don't know. Maybe from their little cousins. Zach and Claire's boys, Oliver and Andrew, have their sister, Isabella. And Joe and Ellie's son Jaime has his sister, Jenni. Maybe they think that is the way it is supposed to be."

"So…" He sent her a mischievous look. She couldn't tell if he was being serious or not. "You'd be up for it?"

Would she?

A thrill went through her, even as she cautioned herself not to want something that might never happen. Casually, she sauntered toward him. He was already looking like he wanted to ravish her again. And she wanted it, too. Especially now that the kids were all sound asleep, their bedroom door shut. "You'd really want more children?"

"With you? When the time is right…" Alex drew her into the circle of his arms and kissed her tenderly. "You bet I would." And giving them no chance to discuss it further, he made love to his wife.

Chapter Fifteen

Alex had just gotten back from dropping the kids off at kindergarten the next day, and had joined Kate in the dining hall for a cup of coffee, when Gabe FaceTimed him.

"I got the initial background check on Tiffany and Paolo," his brother said.

Kate moved to leave to allow the men to speak in private. Alex caught her before she could go and sat next to her so she could join in on the meeting. "You sure?" Kate asked. Normally, he was the kind of guy who needed his space in challenging times.

Just because they were now formally married, did not mean she should intrude.

Alex gave her a compelling look. "Yes. I want you here."

Her heart racing, she nodded in understanding.

With that settled, and when he was sure he had their full attention, Gabe continued reading from the file in front of him. "Tiffany was cut off from her portion of the Phillips family trust. And apparently Paolo was cut off from his as well."

"Any particular reason why?" Alex asked.

"Both of them are from Old Money, and neither of their parents approve of their hasty marriage. Since neither of them work, they are struggling without access to their family funds. To the point, Tiffany had to sell some jewelry and

Paolo one of his sports cars. Plus, Tiffany has gone through all the money she got from her divorce from Alex. So she and Paolo are staying in a month to month studio apartment."

Kate couldn't imagine her old nemesis without tons of money to burn. She had to be desperate.

"Word is she is trying to get her parents to change their minds about her new husband. They have only been married a few months, so their union won't be a deciding factor in the custody fight," Gabe added.

"Then we *did* level the playing field with our marriage," Alex said with a note of optimism. "Since Tiffany and I both now have two parent homes, and both unions are relatively new."

Gabe nodded.

Kate was relieved about that, too. The last thing she wanted to do was cause problems for Alex and the boys.

"We still need to work on the formal response to Tiffany's filing with the court," Gabe reminded his brother. "I've got time this afternoon. Around three o'clock. If you can come in then…"

Alex looked at Kate, clearly as leery of intruding on her as she was on him. "Could you pick up the boys at school at 3:45 p.m.?"

"Sure. I'd have to take your Navigator, though, since my pickup won't fit four safety seats. But if you want, you could take my truck."

He shook his head. "No, I'll take one of the ranch pickup trucks into town."

Kate tried not to feel rebuffed as the call ended, since she knew Alex had traded trucks with his sister in similar situations. Of course, then they'd had to trade back, at a place other than the ranch. And they did have several Rocking M pickups just sitting there, next to the barn.

Deciding she was being ridiculous, she rose and began chopping vegetables for dinner again.

His mind already on the day ahead, Alex said, "Since this is the first time you'll be picking up the kids, you'll have to go into the office, show your ID and then go to the classroom to get them. I'll also have to call and let the elementary school know you are now on the approved list of friends or family who can do pickup or drop-off."

It sounded like a lot. No wonder Alex was so stressed out sometimes when it came to school stuff. "I probably should get there early, then?"

The casual affection in his gaze deepened. "Be a good idea."

Kate knew the last thing either of them wanted was an end to their mutual independence. They were used to running their own lives without unsolicited comment or advice. Still, she had to know. "Have you thought about what your formal response is going to be to your ex's petition?"

"I'm going to ask the court for supervised visitation with Tiffany and Paolo. Since she initially waived all visitation and custody of the boys, and hasn't visited them or even had any contact with them for four and a half years, Gabe thinks at least one session will be ordered by the court. Otherwise, it would be too upsetting for the kids to have to go off with literal strangers."

"No kidding," she muttered.

He regarded her stoically. "And who knows," he continued, "Tiffany might bail on even that, if she has a chance to think much about it."

"So you think, bottom line, this is all about money and her current lack of it?"

He nodded. "Yep."

She looked into his eyes, hanging on to his every word. "Are you going to try and buy her off?"

Frustration tightened the corners of his lips. "Nope. I did that once. It was a mistake. Which is why she is back now. I can't do it again. Otherwise, it will be a never-ending extortion."

She stopped what she was doing and moved closer, inhaling the heady, just-showered scent of him. "What happens if she and Paolo persist and go for a full custody fight?"

His big body relaxed. He reached over to take her hand, as if sensing she needed comfort in this situation more than he did. He met her eyes calmly, his eyes dark and heated. "Then I'll have no choice but to go public with the fact that she lied to me—and everyone else—about her infertility, to get me to hire a surrogate. And have her legal rights as the boys' mother terminated that way—via fraud."

Kate could see that working if Tiffany weren't destitute. But living in a studio apartment in Houston would definitely be considered "subsisting in poverty" to her, and that could certainly provoke her. "You think she won't want that information in court documents?"

His brow furrowed. "The Phillips family reputation is very important to her and her parents. So...would they want it on public record that she is a manipulative liar? Probably not. Is the threat of the ugly truth coming out, enough to stop her from going after me for more cash—via custody of the boys?" He winced. "Only time will tell that."

"And in the meantime...?" Kate straightened, marshaling all her inner strength.

He took her into his arms and held her close. "I intend to drag this out as much as I can, to force her and Paolo to find another way to finance their jet-setting lifestyle." He stroked a hand through her hair. Bent to kiss her temple. "Fortunately,

I'm no longer fighting this alone. I've got Gabe as my attorney, and even more importantly—" he kissed her again "—you by my side."

And that, it seemed, was all he seemed to think he needed.

To Kate's relief, the boys were as delighted as they were surprised to see her walk into their kindergarten classroom just after school dismissal.

They'd been told she was picking them up when Alex called the school. Their teacher had held them in the classroom after the other kids headed out to the bus, parents and car pool lines.

"I'm Sandy Pierce," their fortysomething teacher said, extending a hand after Kate had introduced herself as Kate Taylor...er... McCabe.

She was going to have to get used to saying that.

Although she and Alex hadn't talked about whether or not he wanted her to legally change her last name right away. Though she knew what she wanted. To share the same last name with him and the boys.

"Yeah," Michael said, after all four boys had rushed up to greet her and give her a hug.

He gazed up at his teacher. "This is Kate, our nice new mom. Not the mean one we don't like."

Ms. Pierce was taken aback. She looked at Kate for clarification.

Figuring Alex definitely would not want her to get into that, Kate passed on the opportunity to talk about Tiffany and said, with marked enthusiasm, instead, "Did the boys tell you? Alex and I got married over the weekend!"

"Oh yes," Ms. Pierce said with a conspiratorial wink. "All four boys told everyone in the class how they tried to drive the car to go to your surprise wedding rehearsal, but that didn't work, so their grandparents took them to their Aunt Sadie's ranch to see it instead, but the practice was over by the time they got there.

"Luckily," Ms. Pierce concluded with an indulgent smile, "they got to go to the real wedding the next day."

"Yes, they were all present when Alex and I exchanged vows. Along with the entire rest of the family."

"And we gave her bugs! As a gift!" Matthew said.

"And she loved them all!" Max confirmed.

Kate smiled down at all of them. They were really so sweet. Her heart swelled with love. "Yes, I did."

Mrs. Pierce smiled, too. "The boys seem really happy about having you as their new mom," she said warmly. "And just in time for Christmas, too!"

"I'm happy to be part of their family, too," Kate replied.

They said good-bye and walked out to the Navigator. The boys chatted happily during the drive back to the Rocking M. "How come Dad didn't come pick us up today?" Marty asked.

Kate escorted all four of them back to the dining hall so she could continue prep for the cowboys' dinner.

"Uncle Gabe needed some help with stuff on the computer in his office. I told them I would handle your school pickup and dinner for you and the cowboys." She paused to smile at the boys. "Anyone want to help me set the table?"

Four hands shot up in the air.

Kate kept them busy until the ranchers walked in. Kate had been with the fellas at four-thirty for breakfast, but the boys hadn't seen them since they'd left the previous Wednesday for Thanksgiving.

They all talked about their holidays.

The boys asked lots of questions. Including what their favorite holiday foods were.

Slim loved cranberry sauce. The canned stuff, not homemade.

Buck liked turkey drumsticks.

Rowdy was all about the pies. Coconut, pecan, apple, pumpkin and chocolate chip pecan. He ate them all.

And last but not least, Hector and his grandfather, Luis, waited all year for their family's tamale-fest the day after Thanksgiving.

"What do you like, Kate?" Slim asked curiously.

She had to think about that. "Anything with butter?" she finally said.

They all laughed.

The dinner dishes were a community affair. Everyone helped clear and load one of two dishwashers in the dining hall.

By six-thirty, Kate had the boys back in the main house. She was just feeding Restless when Alex strode in. The boys gathered around and told him about their day while he ate his dinner. After being ushered upstairs for showers, they came back down to say good night to Kate, who was sitting at the kitchen table, a cup of her favorite peppermint tea in hand.

Curious, Max pointed to the picture on her laptop screen. "What's that?"

"Tamales." She turned the laptop so all the boys could see. "I was thinking about making some for the cowboys as sort of an early Christmas present."

"Can we help?" Marty asked.

Kate looked at Alex. He nodded discreetly in approval. "I'd love it," she told them.

"You know, you don't have to ask permission for something like that," he said after they had tucked the boys in and walked back downstairs.

"Technically, I suppose you are right. Since I am still learning all the rules, though, I'd rather err on the side of caution. Speaking of which…when I went to school to pick up the boys today, I met their teacher during the pickup."

"Ms. Pierce."

"Yes. She told me the boys had told everyone in their class today how they tried to drive your car on Friday night to go the surprise wedding rehearsal. Only it didn't work. But they did get to go to that anyway, and then the wedding on Saturday."

Alex groaned and ran a hand over his face.

"I didn't even think about them regaling people with all that," she lamented.

Alex frowned, his anger with himself clear. "I should have."

"You don't think Tiffany will hear about it?" she asked.

"She's not in touch with anyone here in Laramie. Actually, she never even really made friends here while we were married, since the only place she wanted to be was anywhere else than the Rocking M or Laramie County."

Kate bit down anxiously on her bottom lip. "What about the private detective who was following us around a couple of weeks ago, via the illegal tracking device on your Navigator?"

"The civil restraining order against him is still in place."

"But can they hire someone else, who doesn't yet have a restraining order placed against him or her?" she pressed.

"Not without Tiffany's legal team getting in trouble with the court. But even if Tiffany's people were to learn about what happened here Friday night, my parents were here, babysitting that night. Nothing actually happened except the kids hid my keys, used the keypad to unlock the Navigator and climbed into it," he assured her. "And, as you and I both know, they were promptly discovered and safely escorted to the wedding rehearsal. End of story."

"So you think the court would shrug it off."

"Yes."

"I hope you're right," Kate said.

Alex took her by the hand. "The boys are happier than they have ever been. Everyone who knows them can see that. And it is all due to you coming into our lives."

Kate wanted to believe that.

"I know its stressful now but everything is going to work out," Alex promised with his usual Texas confidence.

But what if it *doesn't*? Kate couldn't help but wonder.

What if there were more surprises coming their way? Would he blame her?

His family meant everything to him.

And now they meant everything to her, too.

Chapter Sixteen

"Guess what came in the mail today?" Kate asked a couple of days later.

She and Alex were snuggled together on the big sectional sofa. The kids were in bed asleep. Chores done. Reckless curled up at their feet.

With the Christmas tree twinkling merrily, a cozy fire blazing in the grate, and six identical yuletide stockings hung all in a row, Kate thought how easily she could get used to this. Was this what marriage and family was like?

She might not have an answer to that quite yet, but she knew she was happy. Happier than she had ever been in her life...

Alex turned to her, still trying to guess what had come in the mail. "A special order Shetland pony saddle?"

She rested her head on his shoulder. Loving the way her body felt in the curve of his. "No. Sorry. That has not yet arrived."

"Not supposed to until next week," he admitted with a devilish grin. "But you never know." He stroked her leg, from knee to thigh, the warmth of his hand transmitting through the denim. "So...what arrived?"

"These!" Kate reached behind her and handed over half a dozen toy catalogs. "The boys and I looked through them after school. They remembered you and I promised we would be getting them gifts to open, too. And they all marked their faves." Christmas joy bubbling through her, she showed him some of the selected items that the boys had oohed and aahed over. "I wanted to run their choices by you before I ordered the ones I'm going to give them."

Alex shifted toward her, doing a double take. "You're buying them presents, on your own?" He appeared astonished.

Some of the bliss leaked out of her. She realized she had just made a major mistake. Although in her family, her mom and dad had each given her presents, depending on what she was getting. For instance, her dad never tried to pick out anything like pajamas, and her mom never selected electronics. "Um, yeah." She suddenly felt like a deflated balloon. "Why?" She searched the masculine planes of his face, seeing only wary disapproval. "Don't you think I should?" she blurted out before she could stop herself, doing her best to disguise her hurt.

He tilted his head. "*We* should."

"Oh. Right." They were married now. Hence, when it came to the kids, they should do everything as a team. Made sense.

Feeling marginally better, as well as a tiny bit relieved, she showed him what each of the boys wanted, aside from what they had already asked Santa to bring them. A pirate ship for Max. A basketball for Marty. An elaborate marble run for Matthew. An earth science kit with microscope for Michael. So they could all better look at their bugs, of course. And a height adjustable basketball hoop and net for them all.

Smiling, Alex nodded his approval. "I guess they all are old enough to start playing basketball." Alex got out his credit card.

Kate got out hers, too. "How do you want to do this?" she asked. "Fifty-fifty of the total? Or I buy two and you buy two, and then we split the last?"

Again, he seemed discombobulated. He peered over at her in a way that said he did not want to be challenged or overruled on this. "How about I buy them all?"

She knew they had just been married half a week. Lovers barely longer than that. She should just go with it. Let him do things the way he had always done things. But she couldn't. "You don't want me to pay for any of it," she ventured sadly.

As expected, he did not back down. He regarded her steadily "I'm their dad. I should do it."

What was *she*, then? A babysitter? A glorified maid? A useful pawn in a legal game with his ex?

Clearly seeing where her thoughts were going, he lifted a hand. "You know what I mean," he said hastily.

Kate worked harder to hide her hurt. Was this their first argument? If so, she couldn't let it turn into a Tiffany-sized battle.

She drew a breath, looked down at the catalogs still in her lap and tried to compose herself. Admitting quietly, "I wanted to get them something from me." And if she didn't contribute financially, would any of this really be from her, no matter what the gift tags said?

He covered her hand with his. "And you will be," he reassured her gently. "These gifts will be from both of us. And then they'll have the ones from Santa and the rest of my family."

"Right."

Different families did things different ways.

She told herself that was all this was.

She almost believed it. Until, he went on. "Paying for gifts for the kids wasn't part of our prenup," he said. He slid a hand beneath her chin and waited until she looked at him again before he continued, even more practically, "The reason being,

I didn't want you to be fiscally responsible for this. Everything you're already doing is more than enough."

Was it though? Because right now Kate couldn't help but feel left out. Even though she knew his intentions were in line with the transactional marriage they had entered into with each other. And probably chivalrous as well. At least in his view. He likely thought he was protecting her. Not shutting her out.

But still. That's how it felt.

He dropped his hand, waiting for her to say more. Realizing this was their chance to talk it out, she asked curiously, "What about the two of us? Are we going to exchange gifts?"

His blue eyes remained maddeningly inscrutable. He studied her face. "Do you want to?"

Yes, she most certainly did. But afraid to put herself out there and say what was really in her heart, for fear she would make an even bigger mess of things than she already had tonight, she bit her lip and said instead, "I think it would seem odd if we didn't."

A beat of silence stretched between them.

The idea of how things might look to others was much more persuasive than any emotional argument she might have made.

He nodded in agreement, his expression shuttered.

Stubbornly, she pushed on. "So what do you say?" she asked. "A fifty dollar limit?"

Another pause.

An even stranger look crossed his face. "That sounds fine," he said.

Alex knew he had offended Kate with his insistence that he pay for his kids' presents.

He had been married for his money once.

He didn't want Kate thinking he had married her for hers.

Not that he had any inkling what her finances were. He'd assumed, when he found out her parents owned the Taylor's Sporting Goods chain, that she either had a trust fund or stood to inherit something someday.

Given the rift between Kate and her folks, however—the fact that they had declined to see their only child married, even if it was on short notice to a man with kids they had yet to meet—that might be a false assumption.

He knew what the Rocking M was paying her for cooking for the cowboys. It was a decent salary, especially given the fact it had included room and board while she was here.

But he didn't know what her apartment rent cost.

Or if the eighty thousand custom silver stream mobile kitchen and new Ford pickup truck were paid off. What her professional business expenses were. Or what she charged for her various events around the western part of the state.

Bottom line? He assumed she was fine, financially.

And that was why she had wanted a prenup that said what was his, and what was hers, remained intact no matter how things played out.

So, whether she agreed or not, it was imperative their overall circumstances stay that way. And that they kept to the initial agreement she had asked him for. Even if the gift situation upset the apple cart, just a little bit.

"I was hoping you could help me figure out what I should get Kate for Christmas," Alex said when he met up with his sister in her greenhouse the next morning.

Sadie put down her spade and lifted a brow.

With Christmas less than ten days away, and coming closer every day, there was no time to waste. Alex persisted, "The limit is fifty dollars."

She went down the next row and carefully moved tiny lavender plants into bigger pots, pausing only to smirk. "Wow. Big spender..."

Not amused by the teasing, Alex frowned. He followed Sadie as she worked, allowing in exasperation. "The limit was Kate's idea. And since I don't know what she has available in her budget to spend on gifts this year, I went along with it."

Despite the fact that, had there not been a self-imposed limit, he could have gone to a jeweler and gotten their advice on the best gift for a very new bride.

Not that a gift like that was likely to impress Kate. She didn't seem to covet fancy or expensive things. And though she loved to cook, that was also her vocation, so he couldn't get her any trendy new culinary gadget, either. Because if she wanted it, she would likely already have it. "Besides, it's not the price that counts," Alex continued sincerely. "It's the meaning."

"Which is why you're asking somebody else to figure it out for you?" Sadie's voice dripped with sarcasm. She moved into another row, transplanting lavender as she went.

Alex inhaled. Weren't sisters supposed to help their brothers when it came to things like this? He gruffed out, "You always drop a million hints when it comes to what you want."

Sadie snort-laughed. "Because if I don't, you get me an electric toothbrush!"

He squared his shoulders, indignant. "I thought that was a good gift."

She took pity on him, soothing, "It kind of was. For your sister. Not your *new wife*. What does she like?"

For a gift? Still stumped, Alex shrugged. "I don't know."

Sadie paused at the end of another row. "Chocolate? Perfume? Jewelry?"

"No clue." Not even a hint of one!

Inching off her gardening gloves, she looked at him steadily. "Then I will tell you what I advise everyone who asks me what to get their significant other. It has to be something that means something to that person you are trying to gift. Something that says you know them the way they *want* to be known..." she finished, a little sadly.

Alex studied her. "Are we talking about me and Kate now, or you and Will?"

Sadie made a face at him. "You know he and I are just friends."

Alex picked up on the note of loneliness in her voice. His heart went out to her. It had to be hard for her, especially this time of year. "I know you want me to think you're happy with just that. Tell the truth. You miss him a lot right now, don't you?"

"Of course I do!" Sadie's eyes gleamed moistly. "I don't want him spending the holidays off on some dangerous mission! I would rather he be here with all of us!"

Alex could understand that. "I'm sure he would be here if he could," Alex said gently.

Sadie sighed. "I know that, too. But that's the life of a military guy... Duty to country first."

Alex knew it was. He admired Will's sacrifice, just as he knew his sister did. "In any case, I'm here for you, if you need me," he said sincerely, pulling her in for a hug. "Kate is, too."

Sadie hugged him back. "I know that, too," she said, still sounding a little sad to be without her best friend. "In the meantime, focus on the right present for Kate...!" she advised.

Alex thanked Sadie for her help, such as it was, and thought about what she had said the rest of the day. By midafternoon, he knew. He called Gabe. "You know that private investigator you use for your law firm clients?" he said, sure this would work. If he had enough time to pull it all together, that was. His excitement growing, he asked, "Can you give me her contact information?"

Kate had just finished putting the King Ranch Casseroles in the oven when Alex strode in, boys in tow.

Michael slammed his backpack on the long plank table. "When's dinner?" he asked.

"Dad said if we have more than half an hour we can change into our play clothes and then go outside and look for bugs," Marty declared. "'Cause it's warm enough today."

It sure was, Kate thought. After several weeks of cold, often damp or rainy weather, the temperature today was hovering in the low sixties. "You've got time," she said.

"Take your backpacks to the mudroom!" Alex said.

"'Kay!" they all yelled in unison and dashed off.

He came closer. "Were you in town today?"

She had been, but it wasn't something she could say much about. Not without spoiling the surprise, that was. "Mmm-hmm." She looked up at him innocently. "Why?"

"I thought I saw you coming out of the social services office."

She refused to get sucked in by the blatant sexiness of his gaze. "Oh that."

"Oh that, what?"

Boy, he was nosy today.

Well, she supposed it wouldn't hurt to reveal a tiny bit of what she was up to. Ignoring the feeling that she was oh-so-vulnerable where her new husband was concerned, she went back to prepping garnishes. She picked up a block of cheddar jack and the grater and said, "I had lunch with your mom."

That set him back. He blinked. "Really?"

She wasn't sure if he was happy about that or not.

Although, at this point they had nothing to lose, except

maybe the emotional distance that had sprung up between them when they had discussed gifting the boys, paying for selected gifts—*or not*—and how they were pretty much being forced into buying gifts for each other because of the optics.

Aware he still looked worried, for absolutely no good reason, she said, "I thought, since we're married now, that I should get to know her better. Your dad, too."

There was just something so comforting, so loving and accepting, about Mitzy and Chase. Their kindness reminded her of her late grandmother.

"So next time, if he can, he will join us."

"*Next time*," Alex repeated as if not sure how he felt about that.

Happy she was reaching out to them? Fearful she would tell them more than he wanted them to know? Or just plain left out because she hadn't mentioned it, and he hadn't been invited to join the lunch?

Surprised to find her oh-so-confident husband had any insecurities, especially ones that had to do with her, she met his gaze and—with a playful shrug—asked, "And for the record, what were *you* doing in town that time of day, cowboy?"

It was his turn to hedge and not want to say. "Random errands."

Hmm. He wasn't really a random kind of guy. When he went anywhere, did anything, it was with purpose. Had he been Christmas shopping? *For her?* If so, where? And for what? There was no clue on his handsome face.

Signaling that part of their conversation was over, he sauntered closer. "Something smells really good."

"We're all having Tex-Mex tonight." When he waited for her to elaborate, she said, "King Ranch Casserole."

"Mmm." He rubbed his tummy comically. Sniffed. "Roast chicken. Corn tortillas."

"Cheese. Onion. Peppers. All brought together by a spicy cream sauce. But not to worry. The version I made for the boys is very mild."

He smiled with anticipation. "Mind if I go to my study for a while? I can supervise them from there and get a few things done on the computer."

She lifted an airy hand. "Supervise away. I'll get things squared away here."

As soon as he left, Kate went to her shoulder bag. The information she'd gotten from Mitzy was still there, in a manila folder. She tucked it into the bag and zipped the top shut.

None of it was new to Alex, of course. But it was still important to keep it hidden. She didn't want him seeing any of it just yet.

In the meantime, she thought, as she gazed out the kitchen windows, it looked as if the boys were having a great time hunting for insects in the backyard. They were hunkered down in the mulch around the bushes, checking the ground beneath the slide. As well as going right up to the foundation of the sprawling prairie-style home.

When it began to get dark, as it did around five-thirty every day now, Alex went outside. He called for the boys and Reckless to come inside and wash up.

Instead of heading for him, they ran for the breezeway between the house and the dining hall. Then came racing into the kitchen, with their contraptions in hand. Michael had a handheld trigger with a trap door. Max had a scissor-style scooper. Marty had a vacuum that ushered insects into the adjoining critter barn. And Matthew had Bugnoculars that allowed both magnification and a vented viewing area, where the bugs could stay.

There were insects in all of their contraptions. A group

of ladybugs, a cockroach, an earwig and a little mesquite cicada, according to the boys.

"Wow. You really know your bugs," Kate said, examining them all through the plastic viewing areas.

"Do you like 'em?" Michael asked.

Kate nodded. "I love them. You did a great job finding and catching them."

"But we can't keep them inside, because they will die," Alex said gently. "So you all can show the cowboys, too—" he acknowledged the men filing into the dining hall, ready to eat "—and then we're going to have to take them outside and let them go."

The boys nodded soberly.

Kate could see the bighearted kids did not want their bugs to perish.

The cowboys were equally impressed with the boys' accomplishments and, grinning, praised them accordingly. Alex took the boys back outside. Then into the main house to wash up.

When they returned, dinner was on the long plank table. All of them sat down together. Dishes were passed. Lively conversation began.

Kate smiled as joy bubbled up inside her. She had never felt so much a part of a family. This was, she thought, the way the holiday season was supposed to be. And it was only likely to get better, or so she hoped.

Chapter Seventeen

"What is it?" Kate stepped out onto the porch several hours later.

Alex sank down on one of the outdoor sofas on either side of the front door. He had the papers Gabe had just emailed him, spread out on his lap.

His mouth thinned. "It's an amended petition filed by Tiffany's lawyers."

It shouldn't have been a surprise. Yet it was. "I didn't think you had filed your response yet."

"I haven't. It's not due until December twentieth. The plan was to wait until the last minute and file it then, thereby making any court hearing before Christmas and New Year's Day pretty much impossible."

Something in her went very still. "So what does this one say that's different?"

He scrubbed a hand over his face. Then paused to look her in the eye. "They know about the boys trying to drive my Navigator."

"Oh no."

His expression darkened. "They are asserting that incident—combined with my marrying a woman I barely know—is grounds for an emergency custody hearing, as soon as possible."

Dread pooled inside her. Unable to help but feel this was

all her fault…that she should have left when this situation first started to blow up, she inhaled sharply. "Are they still asking for joint custody and holiday visitation?"

"No." He pinned her with his hard blue gaze. "Now, she and Paolo want full custody. And visitation starting Christmas Eve through New Year's Day. In addition, they would like the case moved out of Laramie County, for fear they can't get a fair hearing here, to Houston where they now reside."

Sadie drove over to babysit the kids, in case they woke up, while Kate and Alex met Gabe at his house in town.

The three of them gathered in the centrally located kitchen of the compact shotgun home. Gabe leaned against the counter his copy of the amended petition in hand, as they began to discuss the situation.

"What do you think we should do?" Alex asked.

Kate sat next to him at the dining table, holding his hand. Not sure who she was trying to comfort more, her new husband or herself.

Gabe shook his head, his expression grim. "Honestly? Everything possible to keep this from going to court."

Kate agreed.

"'Cause if it does…" Alex said.

"It will be ugly," Kate predicted on a beleaguered sigh.

"Very." Gabe measured coffee into the filter of his coffeemaker, poured water into the reservoir and turned it on. "Worse, the kids will be dragged into it, too."

At the thought of the four little boys suffering, Kate felt a wave of panic roll through her. "How do we avoid that?"

Gabe got three mugs out of the cupboard. "You said Tiffany didn't exactly hit it off with them when she and Paolo came out to the Rocking M."

Talk about an understatement, Kate thought, as the scent

of fresh brewed coffee filled the room. "No, she didn't. It was apparent she doesn't like kids."

"Whether she does or not—" Gabe turned to pour coffee "—Tiffany's going to have to do at least one supervised visitation. Given how long it has been since she saw the kids."

Alex got up to help himself to some coffee, fixed a cup for Kate—with cream and sugar just like she liked it—then settled opposite Gabe. "We were going to request she be ordered to do that. In our initial response," he reminded his brother.

Which hadn't yet been filed.

"True. So that doesn't really change anything, about our strategy in that regard, except move up the timeline a bit," Gabe said.

"Does that mean we will go ahead and file our response now?" Alex asked.

Gabe nodded. "Yes. We'll get our answer to both petitions in tomorrow."

Kate breathed a sigh of relief.

Matter of factly, Gabe continued, "We will also be ordered to go to mediation with Tiffany and her lawyer before we ever get a court date."

Uh oh, Kate thought.

"I still want full custody of the boys," Alex insisted.

"And we will still ask for that in mediation and court," his brother assured him. "But we have to give them something if we don't want this to go to court ASAP in an emergency hearing. Or be moved to Houston."

Nodding and listening intently, Kate took a sip of her coffee. Alex's brother was right. Moving the case to Houston would be a tremendous mistake. Especially given the clout Tiffany's very wealthy and influential family had in that city.

"What I suggest is we offer her supervised visitation with

the kids, here in Laramie, at the county social worker's office," Gabe continued reasonably.

"You really think she'll go for that?" Alex asked skeptically.

"Yes, if—in exchange—we set up mediation with them as soon as possible afterward. Before Christmas, if they want. As long as they agree to meet in Laramie."

Alex frowned. "Will we be bound by whatever the mediator decides in this case?" He took a big sip of the strong, black java.

"No," Gabe countered with lawyerly calm. "If you all can't agree what should happen next with the kids, then they'll likely proceed with their request for an emergency hearing before Christmas, and we'll all go to court. And let the judge decide where they will spend the holiday and so on."

"It seems like a lot to put the kids through," Kate said heatedly. "I mean, what if she is as mean and rude to them, during the supervised visitation, as she was when she came out to the ranch?"

"Then it will all be on video, in the presence of the social worker, psychologist and law officer present, and we can argue that Tiffany needs more time and training before she can care for the kids on her own," Gabe said.

Alex grimaced. "Okay. When do we do this?"

"I'll call her attorney first thing in the morning and see what we can work out," Gabe promised.

Alex was quiet on the drive back to the ranch. Kate couldn't blame him. She was rattled, too, by all that had happened in just a few hours.

It was clear that Sadie wanted to be filled in on what Gabe had said. Kate thanked her for coming over, then went on upstairs to get ready for bed, leaving brother and sister to speak privately.

Ten minutes later, Alex joined her in the master bedroom. He came toward her, expression tender. "You okay?" he asked her softly, taking her into his arms.

She snuggled closer and looked up at him. "A better question is, are *you*?"

His face remained implacable. "We'll get through this." He ran a hand down her spine. Tingles sparked, and spread outward through her entire body.

He shook his head in regret. The casual affection in his eyes deepened. "I just wish I had seen the warning signs before my ex and I ever got involved." He wrapped his brawny arms around her, nuzzled her temple. "Although if I had, I wouldn't have the boys, so…"

Kate took him by the hand and drew him over to sit beside her on their bed. "How and when did the two of you meet? You never said."

Their eyes locked for one long second. "I had just graduated from college and taken a job as a junior exec with one of the companies my dad owns."

Kate knew that Chase bought struggling businesses, and turned them around, and over the years had developed quite the portfolio. She hadn't known Alex had ever worked for his CEO dad.

"I was asked to take part in a bachelor auction for a charity in Houston. Tiffany was there and she bid on me." He huffed out a regretful breath. "I was young and I guess I confused physical beauty with inner goodness."

Kate understood. She remembered how charming Tiffany could be—when she wanted to be.

"Did she think you were rich?"

"She knew my dad was well-off. And figured I would be

one day, too. She liked the idea of being part of the famous Texas McCabes."

Kate could see that, too. Status had always been everything to Tiffany and the girls she ran around with.

"So when did the two of you move to the ranch?"

"We came out here a couple of times a month when we were engaged. Tiffany saw it as a retreat since most wealthy Texans have ranches or country estates. Anyway, I didn't actually start running cattle out here until after we married. And to keep bringing in the income I needed to really make a success of ranching, I continued working for my dad's company in Houston, too."

"That sounds like a lot," Kate sympathized.

He nodded, acknowledging that it had been. "I tried living a dual life for a while, but it didn't work. If the Rocking M was going to be a success, I had to be here. So I quit my job in Houston and relocated here."

"How did Tiffany take that?"

"She humored me. Thought I would grow tired of the rural life."

"But…you didn't," she murmured.

"No. I wanted to raise a family. And that was when Tiffany told me the only way it could or would happen was via surrogate."

Kate was aware she was a little fuzzy on the timing of all this. "So you had no idea when you married her that she was supposedly infertile?"

He shook his head. "She said she was afraid to tell me, that if I knew she wasn't ever going to get pregnant herself or be able to harvest her own eggs, or have her own biological children, that I wouldn't marry her. I told her I would be open to adopting. But…she said…if we were going to have a family…bigger than just the two of us…she wanted to go the surrogate route, and have multiple embryos implanted, so I would be sure and have my own biological kids, even if it meant we ended up with more than one baby."

Which statistically usually didn't happen, Kate thought.

"So we did," Alex finished.

"How did she react when she found out you were going to have quadruplets?" Kate asked curiously, remembering how much Tiffany had always liked being the center of attention.

Alex turned contemplative. "I thought she was as happy as I was. I mean, four babies at once! All of them boys! And until they were actually born, I think she was tremendously excited. Mainly because she had this overly romantic view of what parenthood would be like."

Still trying to envision all that, Kate said, "I'm surprised she would have ever wanted to raise the kids here, though."

Alex scrubbed a hand over his face. Looking miserable again. "She didn't. She thought we would live in Houston permanently after the kids were born. Hire nannies. And continue to live as we had, when we were childless, and could do pretty much as we pleased."

"Which meant…?"

"I worked on building a future for us, and she focused on her social endeavors. Trips with her girlfriends. Spa weekends, things like that."

So in other words, Kate thought, separate lives.

"And she pushed for us to use the Rocking M for income, buy a house near her folks in River Oaks and leave the ranch to a foreman to run.

"When I refused to do either that or go back to working in Houston for one of my dad's companies, as an executive, with an eye toward becoming the new CEO and running McCabe Industries when he retired…she said she couldn't continue to live out in the middle of nowhere, away from everything that mattered, and she asked me for a divorce. Offered me full physical custody, in exchange for a hefty financial settlement, which I provided."

"You never thought she'd come back?"

"Initially, I sort of hoped she would want some kind of relationship with the kids, as they got older. I thought that would be better for everyone. But—" Alex shook his head "—if I'm honest, I think I knew from the moment we brought the babies home from the hospital that she wasn't at all maternal. I mean, she tried, at least in the beginning, but she just couldn't seem to bond with them, not the way I did, anyway. I wondered if it was because of the lack of biological connection. And maybe that was it. Or perhaps the day to day grind and stress and pressure of raising quads was too much for her. The way caring for them, and running the ranch, took over all else, and crimped the jet-setting lifestyle she had always imagined for us..."

Alex grimaced. "In any case, she never quite took to motherhood, or ranch life, not the way either of us expected. And that frustrated her, because up until then, she had always been able to achieve anything she set her mind to."

Kate remembered that, too. "So how did you cope with just you and the four babies?" she asked Alex.

"I had lots of help from my mom and dad, Sadie and lots of volunteers from the Laramie Multiples Club."

She imagined all the feeding, changing, and rocking. "Sounds chaotic."

"It was." He smiled fondly, recalling. "I still wouldn't trade it for the world."

She turned toward him, so her bent knee nudged his rock-hard thigh. A comfortable silence stretched between them. "And those kids wouldn't trade you."

"Or you..." he bantered back.

Shifting position, he moved to stretch out on the bed, taking her with him. She loved the way he felt when he held her close and ran a hand lovingly down her hip.

And they made love the way they had every night since they had married. Slowly, thoroughly, tenderly. Until their kisses and caresses reached a fiery crescendo and she clung to him wordlessly beneath the demanding weight of his muscular body. Opening herself up to him, heart and soul.

And Kate knew—this was what she wanted. *He* was what she wanted. Not just for now, but for all time.

Chapter Eighteen

"Kate, when are we going to make tamales for the cowboys?" Max asked when they got back to the ranch mid-afternoon, several days later.

The boys had spent the morning at their Uncle Joe's climbing gym, traversing the rock walls in their full-body safety harnesses. From there, they had gone to Zach and Claire's home to have a pizza lunch with their cousins, Oliver, Andrew and Isabella, who were also enrolled in the Saturday morning climbing camp for kids.

"Yeah," Matthew said, sprawling on the sectional sofa next to his three brothers. "It's going to be Christmas before you know it!"

Kate smiled. "Very true." She had all the ingredients, but the prep would take some time. And of course she had to slow-cook the pork. "We could do it Tuesday after school, if you don't think you will be too tired."

Michael rolled over onto his tummy and rested his chin on his upraised fist. "How 'bout tomorrow?"

She paused. "That is going to be a very busy day, since you have the school choral program in the town square in the afternoon, and dinner at your grandparents' house in town afterward." Every grade would be doing a few songs, from pre-K–12. All the bands and orchestras would be playing holiday songs, too.

"Dad said there is going to be hot chocolate and cookies, just like last year," Max reported.

"I know. It sounds like a lot of fun!" Kate raved. She was surprised by how much she was looking forward to it. Being a mom was really growing on her. Life in a small town, where holidays brought everyone together, was equally satisfying and exciting.

"When is Dad coming back?" Marty asked. Alex had been gone a lot the past few days, as he and Gabe tried to work out the situation with his ex and her legal team. And get mediation and supervised visitation set up.

"When he is done feeding the cattle and horses," Kate replied. She knew the boys sensed something was amiss. Luckily, they didn't know what. Although soon they would have to be told about at least some of it, and she dreaded that.

"I'm bored," Michael declared. "And it's too cold to look for bugs again." He and his brothers sighed in frustration.

"Want to help me wrap some presents for the cowboys?" Kate asked.

All four perked up.

Fifteen minutes later they had everything they needed, including the gift boxes containing the socks for the men, spread out over the coffee table in the family room. Kate cut squares of wrapping paper and showed the kids how to fold it and apply the tape to hold it in place. She wrote the names. They applied the satin bows. "What's in here, anyway?" Max wanted to know.

"A surprise." She heard the back door open and close. "Speaking of which...guess who's home?"

Alex strode in, his face red from the cold. He took off his hat, jacket and gloves and went to the sink to wash up. When he'd finished, the boys led him over to admire their handiwork. He glanced at it, then Kate. Too late, she realized she should have talked to him about some of this first. The last thing she had wanted to do was hurt or exclude him.

His expression careful, he looked at her again and asked, "What's all this?"

The boys jumped up in unison, triumphantly pumping their little fists in the air. "Surprise presents for the cowboys!" they shouted.

Who were luckily off for the weekend, as always. "I wanted to get them something," she said matter-of-factly.

He gave her a thoughtful once-over. His steady regard turned solemn. "I always give the Christmas bonuses."

Except she lived here now, too. And cooked for the hired hands five days a week. That had engendered a certain camaraderie between her and the cowboys. She wasn't going to apologize for her need to give back. Especially when the ranch hands had all been so kind to her. She rose stiffly, handing gifts for the boys to put beneath the Christmas tree. "Well, now they'll have two presents. Three, if you count the tamales the boys are going to make for them Tuesday afternoon."

Alex knew he'd been out of line.

He did not have a chance to really apologize to her until the boys were in bed for the night, Reckless curled up on the floor between their bunks.

Kate was in the kitchen, making cookies for the next day's festivities. She had taken off the Western jeans she had worn earlier in the day and put on black leggings that showed off her long, sexy legs. A long green tunic clung snugly to her breasts and fell to her hips. Her face was flushed, her lips bare, her honey-blond hair in a messy knot on the top of her head. In short, she was gorgeous. And still maybe a little pissed at him for the attitude he had given her earlier.

An attitude she hadn't deserved.

He came closer, inhaling the vanilla and sugar scent clinging to her hair and skin. "I'm sorry."

She turned her amber eyes to his. Still molding the buttery dough into little balls before dipping them into powdered sugar and setting them on a parchment covered cookie sheet.

Nodding stiffly, she turned away. "I know you're under a lot of stress."

"That's no excuse."

She shrugged, continuing to avert her gaze.

He cupped her shoulders gently between his palms, felt her tremble, as he teased, "Don't you want to yell at me, just a little bit?"

A shuddering sigh escaped her softly parted lips as she finally locked eyes with him. "Maybe steal a kiss..."

Now, they were talking.

He hated being at odds with her.

Even just a little bit.

Having her in his arms again, feeling her press up against him as their lips collided, was *so* much better.

"You have got to be the most wonderful woman I have ever met," he rasped, when their kiss ended.

She splayed her hands across his chest. Merriment sparkled in her eyes. "And also the most curious," she confirmed softly. Easing from his arms, she turned and put a pan of cookies in to bake. She paused to set the timer before she turned back to him and asked, "How did things go with Gabe—before you had to go out and feed the cattle?"

Nothing had been as easy as he would have liked. At least when it came to his ex and her barracuda lawyer. "We finally got the supervised visitation set up for Wednesday afternoon. The mediation is Friday at nine a.m. and will probably go all day."

Kate let out a small groan.

He could tell she was worried about the kids. So was he. "You and I can't be there during the visitation, of course, although we are supposed to stay nearby. But we are both requested to be there for the mediation."

Kate looked as if she had figured as much even though she dreaded that, too.

Alex helped himself to one of the finished snowball cookies, then said, "There's no need for the boys to know about the mediation, but I have to tell them about the upcoming visit with Tiffany."

Kate paused, as concerned as ever. "Any idea how you're going to handle that?" she asked gently.

Alex recalled how upset the boys had been after their first encounter with the legal mother they did not remember. He shook his head. "No. Which is why I asked Mom to meet with us, Monday morning, after we drop the boys at school."

"I can't be involved with this situation specifically," Mitzy told Kate and Alex a day and a half later, when she ushered them into her home. "Due to the conflict of interest. But I can give you general advice about how this process works once I ask a few questions." She took their coats and hung them up in the foyer closet.

Motioning for them to follow her, she led the way into the living room. Making Kate feel as welcome as always, Mitzy continued warmly, "First, what do the boys know so far? I'm guessing not much, given how happy they were yesterday at the music extravaganza."

Alex grimaced. He held his mother's level, assessing gaze with one of his own. "All they know is that Tiffany showed up once, before Thanksgiving, and not since."

Mitzy passed around a plate of holiday cookies. "So nothing about the change in custody petition? Or the scheduled supervised visitation on Wednesday?"

Sensing he needed support, Kate slipped her hand into Alex's. He might act all tough on the outside, especially around those like his ex and her new husband who might be seeking to take advantage, but inside he was kind and bighearted. Tender and loving to a fault. The perfect father for his boys, the ideal husband for her. He was good to the rest of the McCabe family and all his employees, too.

Alex squeezed Kate's hand, holding it tight. "No, Mom. I don't want to tell them too soon. All they will do is worry and stress out again."

Mitzy poured tea for all of them, her expression thoughtful. "Agree."

"Because the boys really don't like Tiffany or Paolo," he concluded.

Mitzy did not appear the least bit surprised by that, maybe because she was a veteran social worker and had been through many such difficult family situations.

Calling on her years of social work experience, she told them sternly, "Be that as it may, it is important the kids go into this meeting with Tiffany and Paolo with open minds. Anything otherwise will reflect poorly on the both of you."

Alex furrowed his brow, immediately taking offense. "We didn't create this situation!"

"I am aware, son. This is also the hand you've been dealt. And you have to be strong and calm and purposeful for your children."

Kate remembered how crazy Tiffany's bullying had made her. Luckily, she was older now. More experienced at dealing with difficult people. So was Alex. Whether he realized it or not. She gave his hand another squeeze. "I think we can handle this."

Mitzy sized Kate up over the rim of her teacup. A smile bloomed slowly on her lovely face. "You mean that, don't you?"

Kate sent her mother-in-law a grateful look. "Very much so. The boys need to have as many people as possible around them who love them. Conflict...especially among adults... does not help anything. And that goes double during the holiday season. Which should be about love and joy, hope and faith."

Without warning, her voice caught. She paused, aware she was on the verge of tears. It had been so long since she'd had a joyous, meaningful holiday, too. So long since she had celebrated with someone who really loved and accepted her. "Regardless of how this all plays out...those boys deserve a wonderful Christmas. And Alex and I are going to see that they get it."

He nodded, wrapping his arm around her shoulders.

Mitzy surveyed Kate once again, even more thoroughly this time. With amazement, she observed, "And you say this with such determination—even knowing firsthand, from just one meeting, how difficult Alex's ex-wife can be."

Kate shrugged, guilt sifting through her.

It was more than one meeting... It was four years of high school hell.

Luckily, to her former enemy, Kate was just another in a sea of nerdy wallflowers, whose fate was to be bullied and demeaned by the really popular girls.

She hadn't mattered to Tiffany then.

And Kate would make sure she didn't matter now.

"I have a feeling that Tiffany and Paolo will move on once they see they can't get what they want, which appears to be... money," Kate said.

Lots and lots of it.

"That's my feeling, too," Mitzy said. "Let's hope we are both right. In the meantime, care to hear the plan I suggest...?"

"Definitely," Alex and Kate said in unison.

Mitzy took a sip of tea, then set her cup down before speaking. "Arrange for the boys to take the entire day off from school on Wednesday and then tell them about seeing their 'first' mother again after breakfast the morning of." Pausing, she glanced from her son to Kate. "You both should be there for that, if possible, so you can reassure them everything is going to be okay, and give them a few hours to process it all before taking them to the supervised visitation."

"Knowing everything you know, do you think it will go smoothly?" Alex asked his mom.

Never one to sugarcoat things, Mitzy answered, "For everyone's sake, let's hope so."

"Dad, are you going to be here to help us make our Christmas surprise for the cowboys today?" Michael asked on the following morning, as they were trying to get out the door to school.

Alex, who was taking them today, stopped and turned to Kate. "What time?" The look on his face also asked if she could estimate how long it would take.

She knew how pressured he felt. A section of fence had come down when the last blue norther swept in. The watering ponds had frozen over every night since, which meant the ice had to be broken up the next morning, so the cattle could drink. The cowboys had all been gone over the weekend, as per usual. Which left the Saturday and Sunday feeding and watering to Alex until the crew returned to work on Monday morning.

Plus, most days he had things to do in town, which he didn't seem to want to talk about. She presumed it had to do with Tiffany's amended petition for custody. The history of her negligent mothering when they had been married probably had to be compiled, and witnesses rounded up, in case it ever got to trial.

That had to be tough for him to think and talk about. Especially since he'd thought—erroneously, as it turned out—that he had put it all behind him.

Kate looked over at him. Maybe this was the change of pace her husband needed. "We're going to get started about four o'clock. As soon as they get home from school. I'll have everything prepped, so we can easily put the tamales together and have them for dinner tonight." She paused, taking in the boys' eager faces. "It'll be fun."

The boys all put their hands together and beamed at him hopefully. Alex laughed at their antics. "Sure. I'll be here," he promised with a smile. "In the meantime—" he herded his sons toward the door "—we've got to get a move on, fellas."

To Kate's delight, Alex and the boys were all singing "Jingle Bells" when they marched into the dining hall, hours later.

"Okay. Wash up and we will get started," she said.

At each place setting, she had a stack of corn husks, a bowl of masa with a spoon and another bowl of spiced pork.

Kate showed the boys how to spread the creamy golden masa over the corn husk with the back of their spoon, and then take the finely shredded pork and spread it down the middle.

They folded the edges of the husk over the tamale. She tied them with a string and put them in the steamer to cook.

When they were halfway done, the boys looked at each other. They seemed to be communicating via the secret language only multiples knew.

"You might as well ask her," Marty said.

"Ask me what?" Kate asked curiously.

Michael bent his head over the making of another tamale. "If we can call you 'Mom' now that you married Dad."

Yet something else he hadn't expected and wasn't prepared for, Alex thought. For a second, silence hung in the dining hall. "All the other kids in school, get to call their mothers 'Mom,'" Matthew pointed out.

"And she *is* our mom, so we want to call her that. Also, we don't want the mean mom to come back," Max said.

Alex winced. Talk about bad timing, given that they weren't even supposed to tell the boys about the scheduled supervised visitation for another twelve hours. If the kids were to learn about that this evening, it could cause a meltdown of epic proportions. Not to mention spoil the happy Christmas mood they were in.

"If the mean mom knows we already have a nice mom now, then maybe she won't come here again," Marty explained their thinking.

"I see your point," Kate said, stepping in with her maternal kindness to save the day. Sweetly, she continued, "Would it be okay if your dad and I talked about it first? And then let you know? I don't want to distract the cowboys from all these beautiful tamales. And," she added with a distractingly dramatic sigh that quickly had the boys' full attention, "there is *also* the Santa Claus angle."

Four little faces were instantly consumed with confusion.

Her expression radiating concern, she splayed her hand across the center of her chest. "Santa Claus knows me as *Kate*. I mean, that's what my stocking on the mantel says, right?"

"Yeah…" The boys mulled that over en masse.

"So… I'm thinking…" Kate said sincerely, "as much as I really want you to call me Mom…maybe we should wait until after Santa Claus comes to make that change. Just—" she frowned, perplexed "—so there is no mix up."

The boys nodded. "We wouldn't want Santa to get confused," Marty said. "He might leave everybody the wrong presents."

His brothers agreed that this absolutely could happen.

"We'll wait," Matthew promised. "Till you tell us the time is right…"

That decided, the boys went back to making the rest of the tamales, including a dessert version that was filled with cinnamon sugar masa and diced apples.

Alex met Kate's gaze.

"Thanks," he said gratefully. He wondered, once again, what he had ever done without her.

She smiled. "My pleasure."

Chapter Nineteen

"That was a nice save this afternoon," Alex told Kate later that evening, as they got ready for bed. "When the boys asked if they could start calling you 'Mom.'"

She slipped into the adjoining bathroom and stepped up to her side of the double vanity. "The first part was one hundred percent accurate." She spread cleanser over her face, rubbing it in with her fingertips. Coming out of the bathroom long enough to catch his gaze, she said, "I didn't know how you would feel about that." She hadn't wanted to overstep.

He came into the bathroom and stood, arms folded in front of him, with one ankle crossed in front of the other. Unable to help but think how handsome he looked in just a pair of low-slung pajama pants, she took a moment to admire his broad shoulders and sinewy chest and arms, before returning her attention to his face. An evening beard gave him a sexy edge. A thrill went through her as she imagined how that would feel against her skin when they made love again. As they surely would.

The picture of masculine ease, he told her, "I'm fine with them wanting to call you that. That is, after all, what you have become to them."

Kate swallowed around the sudden lump of emotion in her throat. "I am okay with it, too." *More than okay!* "But..." She had to swallow again before looking Alex in the eye. "I'm afraid Tiffany won't be."

His lips thinned. "Yeah." He exhaled. Frustration edged his low tone. "That notion crossed my mind, too." Straightening, he turned toward the mirror and reached for his toothbrush.

She rinsed her face, then blotted it dry with a clean washcloth and reached for the moisturizer. "I mean...how did you all refer to Tiffany when the kids were born? Did you call her Mommy? Or... Momma? Mom?" Hard to imagine her responding to any of those things, then or now.

Alex looked down as he spread toothpaste on his brush. "She didn't like any of those monikers."

Amazed at how close she felt to him in this moment, Kate began to brush her teeth as well. "Seriously?"

Nodding, he brushed, rinsed, spit. Then reached for the mint-flavored mouthwash. Once finished, he shared it with Kate. "She just wanted to be referred to as Tiffany. Initially, I kind of thought of it as the kind of thing some grandmothers go through. They don't want to be called Grandma or Granny or Grandmother. And instead adopt names like Nana, Mimi, or Gigi."

Kate used the mouthwash, too, then pressed the washcloth to her lips again. "Because it sounds younger or more on-trend." She reached for her lip balm.

He shrugged. "If you say so."

He was standing so close, she could feel the heat emanating from his powerful body.

"I also thought it could have had something to do with the fact they were biologically connected to me and not her, and carried by a surrogate. And that maybe, with time, when she and the babies bonded, she would change her mind."

"But she didn't," Kate guessed.

Alex let out a slow exhalation of breath. "No."

Kate felt his disappointment as silence fell.

She knew he had accepted all this. Still, it had to be hard, and her heart went out to him.

Alex watched her in the mirror in a way that really made her want to soothe away his hurt, all the more. Maybe even... kiss him. "Anyway—" Kate forced herself to continue talking while they still could without interruptions "—I figured it would be better to let this custody petition play out however it is meant to before we let the boys call me that..."

His gaze narrowed as he interjected gravely. "We're going to win."

Kate sure hoped so.

But as Gabe had said, there were no guarantees. In court anything could happen...

Which meant they had to be as careful as could be.

"I pray you're right," she continued soberly, as they both walked back into the master bedroom. Blowing out a breath, she confessed, "But in any event, the Santa thing was just a momentary inspiration to delay the inevitable."

And keep Tiffany from raising objections at this point.

Alex took her into his arms, as relaxed as she was tense. He smoothed the hair away from her face with the flat of his palm. "The important thing is—the gambit worked to distract the kids."

She lifted her chin to meet his empathetic gaze. "Yeah, but was it the right tact to take?" Kate asked, troubled. "Especially with the supervised visitation tomorrow afternoon?"

"My guess is my ex-wife will be on her best behavior, if only as a ruse to get what she wants. But I don't want to talk about that tonight."

He wrapped his arms around Kate, drawing her against him in a manner that left her hot and breathless. "In fact," he murmured, his lips brushing intimately over hers, "I don't want to talk at all…"

"Funny," Kate whispered back, "I don't either, cowboy…"

"Good." He grinned and waggled his brows mischievously. And she laughed as he meant her to. Then his mouth came down on hers. She opened to the probing pressure of his lips and tongue. Loving the taste and heat and sensuality of him. When they were both naked, they slid between the sheets. As they came together, he once again lay claim to her, heart and soul.

And Kate knew, even if Alex didn't yet, that there was no going back for either of them.

She belonged to him, and he to her.

And no matter what the future had in store for them, in her heart of hearts, she knew this was going to be their best Christmas ever.

"How come we're not going to school today?" Max asked at breakfast the next morning.

Kate glanced at Alex, letting him take the lead. "We are all taking the whole day off from work and school."

Michael tilted his head to one side. "Why? The only time we stay home is when somebody's sick and nobody's sick."

Good point, Kate thought, appreciating the boys' superior intellect, as always.

"Because we have something called supervised visitation to go to," Alex said.

He explained that it was in the children's center of the social services building, where Grandma Mitzy worked. And that he and Kate would drop the boys off in a big playroom with a social worker, psychologist and sheriff's deputy there to watch over them.

When they gave him a scared look, he assured them that

everything was going to be okay. They just had to go to the center so Tiffany and Paolo would come in to visit with them for two hours or so. So they could get to know each other and be friends.

The four boys did not think this was a good plan at all. "Why can't you and Kate be there with us?" Marty wailed, his lower lip trembling.

"Because this is the way it works when parents and children don't know each other," Alex continued gently.

"And need to get acquainted with each other," Kate put in. "The same as you all and I had to get to know each other."

The boys considered that for a while. And then, from their brightening expressions, seemed to be thinking it might not be all bad...

Still looking pained by the whole situation, and how much he hated to have to put his children through all this, Alex sent her a wordless look of thanks. He turned back to his boys with an encouraging smile, reminding, "You still have the whole morning to play before we have lunch and then need to get ready to go and drive into town."

The boys looked at each other, their moods suddenly glum again.

"I'll start a new Christmas puzzle with you," Kate offered. Since they had just finished the second one.

"Or," she tried again, still attempting to cheer them up, "we can watch one of the holiday movies that you like..."

More looks were exchanged between the boys. They were back to communicating without words again. All four crossed their arms in a posture of defiance. "We want to go outside and look for bugs," Michael said.

The one thing they really shouldn't do. Of course.

Wincing, Kate warned, "It's really cold outside. Below freezing."

Shrugs all around. "We don't care if we find any or not, we just want to look!" Marty said.

Kate looked at Alex for direction.

He seemed to understand this was as comforting to the boys, as relaxing in front of the fire was to him and Kate.

"Okay. If you bundle up nice and warm, you can go outside to play," he told his sons. "But you stay in the backyard with Reckless. And when we call you to come in, you come in. No arguments."

The boys murmured their assent and ran upstairs to get their assorted bug catchers. And warm clothes on.

"I'll keep an eye on them," Kate promised, realizing all over again just how much she liked being a mom, even if they couldn't call her that yet.

Alex paused. As if worried he was overstepping. "You sure?"

She flashed him a reassuring smile. "Positive."

While Alex went into his study to work on payroll, Kate hung out in the kitchen. An hour and a half later, the boys came in, their cheeks ruddy with the cold, lips chapped.

"Find anything?" she asked.

They shed their coats, gloves and hats in a big pile on the mudroom floor, dropped their bug catchers on top of that, and marched sullenly into the kitchen. "No!" was the resounding answer. "Nothing!"

"Well, I'm sorry to hear that, fellas." Kate poured hot cocoa into mugs. "But maybe it's a good thing."

They looked at her curiously.

"If the bugs did come outside in this frigid weather, they would probably get super cold—because they don't have coats and hats and gloves and stuff. So, if they stay underground, all cozy and warm, then they'll be fine and able to come out next spring, so you can see them."

"Instead of dying," Michael said.

Kate nodded. "Right. Anybody want mini-marshmallows in their cocoa, or on their plate?"

Four hands shot up.

Turned out everyone wanted them on their plate, so they could eat them plain or dunk them in the cocoa, or do both.

Kate added shortbread cookies to their snacks. They munched on them happily and began to relax. Apparently with their dad not there, they felt free to speak their minds. "How come we have to go see the mean mom?" Max said. "We don't like her!"

"Because she is your first mom," Kate said gently.

"But we want you to be our first mom!" Matthew harrumphed. "Not that other lady!"

"I know you all feel that way now, but maybe that is because you don't know her and Paolo very well. This meeting today could change that."

At least, in this season of Christmas, Kate could hope. Especially if Tiffany was at her charming best.

She sat down with them at the island, moving her stool so she could see all four of them at once, and they could see her. "In any case, kids can have more than one mom. Like… when parents get divorced, the way your dad and your first mom did. Then, later on, if the dad marries someone else, the way your dad married me, you can have a second mom, called a Bonus Mom."

Wordlessly, Michael absorbed that. "So you are our Bonus Mom?"

Kate encompassed them with a reassuring glance. "Yes, I am."

Max shrugged. "Having two moms could be kind of awesome."

"In any case, you four boys need to be as nice and polite as you can to Tiffany and Paolo today. As nice as you've been to me."

Matthew squinted. "Like when we gave you our bugs for a wedding present? And showed you the real ones we caught before we let them go again?"

Kate nodded.

Michael frowned. "Except we didn't get any bugs today. It was too cold. So we can't give her any."

Kate handed out wet wipes so they could wipe their faces. "You don't have to give someone presents, guys, for them to like you."

They seemed confused.

"I'm just talking about not spraying her with your water toys like you did that first time you met her. When you got her—and Paolo—all wet. If you don't do anything rowdy or silly like that, you'll be okay," Kate promised. "Your dad will be very happy with you."

Marty tilted his head to one side. "What about you? Will you be happy with us if we are really good today?"

"If you are as nice to Tiffany as you are to me, then yes, I will be very happy," Kate vowed. Because that would go a long way toward disproving Tiffany's allegation that the boys were out of control and suffering from a lack of maternal influence in their lives.

The boys looked at each other, sighed, then finished their hot cocoa in thoughtful silence before heading upstairs to get ready to go.

Kate knew this wasn't what the kids wanted.

It wasn't what any of them wanted. But sometimes life dealt you a difficult hand, and you just had to play.

All she could do was keep a low profile, so Tiffany would not recognize her, and be there for Alex and the boys in any and every way she could. And hope it was enough.

"How do you think the kids are doing?" Alex asked, several hours later.

He and Kate walked through the town park, which was several blocks from the county social services building.

Kate knew Alex was worried.

She was worried, too.

"It's probably going to go one way or another," Alex predicted gravely, without waiting for her reply. "Tiffany is either going to lay on the charm to try and demonstrate that she is the better parent after all. Which is actually what I expect. Or she'll needle them just enough to get them to misbehave, thereby proving her point that I haven't been a very good parent to them."

"Hey." Kate swung around to face her husband. She clasped his arms, holding him in front of her, offering him every ounce of moral support she had. "You are a terrific dad. Make that terrific *single father*, which is much harder. Are the boys perfect? Of course not. They're kids. But they love you and they're generally happy..." She stopped talking as his cell phone buzzed.

He pulled it out of his pocket and looked at the screen. Swore.

"What happened?" Kate panicked, already fearing she knew.

"The visitation is being cut short. The boys are hysterical. They want us there right away."

Minutes later, when they walked into the visitation room, Tiffany and Paolo were just walking out, their expressions angry and resentful. She glared at Alex. "You know, fool that I was, I was hoping for the best today, for all our sakes.

But the reality is, your children do not know how to behave. At all."

Kate noticed Tiffany said, *your* children. Not *my* children. Or *our* children. Yours.

Technically, it was correct. The birth mother was a surrogate. The eggs donated by an unknown person. Of all of them standing there, only Alex had a biological connection, via his sperm, to the four boys. Unhappily, Tiffany still had a legal one. And like it or not, that made her their official mother.

"Fortunately, I know Paolo and I can do better when it comes to raising them. So if this was some sort of scheme to get me to back away," she announced haughtily, "it has failed miserably."

"What are you talking about?" Alex demanded.

Tiffany turned a dismissive glance to Kate. "Ask the Bonus Mom, why don't you?" Her tone turned even nastier. "I don't know what it is about you. You remind me of someone, something..."

Kate froze.

"Repugnant. And or... I don't know. Trashy. Disrespectful."

"That's not Kate," Alex growled. "Watch how you talk about my wife."

"Well, it certainly *is* your four boys!" Tiffany snarled, before stomping off, her spike heels clicking on the tile floor.

Behind them, the social worker emerged. "Mr. and Mrs. McCabe? Could you come with me, please?"

She led the way through the visitation area, to a small private room with a settee and upholstered chairs. The four boys were huddled on the sofa, their faces tearstained, their expressions sulky.

As soon as they saw Kate, they ran toward her, arms outstretched, and gathered her close in a group hug. She wrapped her arms around them, too, her heart aching for them as they began to sob. "W-w-we didn't mean to be bad! We were trying to be nice, like you told us to be," Max claimed. "So we showed her our bugs, and the mean mom thought they were real and she started to scream. And she knocked them away."

"Were they dead bugs?" Kate asked in confusion. She knew they didn't find any outside. Which didn't mean they didn't have some stashed somewhere.

"No. Plastic. The toy kind." Matthew pulled out a handful from the pocket of his cords.

"Oh," Kate said. They were lifelike, especially if you just assumed they were real.

Alex scrubbed a hand over his face. "Why would you do this?" he asked them miserably.

Max explained, "Because Kate told us to be nice to the mean mom, like we were nice to her, and she also said bugs were a good gift when we gave her some. So we were trying to be fair and give the mean mom some, too."

"Well, this explains a lot," the social worker said. "It didn't seem like an act of mischief, but things got out of control so fast..."

"I understand," Alex said with a heavy sigh. He ran his hands over his face again. Straightened. "So what next?"

The social worker gestured unknowingly. "Since this was voluntary, not court-ordered, it is up to your lawyers to decide."

"We're sorry, Dad," Marty said. They all walked together toward his Navigator. Michael and Max held Alex's hands while Marty and Matthew held Kate's.

"I know," Alex replied wearily. "Me, too."

"Are we going to have time out?" Michael asked.

Alex sent all four of his sons a compassionate glance. "I don't think so. You were trying to do what you were asked.

It just didn't work out the way you expected that it would." He cleared his throat. "I do want you to remember one thing, though. You can't hide toy bugs in your pockets when we go somewhere. If you want to do it at home, that's fine. But no scaring people with them, even accidentally, okay?"

The boys nodded.

At home, they settled in front of the TV to watch a Christmas movie. Meanwhile, Kate and Alex went into the kitchen to make some coffee.

"Well, that did *not* go well," Alex muttered.

"No, unfortunately, it didn't." Worst of all, Tiffany had started to remember Kate. Or at least niggling feelings of repulsion related to their prep school years. Which made Kate wonder if she had done the wrong thing in keeping the truth from him.

Alex caught her hand and drew her close. "If you think I blame you for what happened, you're wrong. I don't. The boys could easily have done this on their own, without any misinterpreted encouragement from you."

But they hadn't.

Which made Kate wonder.

What would happen between her and Alex if she were at fault for him losing custody of his sons? Would he forgive her so easily then?

Chapter Twenty

"Dad! Come look at us!" Marty said, early Thursday morning.

Alex walked into the kitchen. His boys were still clad in their pajamas.

Kate was there, too. In a long, festive red tunic, jeans and cowgirl boots. Her hair was caught up in a bouncy ponytail high on the back of her head. Merriment—that matched his sons'—flashed in her amber eyes, and her lips were curved into a mischievous smile.

"Good morning, Alex," she said. "Do you want to join us for pancakes and bacon?"

"You can decorate them any way you want!" Max pointed to the Santa-, reindeer-, Christmas tree- and ornament-shaped pancakes.

Loving the warm camaraderie Kate managed to imbue, wherever she was, Alex squinted his approval. "I see." Times like this, he wondered how he had ever managed without her. She made all their lives so much better.

"It's kind of like finger painting," Matthew explained, "except we got strawberry jelly, whipped cream and chocolate syrup for decorating."

"Raisins and dried cranberries and vanilla chips, too," Kate said.

Alex moved to her side. He wrapped an arm around her

and pressed a kiss on her temple. "Good morning, wife," he whispered huskily in her ear.

"Same to you," she murmured back, leaning into him with a happy sigh.

Now that they were married, PDA was no longer disallowed. And right now, he needed all the comfort and support Kate could give him and the boys.

"Looks good, but I have to check in with the guys. They're over at the Knotty Pine, taking care of that herd this morning, and they want me to take a look at some of the fence. See if it all needs to be torn down and replaced, or just repaired here and there. Then I've got a business meeting on the other side of Laramie County."

"Busy day." Her voice was low and soothing.

He cuddled her even closer, inhaling the sweet lavender scent of her. "Yeah. I was going to ask if you could take the boys into town and drop them at school this morning."

"No problem." As usual, she didn't hesitate to help. The gentle affection in her smile was mirrored in her eyes. "I can get them this afternoon, too."

"But you should come home early, Dad," Matthew informed him. "Because we're making a gingerbread house after school today!"

"Now that sounds fun." Alex let go of Kate reluctantly and went to pour himself a travel mug of coffee. How was it that the world always felt a little brighter when he was with this woman, and a little bleaker when he wasn't? "I'll try to be here, at least for the last bit," he promised.

The boys beamed at him, their little faces and hands covered with pancake and toppings.

"See you later, Dad!" they called in unison.

Alex tipped his hat at them, then went over to give Kate a final quick kiss, which she sweetly returned. Then he headed out the door, his heart a little lighter than it had been last evening.

He had expected the kids to be as glum this morning as they had been after the supervised visitation the afternoon before.

Instead, they seemed happier than ever.

Part of that was Kate—and the entertaining breakfast she had prepared for them, and the promise of the activity she'd planned to keep them even busier later that afternoon. The rest was likely the fact that they had concluded that Tiffany really didn't like them and, because of that, would not be back to claim them.

Had their legal mother not been broke, that could very well be true. But Tiffany was. Which meant he was going to have to see her privately today, like it or not.

"I had a feeling you'd call," Tiffany said a few hours later.

The two of them were in a cozy private dining room at the Laramie Country Inn, where she and Paolo were staying. It was a nice place, but not nearly as swanky as the hotels Tiffany preferred. The food was really good though. The overnight accommodations on the second floor were limited to half a dozen en suites, which were usually fully booked and occupied by business folks visiting the area during the week. Because the main dining room wouldn't open to the general public for lunch for another hour, the inn was exceptionally quiet.

Hoping the solitude might enable them to talk openly and honestly, Alex sat opposite his newly married ex-wife.

She was as beautiful as ever, from a cosmetic standpoint, but there was a new brittleness to her personality that told him life was not being as kind to Tiffany as she had always expected.

And that was a shame.

He had the feeling that if she were ever truly satisfied with what life doled out to her, she might be a different person. One worth knowing. Luckily that was no longer his responsibility. The only thing he had to do was take care of his family. Prevent her from hurting the boys.

He waited until their continental breakfasts were served and their coffee cups filled. When the waiter left, and closed the door behind him, he said, "This isn't about the kids. You know it. I know it. What you want is money."

Tiffany's chunky gold jewelry glinted in the sunlight, pouring in through the windows. She ripped off a corner of her croissant, tore it into shreds, then looked up at him slyly. "Are you saying you'll give me some?"

He saw the desperation she was working so hard to hide. Felt nothing but pity. To have a life that was only about how much cash you had was just damn sad. He took another gulp of coffee. "There's nothing to give."

Temper flared in her heavily made-up eyes. She brushed an imaginary speck of dust off the V-neckline of her ecru silk dress. "Come on. I've seen the Rocking M. How many acres do you have these days, if you don't count the land you use on the Knotty Pine?"

Getting a little tired of his ex's greed, Alex gave her a long, level look. "That's not mine. It belongs to my parents."

"But it likely will be someday since none of your siblings are interested in ranching."

Fuming, Alex fell silent.

"Not going to tell me?" Tiffany looked at him like he was a day late and a dollar short. She leaned across the table. When she spoke again, it was in a much more conciliatory tone. "Okay, my dear ex-husband, I'll tell you. The Rocking M has ten thousand acres, roughly a thousand head of cattle and, of course, that very nice modern ranch house you built a few years back."

"The boys and I live there, and I make my living raising the aforementioned herd of cattle on that land."

"So what?" Tiffany flashed a winning smile. "Sell it and go back to working in the city. You'd probably be much happier. I know our boys would."

Our boys. What a crock of malarkey.

Seeming to realize she had crossed a line, Tiffany shrugged. "Or...get a second mortgage on the Rocking M and stay there with the boys."

Hanging on to his temper by a thread, Alex retorted, "And then what?"

She took a small sip. Gave him a dazzling smile. "Paolo and I will go to Europe for a while."

Aware his ex would like nothing better than to see his life blown to smithereens, he told her flatly, "I'm not paying you off. I did that once. Clearly, it was a mistake."

Tiffany drew herself up like a rattler about to strike. "Yes," she said icily, "it was an error in judgment on my part, as well. I should have asked for more than just what was left of your itty-bitty trust fund."

He ignored her snide insult. Although she had a point—the money his mom and dad had given him and his four siblings had been enough to start a life or a business. Not a fund to live on, so they would never have to work a day in their lives.

Hard work was valued in the McCabe family.

Whereas her Old Money fund, derived from the oil and gas profits of her family's business, was close to two hundred and fifty million.

Enough so she and Paolo would never have to work a day in their lives, if she could ever get access to it that was.

Unfortunately for Tiffany, her parents had never seemed to want to stand around and watch her foolishly deplete it.

He leaned toward her urgently. "Listen to me," he warned in a low, serious tone. "Continuing down this path will hurt the boys and us. If it goes to court, everything that has happened between us to date will come out, and it will be public record. And there are things that I know about you...like how you lied about being infertile...that won't play well in Houston society. Especially since your parents felt they had no choice but to continue on with that misconception when we arranged for donor eggs and hired a surrogate to carry my children."

Tiffany shrugged, cavalier as ever. "They'll be able to handle it."

Alex doubted that. The Phillips family reputation meant the world to them. Just as Tiffany's rep was everything to her. She might be mean as a viper behind closed doors, but in public...she wanted to be seen as a charming socialite and jet-setter, nothing less.

Alex had let her paint him as the bad guy, when they had split up, for two reasons. First, he wanted his freedom from a life of duplicity. And second? He had wanted her away from the kids that she would never love. Or care for.

Both of those motivations still stood.

Only now it wasn't just his sons he was protecting, but his new life with Kate. And the family they were building.

The only hitch was that Tiffany refused to be reasonable. Which meant, Alex thought—no less determined to emerge the victor—they were going to have to do this the hard way.

"Ready to go in?" Alex asked Kate as Gabe approached them on the courthouse steps on Friday morning.

She took his hand and nodded. Trying not to show the fear she felt.

Gabe signed them in, and they were led to the appropriate room on the mediation floor.

Tiffany, Paolo and their lawyer—a stern, standoffish woman with perfectly chiseled facial features...the kind that seemed heavily Botoxed—were already there. As was the mediator, a young cordial guy barely out of law school.

The mediator went over the rules and confirmed this was a voluntary mediation that could be opted out of at any time. If the parties involved did so, however, they would likely face a full court-ordered mediation before anything was heard by a family court judge. So it behooved the parties to make the best of this meeting.

The mediator let the petitioner begin, with a summary of the complaint, read by Tamara Marshall.

"Alex McCabe has been caring for the four quadruplet sons for the last four and a half years. It has come to our client's attention that he is an unfit parent."

Like hell I am, Alex thought.

"This was confirmed when Tiffany Phillips McCabe Delucca and her husband, Paolo Delucca, drove to the Rocking M Ranch Thanksgiving week, to check out the situation in a surprise visit. They were greeted by four extremely hostile children, a woman—Kate Taylor, Alex McCabe's new ranch chef and girlfriend—and Alex. The children were sent away, but returned with loaded water toys and promptly attacked their mother and her new husband."

Only because they felt threatened, and rightly so!

"Later that week, while under the highly distracted care of Alex and his new girlfriend, the boys went missing at the Laramie County fairgrounds. An announcement had to be made on the loudspeaker before they could be found."

Alex grimaced. That had been scary. And had been a moment he was not proud of. He—and Kate—should have done better.

"A week later, when Alex impulsively decided to marry his ranch chef, the boys tried to steal his Lincoln Navigator to drive to the wedding themselves. They were unable to get the SUV started, which was the only thing that saved their lives that night."

Talk about a complete exaggeration!

Although he and Kate shouldn't have shut the boys out of their decision to marry...

"Then, finally, at the supervised visitation Alex McCabe insisted Tiffany and Paolo attend prior to this mediation, Kate instructed the boys to terrify Tiffany with realistic looking insects."

Definitely not true! Alex fumed.

"Tiffany did not initially realize the bugs were plastic and screamed in fear. The visitation erupted in chaos and was promptly ended unfairly."

Tiffany's lawyer glared. "In summation, the boys are being raised in a half frat house, half bunk house atmosphere and need to be removed from their father's care immediately. Hopefully, before Christmas."

Kate was stunned by how bad that all sounded. There were explanations for everything, of course. Gabe had promised them he would go through any accusations, one at a time, and clarify with the full facts and the truth. But still, on the face of it, she couldn't help but think that Tiffany had more of a shot of assuming custody of the boys than Kate had allowed herself to believe.

If the grim expression on Alex's face was any indication, he was thinking the same.

Then Gabe started his opening recitation. "Tiffany Phillips McCabe Delucca married Alex McCabe under false pretenses. She told him she wanted to be a ranch wife and have his children. Her only problem, she declared, when it came time to deliver on that promise, was that complex gynecological problems in her teenage years left her unable to get pregnant or carry a child to term, but she stated she was very willing to have his children by surrogate. She even knew doctors that could help them.

"It became clear after the birth of the four boys, that she had no interest in personally caring for the children, and as time went on, had less and less to do with them. When they reached their first birthday, she demanded a divorce from Alex, and a large financial settlement, which he gave her. At that time, she kept legal custody of the children, even though she had no biological ties to them. Alex allowed it because he thought she might eventually change her mind and want to be a mother to them.

"Unfortunately, she did not. In fact he did not hear from his ex-wife at all until three and a half weeks ago."

What a day that had been, Kate thought.

"When she suddenly appeared, with little warning, demanding she wanted the children for the holidays.

"The boys were frightened by her aggressive demeanor and acted to defend themselves and their father, in a way only kindergarten students would think reasonable."

"More likely they were simply undisciplined ruffians!" Tiffany said.

On the contrary, Kate thought furiously, they were sweet, lovable little boys!

The mediator silenced Tiffany. "You'll have your time to respond to your ex-husband's claims. Just as he will have an opportunity to respond to yours." He looked at Gabe, with a nod, indicated he should go on.

With a frown, Gabe continued, "The four boys also tried to give their legal mother a chance to get to know them, and vice versa, which is why they took the bugs to the supervised visitation. They had had great success showing their stepmom their collection, and becoming closer to her in the process. They expected the same reaction from Tiffany. And became very upset when they did not receive it.

"In conclusion, Tiffany accepted a million dollar settlement from Alex McCabe four and a half years ago to start her new life. She has since depleted it. She also married Paolo a few months ago, against both their wealthy parents' wishes. In response, both parents cut off access to the financial trusts of their adult children." Gabe cleared his throat, then said with conviction, "Tiffany is back in Laramie County, to extort more money from her ex-husband. He is refusing to give it to her. So she is using custody of the children as a bargaining tool. And that is the only reason why we are here today."

Tiffany glared at Alex. Then Gabe and Kate. "Lovely," she muttered. "Just lovely."

A knock sounded on the door. A uniformed officer stepped in. "Sorry to interrupt. Tiffany's parents are here."

Tiffany looked genuinely shocked. She stared at the officer. "They came all the way from Houston?"

The uniformed officer nodded. "There is some sort of family emergency. They need to see you and your husband right away."

"Of course, you should go," the mediator said.

"I still want to finish!" Tiffany whined.

Alex lifted a hand, said graciously, "Not to worry. We will wait."

Looking equally confused and concerned, Tiffany and Paolo swept out.

The mediator went on break and left the room. A stressful silence fell. "This is horrible," Kate whispered. Already so much worse than what she expected.

Hurtful in literally every way.

"Yeah," Alex agreed glumly. "It is. Custody battles always are."

And they were in one that was just getting started, Kate thought anxiously. What kind of damage, collateral or otherwise, was it going to do?

Tiffany and Paolo returned thirty minutes later, their lawyer in tow.

Kate had expected them to be worried or upset. Instead, Tiffany and Paolo looked surprisingly happy and victorious.

Her attorney informed everyone that Tiffany was withdrawing her petition and, further, had signed away all legal rights to the children, at her parents' behest. In exchange, she would be getting full access to her trust starting immediately.

"Wow..." Kate hadn't meant to say that but she did.

Alex's jaw set. He stood to face off with his ex-wife. "I guess I was right all along," he said bitterly.

"Oh, you think so?" Tiffany tossed her head, clearly stung by Alex's assessment of her. "You think I'm horrible and that—" she turned to Kate and waved her hand as if at a pesky insect "—*traveling chef* you're married to is heaven's gift?" She swung back to face Alex, resolved to inflict as much damage as she felt she had suffered from him! "Well, let me tell you something, my dear ex-husband. Katherine Taylor is *no angel*. In fact, she's had an agenda for years now that you just stupidly happened to fulfill! And you know *how* I know that? We went to prep school together!"

"Oh no…" Kate said before she could stop herself.

Tiffany gave Kate a snide look. "Yeah, I did remember. The only reason I initially *didn't* is because you went by the name Katherine back then, not Kate, and because you are lot more put together now than you ever were then."

Alex turned to Kate, looking like the air had been knocked out of him.

She had no idea what to say or where to start, so she remained silent as the heat of utter humiliation filled her face.

Alex continued to stare at her, still waiting for her to explain her way out of the nightmare that she thought she—and her parents—had put behind her years before.

She could tell he still wanted to trust her.

Like she still wanted to trust him with all her heart and soul.

Tiffany snorted, the way she always did when she hadn't yet managed to inflict the desired damage. "I can tell you don't believe me, so…" She whipped out her phone and typed something in.

Almost immediately, Kate's and Alex's phones signaled identical incoming texts had been received.

Kate's heart sank.

Smirking, Tiffany swung back to taunt Alex. "Take a look at this video," she dared. "And then tell me you know all about this cowboy-hunting gold digger you just married. Not that she is the only one apparently keeping secrets…" Tiffany let out an evil laugh.

"I mean—" she paused to give Kate a pitying look before resuming her dressing down of Alex "—you didn't tell her about our intimate breakfast for two yesterday, did you?" She sized Alex up like he were the lowest reptile on earth. Gave an even more sinister sounding laugh, before concluding haughtily, "I didn't think so." Damage done, she turned on her heel and walked out.

Chapter Twenty-One

"What is she talking about?" Kate asked. A private breakfast for two? Alex hadn't said anything about that!

"You know what?" Gabe gathered up their copies of the papers that had been signed. The mediator and opposing lawyer did the same. He sent Kate and Alex a look, practically begging them to work this out. "I think we should let these two have the room. It's reserved for another few hours, anyway, and they need to talk privately."

They sure as hell did, Kate thought furiously.

How was it she had been maliciously unmasked by her former nemesis and betrayed by the love of her life all at the same time?

In the meantime, Alex had opened the file Tiffany had texted him, and there it was on his cell phone screen—Kate's public humiliation in all its poorly video-recorded glory.

His brow furrowed in confusion. He was so still he could have been playing a game of statue. "What is this?" he said, in a low, gravelly tone.

He sat down at the conference table.

She sank into the chair beside his.

And still he didn't start the video. It was as if he instinctively knew that pushing play was going to change things between them in a way that his ex-wife wanted and the two of them didn't.

Her cheeks burning, she swallowed around the rising ache in her throat. If only she could go back and rewrite the past! She forced herself to look into his eyes. "It is a copy of my senior year speech to the entire school assembly." Teachers. Kids. Parents. Everyone.

Alex rubbed his hand across his jaw, as if it were taking everything he had to contain himself. He looked at her even more closely. Acting like if there were something bad about her, he really didn't want to know about it. Which made two of them because she really didn't want him to know about this, either.

"So what is supposed to be so bad about it?" he asked slowly.

She looked away and released a long exhalation of breath. Doing her best to revisit what had been the most mortifying event of her entire life. One she had sadly and foolishly brought entirely on herself.

"Honestly?" She forced herself to meet his gaze yet again. Like it or not, they'd been brought to this place by his ex, and now they had to get the big reveal over with. "Pretty much everything."

He took her hand in his. "I'm listening."

Appreciating the compassion and kindness he had always shown her, she relaxed into the comfort of his grip, continuing, "It was a tradition at my all-girls school for every graduating senior to give a farewell speech before she graduated. We were to talk about what we had learned going to the Westchase Academy for Girls, and what we expected our future would look like."

"I don't get it." He sat back in his chair, his broad shoulders relaxing. Tenderly, he encouraged her to go on. "How can that be bad?" He shook his head, as if that would bring new light to the situation. "Did you get stage fright or something? Did everyone laugh at you? Or make fun?"

Kate winced, wishing it had been that simple. She drummed her fingertips on the glossy conference table. "No, I had complete control of my faculties that day." Which somehow made it all the worse. Because she had known full well what she was doing every second. She had planned it. "It was my *anger* at having been mercilessly bullied and disrespected for all four years as a student there that was out of control."

Alex sent her a confused look.

Unable to sit still a second longer, Kate got up and began to pace. She ended up at the window, overlooking the quiet Laramie streets. Taking solace in the peace and acceptance she had found here, she pivoted back to face him, her spine resting against the chill of the window. "All my fellow students were talking about the social connections they had gained at the prep school that, along with their family clout, would pave their way to unimaginable success. One predicted she would be an Oscar-winning actress. Another, president of the United States. One girl thought she would be a CEO of a Fortune 500 company. Another, a supreme court justice."

Alex threw up his hands as if to say, "Okay, high school students have big dreams. Perhaps even illogical ones." He stood and came over to stand next to her "I still don't see what the big deal is."

Kate drew a bolstering breath and, pushing past him, began to pace again. "I went on a rant about the Old Money snobs pitting themselves against the hardworking New Money and scholarship students. And I also listed some of the things that had been done to bully and discourage me and make sure I did *not* achieve the connections the rest of those girls had."

A muscle ticked in his jaw and she could only imagine what he was thinking. "Like...?"

"At first it was silly things, like jamming my locker so when I opened it, literally everything came tumbling out onto the floor," she divulged. "Then they started writing my name and phone number on bathroom walls in public places. You know, 'For a good time, call Katherine…'"

"Oh man…"

"Then they filled my backpack with condoms and jerry-rigged it so when I stood up, they would fall all over the classroom floor."

His blue eyes narrowing, he bit out, "No teachers or counselors intervened?"

"I think they believed the stories Tiffany and her ilk were circulating about me being a slut. And, in any case, any academic award or starting slot on an athletic team always went to the Old Money girls because it was their parents who funded their trips and donated new equipment to the school science labs. I mean, I was an A student, but for the most part an unrecognized one."

Alex put his arms around her and held her close. Stroking her hair, he rubbed a hand down her spine and asked, "Did you tell your parents?"

Kate rested her face against his shoulder, his strong male presence like a port in the storm. "Only that I was unhappy there and didn't really have any friends. I was too embarrassed to say anything else." She released a shuddering breath. "I was such a wallflower back then, Alex, and had no idea how to handle those vicious rumors circling around. No big sister to go to…no one on the faculty I trusted."

He drew back, his gaze and touch gentling all the more. "So you pretty much suffered in silence your whole four years there."

"Yep. Until I spilled all during a school assembly."

His lips formed a sober, downward curve. "I'm guessing that didn't go over well with the audience."

The tsunami of emotions she had felt back then returned, full force. "Actually," she admitted, feeling more embarrassed than ever, "a lot of the girls loved it! They thought I just proved what unsophisticated trash I was. And always would be. Unbeknownst to me, they were filming it on their phones."

Alex groaned, sharing her pain. "Then what happened?"

"I grew sarcastic, and yeah, while I'm not proud of it I lowered myself to their level."

"How so?" he asked."

"By lashing out at them, saying I would have to work very hard to be successful in college. But unlike them, my grades would not be bestowed upon me because my parents had just done something shady or donated a new library to the university.

"Not that my family had that kind of money," she admitted to Alex. "But I did know what brilliant businesspeople my parents were and, in my speech, I mockingly predicted that strings would be pulled for me, too. Sooner, rather than later. And that then I would likely be guilted into joining the family retail business. At least for a while. And that like most of those girls, I too had a generous trust fund that I would have access to when I was married and had children of my own."

Alex frowned and she could tell it was dawning on him that she hadn't ever mentioned this to him, either.

With effort, Kate went on summarizing her speech. So Alex would be prepared when he finally did watch the video of a person she didn't recognize then, or now. "Hence—" she pushed away the immense pain she had felt at the time "—I went on to say, I planned to work just long enough to snag a wealthy Old Money husband. No old men for me. Even if they did own properties all over Europe. I wanted someone handsome and very sexy, who was my own age. 'A real Texas cowboy,' I said."

He stared at her, shock and disappointment on his face.

Knowing that was exactly what she had found with him, Kate forced herself to go on.

"We'd buy a ranch to live in on the weekends, and have a dozen kids and live happily ever after. And I would forget my days at the prep school ever happened."

Kate went back to the table, reached for his phone, hit the play button, then handed it to him. "But no need to take my word for it. Here. Listen for yourself."

Alex watched the video on his phone. Kate wore a frumpy dress that practically screamed wallflower. Her honey-blond hair was a frizzy mess that obscured much of her pretty face.

Her voice was filled with emotion, strength and hurt.

And not surprisingly, her emotional speech was pretty much word for word what she had described for him.

Which made him wonder—how many times had she listened to that rant in her head? What must it be like for her to have it haunt her again now?

Had she in some way used him to make that dream come true, he wondered, before immediately pushing the notion away. He knew the kind of woman Kate was. That she would never use anyone. Even if she had made a huge mistake, keeping all of this from him, when he was in the midst of an ugly custody fight with his ex. Who not only would—but had—used it against them.

With a grimace, he shut off his phone. Not surprisingly, Kate still looked as if she felt incredibly guilty for blindsiding him this way. She had told him bits and pieces of her story before, but not the whole thing. "So how does Tiffany have the video of your speech?" he asked stonily.

"I don't know." She balled her hands into fists at her side. "Briefly, of course, it went viral among the students, but my parents and the administrators at the prep worked very quickly to get it taken off the internet. So, as far as I knew, at least until this morning, it had been completely deleted."

Alex shoved a hand through his hair. "Obviously, someone still had a copy."

Kate nodded, looking as distraught as he imagined she had been back then. "And once she realized who I was, Tiffany would have known who to contact for the worst graduating senior speech that was ever given in the history of Westchase Academy for Girls."

"What was your parents' reaction to it?" he asked, still trying to wrap his brain around the bombshell that his ex and current wife had a history together.

And an ugly one at that.

"Twofold. They were sorry they hadn't realized how bad things were for me and wished they'd agreed to move me to another school when I first told them how miserable I was. And they were furious with my behavior, and the fact I was nearly expelled—at least until my parents gave the school a huge endowment to make up for the calamity caused by me.

"Anyway, it was a huge lesson for me. I spent nine years paying penance. Trying to make up for what I had almost done to my parents' reputation and business." She released a gusty sigh. "Until one day I woke up and finally realized I had paid my debt, and would never be happy unless I followed my *own* path. Which was what led me here, of course."

Silence fell as he thought about how this all could have blown up both their lives. Still reeling, he asked, "Why didn't you tell Gabe and me about this when he was asking you about your background, and to divulge anything that might hurt my chances of keeping sole custody of the boys?"

"Because I was trying to *protect* you! Please tell me you understand that." Her eyes glimmering with tears, she gave him an imploring look that let him know just how long this secret had been weighing on her. "You have to know, Alex, that the last thing I wanted was for any of this to come out." She clamped her arms beneath her breasts. "And I honestly thought all copies had been destroyed," she said in a low voice trembling with remorse.

Disappointment churned in his gut. "But, as we now found out, they *hadn't* been. What if Tiffany's parents hadn't come through with access to her trust today?" he countered bitterly. "And she had continued to go after me, blindsiding me with her claims that you are a gold digger in pursuit of a rich cowboy and a passel of kids?" Jaw set, he looked her in the eye and said, "If we had been prepared, we would have had a strategy to deal with it. As it was…"

Flinching, she took a step back. "Like the strategy to deal with all the pictures of us kissing? The get-married-quickly plan?" Her expression was taut with pain and regret.

He forced himself to calm down and corral his own hurt. "You know how bad her lawyer's recitation of everything the boys have done since Tiffany came back into their lives sounded today," he told her, refusing to let her run away. "You were supposed to be the stabilizing grace."

"*Supposed* to be?" she asked in a low, strangled voice.

"This video would have undermined everything you have presented yourself as, or mean to me and the boys, and completely negated any positive influence you've had on our lives."

"Meant? As in past tense?" She squared her shoulders and locked gazes with him. Suddenly frustrated and angry now, too. "Why don't you say what you really think?" she bit out eventually.

"Fine. You want to know the truth?" He crossed his arms and glared down at her. "I'm ticked off you kept this social media catastrophe from me, knowing what a disaster it could have turned into." He'd thought they weren't just married, but in a committed relationship. One where they shared everything important and were able to count on each other, even in the hardest of times, too.

"I'm sure that's part of it." Her voice quavered, yet took on a low, accusing timbre at the same time. "What's the rest?"

"I have no idea what you're talking about," he retorted.

She spun away. Then, huffing out a breath, turned back and sent him a withering glare. "Is it possible that now that you have permanently won the battle with your ex over the kids, that you are suddenly regretting marrying me, and are looking for a way out?"

He reeled, as if she had delivered a physical punch.

She slowly looked him up and down. "Or did you keep your meeting with Tiffany secret from me because you didn't *trust* me to support your plan to see her alone? Or thought I would get jealous and insist on coming with you?"

Yeah, maybe he shouldn't have hid his plans to meet with Tiffany from her. But at the time, he'd felt he had no choice because he'd known that if Kate *had* known and wanted to come, he would have let her. Which wouldn't have worked, since his last-ditch effort to deal with Tiffany had had a better chance of succeeding one-on-one. But there was no reason for Kate to be jealous. She had to know that! "This is ridiculous, Kate. After what happened today, I'm the one who should no longer trust you. Not the other way around."

Her guard went up. Twin spots of color blooming in her cheeks as her hurt and anger intensified. "Maybe we just shouldn't trust *each other*," she choked out. "As I said in the beginning, this has all happened way too fast…"

Her betrayal had stung. But her willingness to just write him off hurt even more. Unexpected sorrow roiled in his gut. "Whether it has or it hasn't is inconsequential, now that the boys are involved." He forced himself to temporarily push aside their mess of a relationship and act like the devoted father he was. "We *can't* ruin their Christmas, Kate."

A myriad of emotions came and went in her eyes. She shoved both hands wearily through her hair, the unbridled love they both felt for his sons hanging in the air between them. "Agreed." She stared at him a long moment, then dug in all the harder, becoming as magnanimous as he had always expected her to be. "They *deserve* to have a happy holiday. And much more, actually."

At least they agreed on that, Alex thought wearily. He inhaled sharply, asked, "So how are we going to achieve that?"

She shrugged. The wife who had made love to him so tenderly, the woman who'd begun to share everything with him, now nowhere to be found. A shield was up around her heart that he wasn't sure would ever come back down.

Quietly, she said, "By going back to the plan we had at the very beginning. We return to the solely platonic, transactional relationship we had when I first came to the ranch."

It was one thing to screw up and not know how to fix it. Another to simply call it quits. Pretend no feelings had ever existed. "Except we're married, Kate." They'd been intimate. They knew how good things could be…

"And we can *stay* married as long as you want." Kate lifted her hands, palms up. "We've got a prenup, remember? One that states what is yours is yours, and what is mine is mine. Including our separate businesses."

Even if they hadn't had a signed legal document spelling everything out, finances would never have been a problem between them. Trying not to feel like his life was going to hell, he demanded curtly, "What about the rest of it?"

Releasing another long sigh, Kate slumped her shoulders in defeat. "I'll go back to sleeping in the guest suite," she said. "Keep cooking for the cowboys. We'll be polite to each other and be respectful at all times. If we work hard enough to be as considerate and kind to each other as always," she predicted, "the boys will never know anything is amiss."

He studied her, his emotions locked down as irrevocably as hers. "You could do that?" *Could he?*

"For the kids?" Kate's voice trembled with emotion, and then broke, as surely as his own heart. "Absolutely."

Chapter Twenty-Two

"Where's Kate?" Gabe asked Alex the following day. They were at the Laramie Climbing Gym, where the Saturday morning youth camp was going on.

He waved at all nine of the McCabes. Claire and Zach's triplets were with the pre-k kids, Alex's boys the kindergarten class and Ellie and Joe's two toddlers with the beginners group. All wore full-body harnesses and were having the time of their lives, moving from rock to rock on the brightly colored wall. Teenage coaches were at their sides.

Alex paused the video function on his phone, then moved out of earshot of other observing parents. "She went with Mom to get things ready for the family lunch today, over at Mom and Dad's house."

"So... Things are fine between the two of you?"

Alex couldn't exactly say that. Actually, they'd gone all to hell in private. In public, it was a different story. He walked over to get a vitamin drink at the canteen. Gabe got one, too.

"We worked out a plan for at least the next month." Hopefully longer, if things calmed down and he and Kate could go back to being at least friends. If not ever lovers again.

Gabe untwisted the cap. "Meaning what?" He squinted at Alex, then took a drink. "You haven't forgiven her for a mistake she made in high school?"

Alex moved to another quiet spot. Where they could watch

the kids, but not be overheard. "It's more than that. You know what her secrecy could have cost us all."

"But it didn't."

Thank God for that. Alex sighed in frustration, explaining, "Which is why we are still trying to figure out a way forward that will meet the kids' needs and expectations." And still give Kate the family she always wanted. Because regardless of what was going on between him and her, she had become the mother the boys had always deserved, and they had become beloved sons to her as well.

He'd have to be cruel beyond measure to break that up, never mind at Christmastime. So what if *he* didn't get what he wanted and needed? His kids, and Kate, would be happy, and that had to count for a whole hell of a lot, didn't it?

Gabe stared at him, seemingly unable to understand. "And you're okay with a sham of a marriage and a family in name only?" he prodded, stunned.

The criticism rankled. It wasn't as if his brother had made it work with Lauren, the love of his life, from his college days. They had broken up when Gabe had refused to get married while still in law school, and Lauren had not wanted to wait to start living their life. They had moved on, to disastrous result. "Of course it's not what I want."

Gabe frowned. "And yet you're allowing it to happen."

He tensed, the pain of the past mingling with the hurt in the present. The only thing he knew for sure was that he couldn't keep making the same mistakes over and over, when it came to choosing women, and expect that he would ever be happy.

Not that Kate was anywhere near his malicious, money-grubbing ex-wife.

No, she had so many good qualities.

So. Many.

Still... He turned to his brother. "I need a woman I can trust not to lie to—or keep things from—me." He figured, as a lawyer who had handled plenty of divorces, Gabe should understand that.

Gabe lifted a skeptical brow. "Not lie to you? Or not make a mistake? Because if you're looking for someone who is perfect, bro, you're going to be looking for a long, long time."

Mitzy basted the spiral sliced ham and put it back in the oven to finish baking while Kate rinsed and trimmed the green beans.

"Did you get Alex's Christmas gift finished?" Mitzy asked.

Yes. The question is, will he even want it now, given that it's from me?

Kate nodded glumly.

Mitzy stirred sugar, orange zest and water into the cranberries and set the saucepan on the stove to cook.

Aware it was killing her to pretend everything was normal, when it wasn't anywhere near close to that, Kate turned to her mother-in-law. "You know what happened at the mediation yesterday?"

"Are we talking about the video from your high school days? The one that briefly ended up on social media before it was taken down in a joint effort between the prep school and your parents?"

"That would be the one," Kate said miserably. She set the green beans in a bowl next to the stove, ready to sauté, then returned to the island to dice apples for the cranberry compote.

But she could barely concentrate on her task because the suspense was killing her.

"Did you and Chase see it?"

Mitzy put two large casserole dishes in the second oven to bake—sweet potato, and potatoes au gratin. Both looked delicious. "Alex sent it to Sadie and Gabe. And yes, Sadie showed it to us," Mitzy continued, explaining gently, "but only because she was worried how it resurfacing might affect you." Mitzy surveyed her closely. "Are you okay?"

Anxiety welled. "Honestly, I don't know..."

"You must have really been bullied by those girls to make fun of them like that."

Kate sent Alex's mom a surprised look. "How did you know about that?"

Mitzy began putting together individual fruit cups for the grandkids. "I grew up in Dallas and went to a similar all-girls prep school. It was tough if you didn't want to run with the popular girls—who were also mean as could be to anyone not in their clique." She made an exasperated face. "And you can imagine how well I fit in since I was the only daughter of a Dallas socialite...who had very little interest in material things and wanted to be a social worker when she grew up."

"Oh. Yeah. The majority of your classmates would definitely not have understood that." Kate stood and took the diced apples over to the pot of cranberries simmering on the stove.

She returned to help Mitzy with the fruit cups.

"Fortunately—" her mother-in-law smiled as she cut red and green grapes into bite-size chunks "—I spent a lot of summers and holidays with my dad, who lived here in Laramie and owned a saddle-making company. So even though I was torn between two worlds, I was also very grounded. Which made it hard to put up with the style-over-substance crowd." She hesitated for a beat before saying, "I'm guessing, because your parents built their business from the ground up and you saw for yourself how hard they worked, that you found it as difficult as I did to just go along to get along. I mean, you can do it for a while, but eventually..." Mitzy stopped and shook her head. "You just *can't* do it anymore..."

Guilt flashed through her. "Which is why I came up with that juvenile plan to mock the school and everything it stood for and everyone who went there. I thought I'd shame them into waking up, seeing who they had become. Instead, all I did was destroy my own reputation... And now, that awful moment of poor judgment is back...and Alex can't forgive me."

Mitzy tilted her head. "Is that what you think marriage is? One mistake and you're done?"

Clearly, her mother-in-law didn't, Kate thought. "Well, it's sort of been that way with my parents and me."

Like the veteran social worker she was, Mitzy noted, "They're not happy with your choices. But they are still taking your calls? Yes?"

Kate bit her lip in confusion. "Meaning...?"

"With time, and patience, there is still hope for the future. Especially this time of year."

A new wave of sadness swept through her. "Because they are in retail, my parents don't really celebrate the holiday."

"But Alex does, Kate. He's all heart this time of year. He wants everything to be wonderful. Happy and joyous. His emotions run high."

Kate had seen that. Basked in it in fact.

"He's also practical, though. A guy who is very grounded in the reality of situations. And Chase and I both think that he'll eventually get over the fact you kept something from him, because you didn't think it would ever come out, and you were trying to protect him and the boys, and see what we did when we watched the speech you gave. Which was someone who had been bullied, who had finally had enough and hit back, lashing out in kind. Problem is…as you said…you didn't hurt the mean girls at all. You hurt *yourself*. And inadvertently, those you loved most…"

"So what do I do? How do I fix this?" Her relationship with her parents was still a work in progress. Going to take time. But the situation with her marriage was much more dire. How could she get Alex to forgive her so she could win him back? Was it even *possible*? Her heart lurched as she worried about what the future held for the two of them.

"First, you have to forgive yourself for the mistake—because that's all it was. *A mistake*. Then and now. And then you have to ask yourself what are you going to do differently the next time you're in a hurtful situation? Are you going to pretend it doesn't exist? Lash out? Run away? Or find another path?"

Mitzy took Kate's hands in hers. "Come up with a workable strategy, sweetheart, and I guarantee you that you'll find your way. And this Christmas will be better than ever."

Kate thought about what Mitzy had said to her the rest of the day. All through the boisterous lunch with the family. During a yuletide crafting session at the community center. And at dinner out with Alex and the boys.

By the time they got back to the ranch and Alex took the boys upstairs to put them to bed, she knew exactly what she had to do. And why.

But first she had to put the finishing touches on the present that she hoped he would treasure as much as she had loved making it for him.

It took a little longer than expected.

When she finally came out of the guest suite, she saw him walking down the hall toward her. He looked solemn. "Everything okay?" she asked.

He nodded. "Boys have been asleep for about an hour now."

Alex walked her back to the living room where a fire blazed in the grate. The tree lights were on, giving the room a romantic aura, or maybe that was just wishful thinking on her part.

"I thought right now might be a good time to talk," he told her.

A whisper of attraction coursed through her, followed swiftly by a flood of suppressed emotion and longing. Wishing they could bypass the reckoning and go straight to the making up, Kate drew a bolstering breath. "I was thinking the same thing." As she set the gift-wrapped present under the tree, she saw another one, roughly the same size, also gift-wrapped. It had her name on it.

A good sign?

Or a hint of the end?

Didn't matter.

Kate had already decided what she was going to do. She wasn't surrendering to fear and weakness now. Not after they had come this far.

She turned to face him, mustering all her courage and strength. "I want to go first, though." She met his searching gaze and drew an enervating breath. "I need to apologize."

"Kate..."

She held up a staying hand. "I do. I should've told you I knew Tiffany from the start."

He looked at her uncomprehendingly. "Why didn't you?"

"I was so stunned to see her that first morning. Never mind find out she was your ex-wife and that you had quadruplet sons. And then..." Kate knotted her hands together. "I was only going to be here a few days. And even though your ex'd made my life sheer hell for four years of high school, she didn't remember any of it, which suited me. I just wanted to put the bullying behind me." Kate shook her head in regret.

"And then things got complicated. And I thought I could pretend none of it had ever happened and you'd never be hurt by any of it."

"Because you thought the internet had been wiped clean," Alex sympathized.

Tears pushed at the back of Kate's eyes. She struggled not to let them fall. "But, of course, it never really is," she said thickly. Fearing that if she let her emotions rule her, she would never get through everything she needed to say, she took a deep breath and gazed at him earnestly. "Anyway, I should have told you everything instead of running away from my mistakes, the way I always do."

"So what changed?" he asked in that husky voice that had every feminine inch of her wound up tight with anticipation. Gently, his gaze roved her face. His ocean blue eyes turbulent, serious, compelling. "Why did you decide to stay married to me," he asked, resting his hands on her shoulders, "when you could have walked out?"

Kate splayed her hands across the solid warmth of his chest. It had only been a day since they touched, yet she had missed the feel of him so much. Though it wasn't clear, from the implacable look on Alex's face, what he felt. Except sorrow that it had ever come to this. A place where it would be way too easy to lose everything they had gained.

As resolved not to let that happen as ever, she forced herself to remain calm as she confessed quietly, "I realized I finally had something worth fighting for. You and the boys. So that's what I'm going to do." Her eyes filled again and her voice quavered. "If you'll have me, I'm going to stay, and hope we can move on. Start fresh…"

Briefly, his expression turned formidable. "I'd like nothing more. But first, I owe you an apology, too." His sensual lips compressed in regret. "I should've told you about my meeting with Tiffany on Thursday."

Her pulse pounded. Beneath her fingertips, she could feel his heart beating as hard as her own. "Why didn't you?"

"I wanted to spare you any ugliness and, as you have experienced yourself, it's always ugly when Tiffany doesn't get exactly what she wants, when she wants. Anyway, I had hoped talking reason to her would make her realize there was nothing to be gained from continuing the custody fight. Or going to mediation. That she'd gotten all the money she was ever going to get from me."

"And it didn't work."

"No, it didn't. Because although none of us realized it then, I wasn't the target. Her parents were. I did some more digging and found out that despite pretending otherwise, for social reasons, her folks had never been keen on being linked to kids not of their bloodline and were secretly happy when Tiffany and I divorced. So to have the children back in Houston, still legally Tiffany's and reportedly very out of control at that, was more of a nightmare to them than her impulsive marriage to Paolo."

Understanding dawned and Kate began to relax. "Hence the deal they made regarding Tiffany's access to her trust."

"Right." He inhaled and drew her closer, wrapping his arms around her waist. "In any case, I sensed all along that Tiffany would try and use you to hurt me, just as she was already using the boys, and I told myself I was protecting you by not involving you in the last-minute effort to talk sense into her."

That made sense, Kate thought.

"In retrospect, though..." Silence fell, emphasizing all

that was at stake. His jaw clenched. "I think I was really just protecting myself."

Here was their chance. To open up their hearts. Go for broke. "From?" she rasped. When she would have drawn away, he held fast.

"All the feelings I was beginning to have for you," he confessed gruffly, wiping away her tears with the tip of his finger. His regret over mistakes made was clear. "We promised each other we were going to have a transactional marriage that would give us both the complete family and loving home we wanted."

She remembered how simple it had all seemed.

"And here I was—" Alex shook his head ruefully "—breaking the deal within our very first month together by falling in love with you."

The words echoed within her. Surprise turned to joy. Then bliss unlike anything she had ever felt. Kate blinked. "You love me?" she repeated hoarsely.

Alex brought her closer. Kissing her passionately and evocatively. Until her knees wobbled and her toes curled.

"I do. With all my heart and soul."

Talk about holiday dreams coming true! "Oh, Alex," she whispered reverently. "I love you like crazy, too."

They kissed again, then pulled back, their gazes locking as readily as their smiles. "I want us to have a real marriage in every sense," she confessed. "Starting now. One where we can and *will* tell each other everything." The strength of his embrace imbued her with warmth.

"I want that, too, darlin'." He kissed her again, even more sweetly this time.

"And to that end… I have something to give you," Kate said. She eased away from him and brought her present out from under the tree. Seeing where this was going, Alex picked up his for her.

They settled side by side on the sectional. "You first," he said.

She undid the wrapping, opened up the box and saw an album nestled inside. It contained photos of herself and her grandmother—the house they had lived in together, the elementary school she had attended until she was seven, even the cafeteria two blocks away where she and her grandmother had walked for their holiday meals!

"Oh, Alex, how did you get all this?" Happy tears blurred Kate's eyes.

His grin widened. "I had help from the investigator Gabe uses on cases and then I took it from there, contacting the neighbors who lived next to your grandmother. When they understood what I was trying to do, they were very helpful."

"Looks like!"

He put his arm around her, pulling her into the curve of his body. "I was thinking, since we have time over Christmas break, we might drive down there with the boys, visit the old neighborhood and show them where you went to elementary school, where your grandmother lived and maybe even have a meal at the cafeteria that you loved so much. It's still got a four-star rating and is a community favorite, you know. I checked!"

Blown away by his thoughtfulness, Kate paused. "I would love that. Truly. Would you mind stopping in at Taylor's, seeing what my parents have built, and hopefully meeting them? I'd really like them to get to know you and the boys."

"The boys and I'd love that, too."

"Wow." Kate looked down at the gift that meant so much, which was still on her lap. "Now I'm not sure my gift is going to measure up. Although it does prove *something*," she said mysteriously, resisting the wild urge to giggle. She handed over her present to him. "Here goes, cowboy..."

With a quizzical expression, he opened his gift. Seeing what was inside, he began to laugh. "Great minds think alike, right?"

"You betcha." She watched him remove the album she had compiled for him, with *The History of the Rocking M Ranch* emblazed across the front.

"How did you come up with this?" he asked with an impressed look.

"I got to thinking about what you told me. About your mom always saying...all the memories you take for granted and don't think you need to memorialize now will mean so much to your kids one day. So when I realized I hadn't seen anything in the attic or your study that memorialized the Rocking M, I talked to your folks and they helped me put together a history of the Rocking M Ranch, so far."

He looked through the pictures of the property he had bought in its initial rundown shape. The way it had grown and expanded over the last ten years. There were pictures of the kids, the cowboys, the horses and the cattle. Reckless. And him.

"Only one thing missing," he said, shutting the album. "Your picture needs to be in here, too, Kate Taylor McCabe. Because you turned this place from a ranch house to a home and infused it with Christmas cheer, love and joy, and *family*. And that," he said, kissing her again, even more tenderly this time, "is the best gift of all."

Epilogue

December, one year later

"Everybody ready to get started?" Kate asked.

Alex and the four boys gathered around the kitchen island. Christmas-tree-shaped vanilla cakes, bowls of pine green buttercream frosting and appropriately sized offset spatulas were in front of them.

"We're ready, Mom!" the boys said in unison.

"Okay, the first thing we are going to do is put a layer of green frosting on each of these cakes." Kate demonstrated.

The boys had spent so much time in the kitchen with her the last year, they had no problem smoothly coating the full-size "tree" cakes.

Alex was a little less handy.

Or maybe he just wanted her to come over and stand close to him and put her hand over his, to show him the appropriately smooth motion.

"Getting the hang of it, cowboy?" she whispered in his ear.

"Almost," he teased right back. "Although I think it wouldn't hurt for me to have a little more help."

"She's a good teacher, Dad!" Matthew declared.

"She certainly is," Alex agreed, giving her a look only she could see. One that promised lots of love coming her way later.

"Mom, do you think all the cousins and grownups are going to like the dessert we are making for the party at Grandma and Grandpa's house tonight?" Marty asked.

"I do," Kate said. "And it's a really nice thing to do for them. Especially at Christmastime."

"Do you think we should make some for the cowboys or tamales again?" Max asked.

"I think we should probably ask them if there is anything special they want this holiday season," Kate said.

"Are we ever going to get a sister?" Michael asked, completely out of the blue.

Kate and Alex exchanged glances. This was not in the plan for today! Nevertheless, she could not stop blushing…

"Why do you ask, son?" Alex said.

"Because all of our cousins have a sister. Andrew and Oliver have Isabella. Jaime has Jenni," Michael explained as studiously as ever. "And besides," he added slyly, "we might have heard something about a baby if we had been eavesdropping…and we weren't."

"Seems like the surprise is out of the bag," Alex said, their plans to make the big announcement to the kids that evening, before they left for the family dinner, suddenly derailed. They'd held off saying anything until they'd had the eighteen-week ultrasound and knew all was well. He looked at Kate, teasing, "Shall we tell them? Or leave them waiting painfully in suspense."

The boys groaned impatiently, then turned pleading eyes to her.

Kate smiled. "You all are right about getting a baby sister. Your dad and I are having a baby girl. Who is in my tummy right now!" Kate went and got the ultrasound photo she had put in her purse. She and Alex both grinned as the boys *ooh*ed and *ahh*ed and decided, after some conversation, that their sister looked "pretty squiggly" right now.

"Not to worry, fellas. She will look like a newborn baby when she comes out," Kate reassured them.

"And she will be here next April. Right in time for Easter break," Alex added.

"Does she have a name?" Matthew asked.

Kate and Alex shook their heads. "Not yet," she said.

"Does everybody know?" Michael said.

"No. We haven't told anybody yet. You boys are the first to know. But we probably will tell everyone at the family dinner this evening. Okay?" Kate piped white garlands on each of the cakes, then handed out different colored candies to act as ornaments.

Already engrossed in the next big thing, making their confections look like fancy decorated Christmas trees, the boys went back to work. Reckless hung around next to them, watching.

Alex joined her at the sink when she went to wash her hands. "I hear congratulations are in order, Mrs. McCabe," he teased, leaning over to kiss her cheek.

"I'm sure you know all about it," Kate whispered back, just as humorously.

He dried his hands, then tucked a strand of hair behind her ear. "Have I told you what a great wife and mother and all-around chef you are?"

"Many times." She went up on tiptoe and put her lips against his ear, murmuring, "I think I might have mentioned you are a superb dad and husband and cowboy, too."

Eyes locked, they sighed together contentedly. "Seems like we're the perfect couple then," he said.

Kate felt the familiar bliss well up inside her. "And family, with another on the way..."

The boys turned to see what they were doing. "Hey, Mom and Dad! If you're going to kiss," Max yelled mischievously, "you better find the mistletoe!"

Which, as it happened, had been hung by Alex and the boys—just above the kitchen sink. A place where they knew she would be one hundred times a day. And hence would be an easy target for all their familial joking around.

"We know you're in love!" Matthew pretended to play the violin.

"'Cause you're married!" Michael said, flapping his hands, like bird wings, over his heart.

"And living happily ever after!" Marty concluded with a howl of super silly laughter that soon had his brothers joining in.

They sure were living the dream, Kate thought. She had never imagined her life could be this full. And utterly wonderful.

She had adopted the boys the previous summer. And was now officially their mom, forever and ever.

She still cooked for the cowboys, five days a week, via a contract between her company and the ranch, and she took occasional gigs in the area.

But it was the cooking and successfully running a business she loved, not the travel, or dealing with endless strangers.

It was being Alex's wife, mother to the boys and a member of the McCabe clan that truly brought her the most joy and fulfillment every single day.

And that was bringing her closer, albeit slowly, to her own parents.

For which she was very grateful. And wasn't that what Christmas was all about? Hope and love, joy and faith…? Giving yourself to others?

"This is shaping up to be yet another great Rocking M

Ranch Christmas," she told her five guys, looking at each of them and meaning it with all her heart.

Alex kissed her beneath the mistletoe once more, looking every bit as happy and content as she felt, while their sons cheered them on, then came over to hug them, too. "It sure is…"

* * * * *

*Watch for the next book in
A Marrying a McCabe Romance miniseries,
where Sage and Will find their happily ever after!
Coming soon, only from Harlequin Special Edition.*

Get up to 4 Free Books!

We'll send you 2 free books from each series you try PLUS a free Mystery Gift.

FREE Value Over **$25**

Both the **Harlequin® Special Edition** and **Harlequin® Heartwarming™** series feature compelling novels filled with stories of love and strength where the bonds of friendship, family and community unite.

YES! Please send me 2 FREE novels from the Harlequin Special Edition or Harlequin Heartwarming series and my FREE Gift (gift is worth about $10 retail). After receiving them, if I don't wish to receive any more books, I can return the shipping statement marked "cancel." If I don't cancel, I will receive 6 brand-new Harlequin Special Edition books every month and be billed just $6.39 each in the U.S. or $7.19 each in Canada, or 4 brand-new Harlequin Heartwarming Larger-Print books every month and be billed just $7.19 each in the U.S. or $7.99 each in Canada, a savings of 20% off the cover price. It's quite a bargain! Shipping and handling is just 50¢ per book in the U.S. and $1.25 per book in Canada.* I understand that accepting the 2 free books and gift places me under no obligation to buy anything. I can always return a shipment and cancel at any time by calling the number below. The free books and gift are mine to keep no matter what I decide.

Choose one:
- ☐ **Harlequin Special Edition** (235/335 BPA G36Y)
- ☐ **Harlequin Heartwarming Larger-Print** (161/361 BPA G36Y)
- ☐ **Or Try Both!** (235/335 & 161/361 BPA G36Z)

Name (please print)

Address _____ Apt. #

City _____ State/Province _____ Zip/Postal Code

Email: Please check this box ☐ if you would like to receive newsletters and promotional emails from Harlequin Enterprises ULC and its affiliates. You can unsubscribe anytime.

Mail to the Harlequin Reader Service:
IN U.S.A.: P.O. Box 1341, Buffalo, NY 14240-8531
IN CANADA: P.O. Box 603, Fort Erie, Ontario L2A 5X3

Want to explore our other series or interested in ebooks? Visit www.ReaderService.com or call 1-800-873-8635.

---

*Terms and prices subject to change without notice. Prices do not include sales taxes, which will be charged (if applicable) based on your state or country of residence. Canadian residents will be charged applicable taxes. Offer not valid in Quebec. This offer is limited to one order per household. Books received may not be as shown. Not valid for current subscribers to the Harlequin Special Edition or Harlequin Heartwarming series. All orders subject to approval. Credit or debit balances in a customer's account(s) may be offset by any other outstanding balance owed by or to the customer. Please allow 4 to 6 weeks for delivery. Offer available while quantities last.

Your Privacy—Your information is being collected by Harlequin Enterprises ULC, operating as Harlequin Reader Service. For a complete summary of the information we collect, how we use this information and to whom it is disclosed, please visit our privacy notice located at https://corporate.harlequin.com/privacy-notice. Notice to California Residents – Under California law, you have specific rights to control and access your data. For more information on these rights and how to exercise them, visit https://corporate.harlequin.com/california-privacy. For additional information for residents of other U.S. states that provide their residents with certain rights with respect to personal data, visit https://corporate.harlequin.com/other-state-residents-privacy-rights/.

HSEHW25